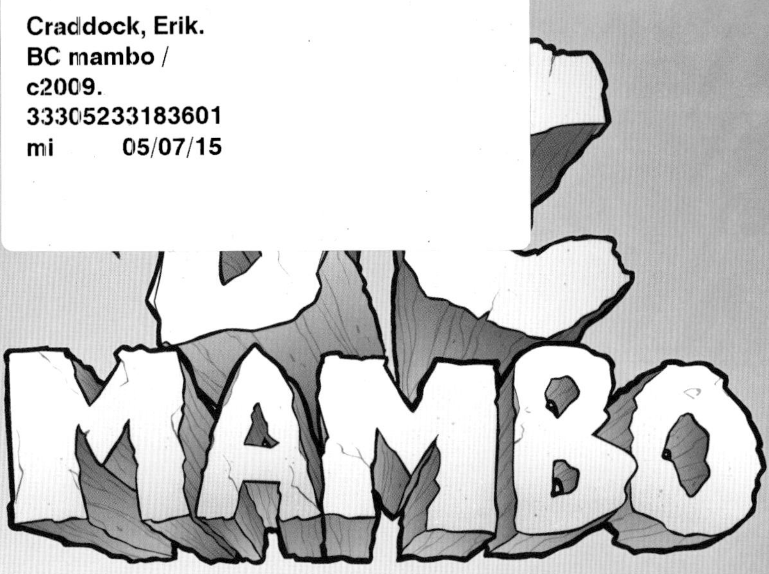

BC MAMBO

By Erik Craddock

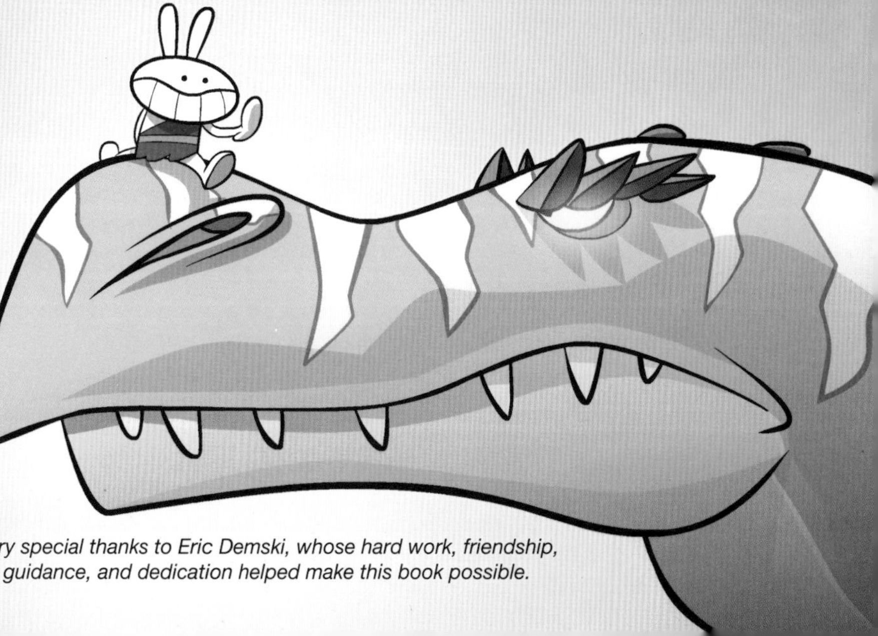

Very special thanks to Eric Demski, whose hard work, friendship, guidance, and dedication helped make this book possible.

Published in the United States by Random House Children's Books, a division of Random House, Inc., New York.
Random House and colophon are registered trademarks of Random House, Inc.

Visit us on the Web! www.randomhouse.com/kids

Educators and librarians, for a variety of teaching tools, visit us at www.randomhouse.com/teachers

www.stonerabbit.com

Library of Congress Cataloging-in-Publication Data
Craddock, Erik.
BC mambo / by Erik Craddock. — 1st ed.
p. cm. — (Stone Rabbit ; bk. 1)
Summary: After Stone Rabbit is transported back to prehistoric times, his bottle of barbecue sauce becomes the key ingredient in a power-hungry Neanderthal's plan to dominate the world.
ISBN 978-0-375-84360-0 (trade) — ISBN 978-0-375-93922-8 (lib. bdg.)
1. Graphic novels. [1. Graphic novels. 2. Rabbits—Fiction. 3. Prehistoric peoples—Fiction. 4. Time travel—Fiction. 5. Humorous stories.] I. Title.
PZ7.7.C73Baak 2009
[Fic]—dc22 2008000681

MANUFACTURED IN MALAYSIA

10 9 8 7 6 5 4 3 2

First Edition

Random House Children's Books supports the First Amendment and celebrates the right to read.

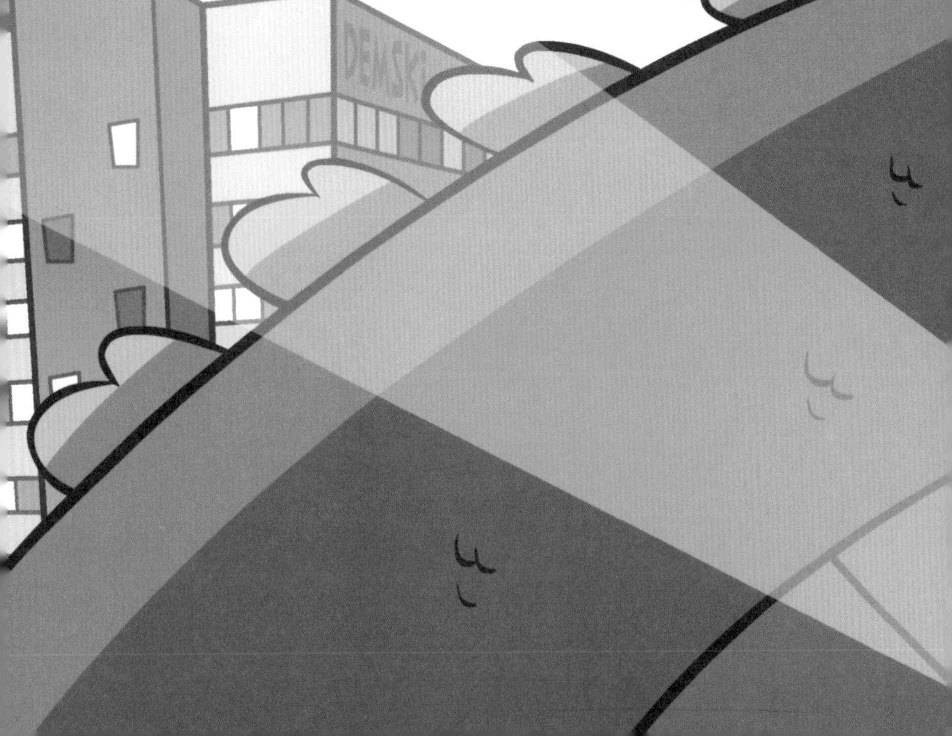
DEMSKI

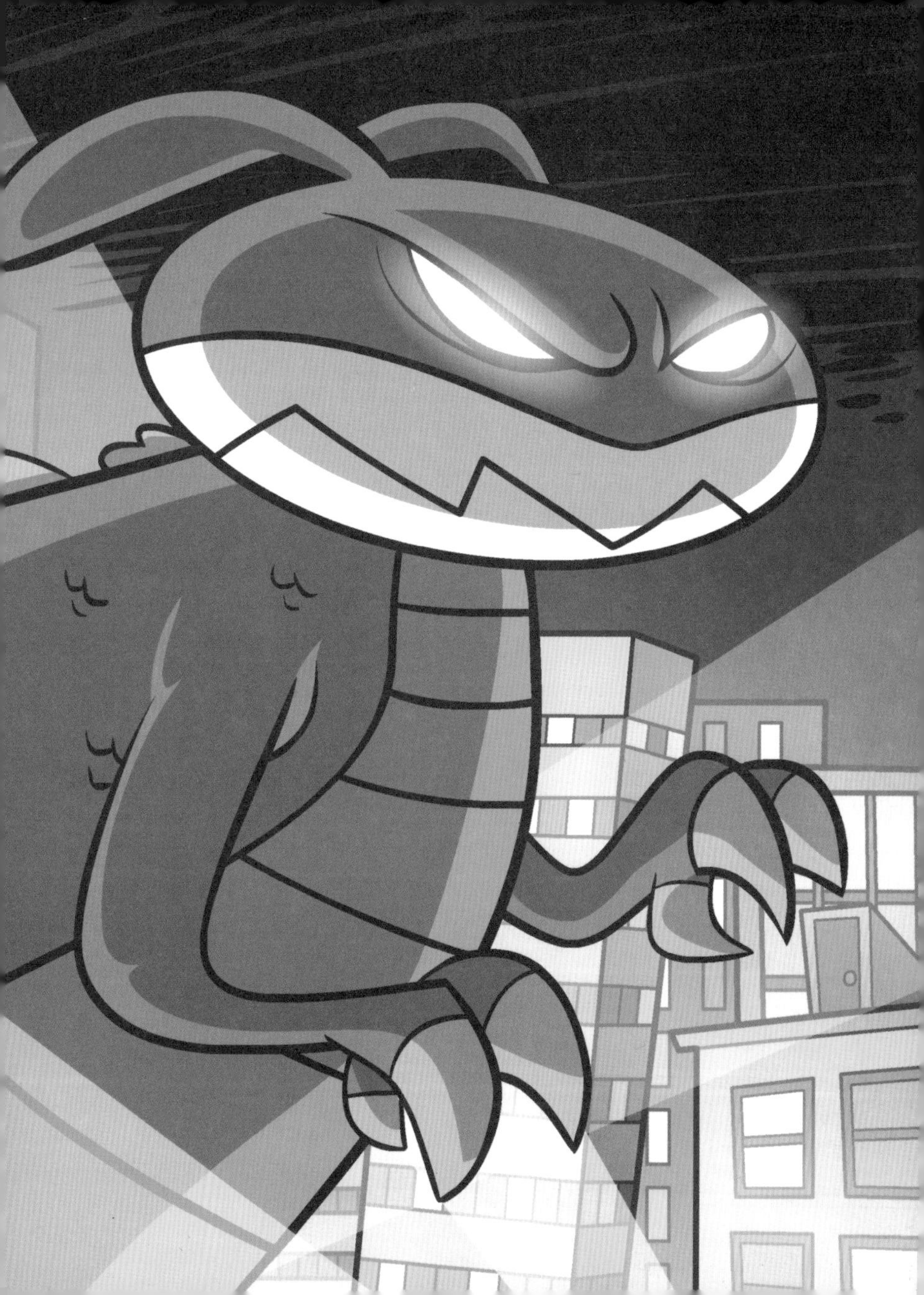

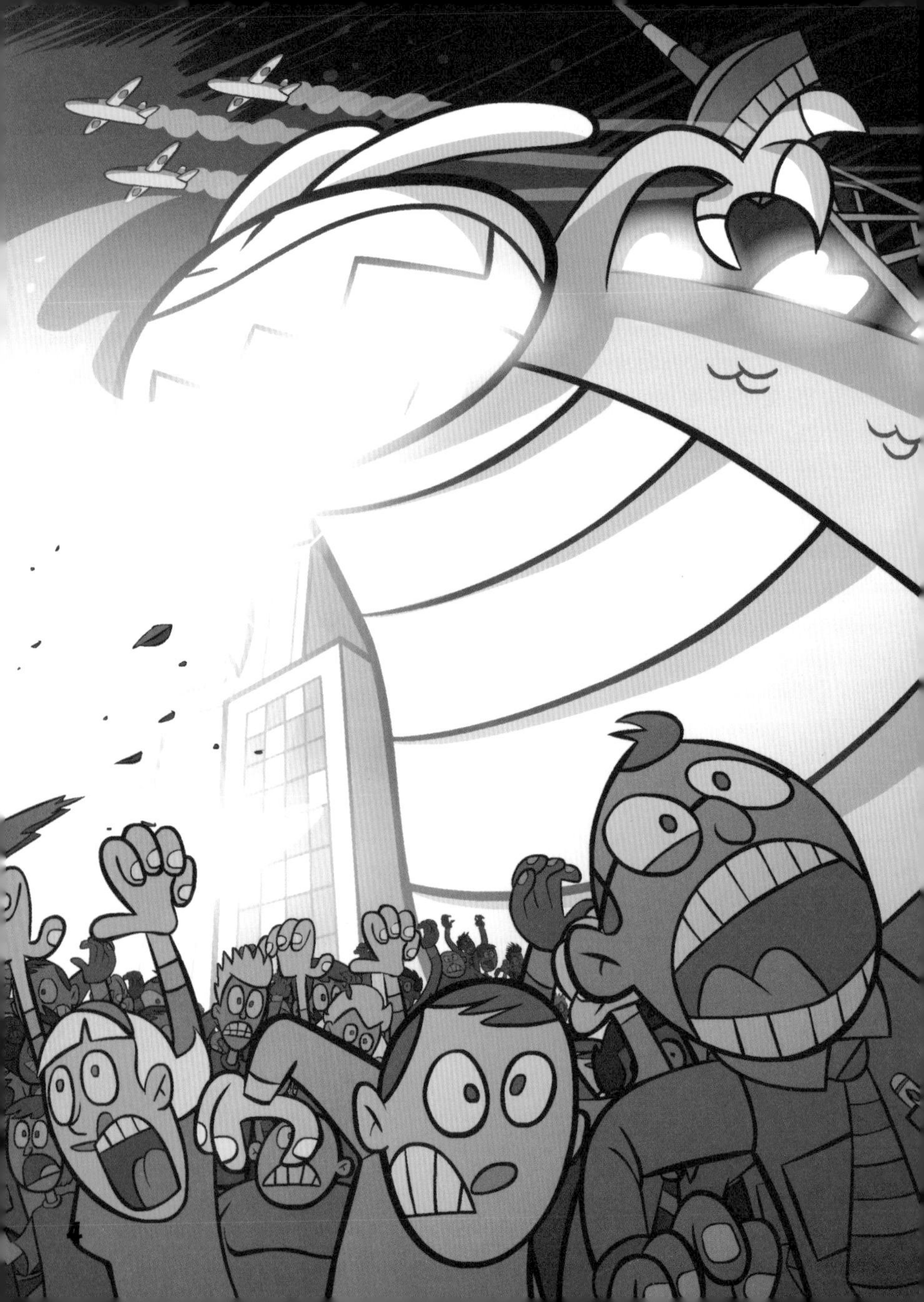

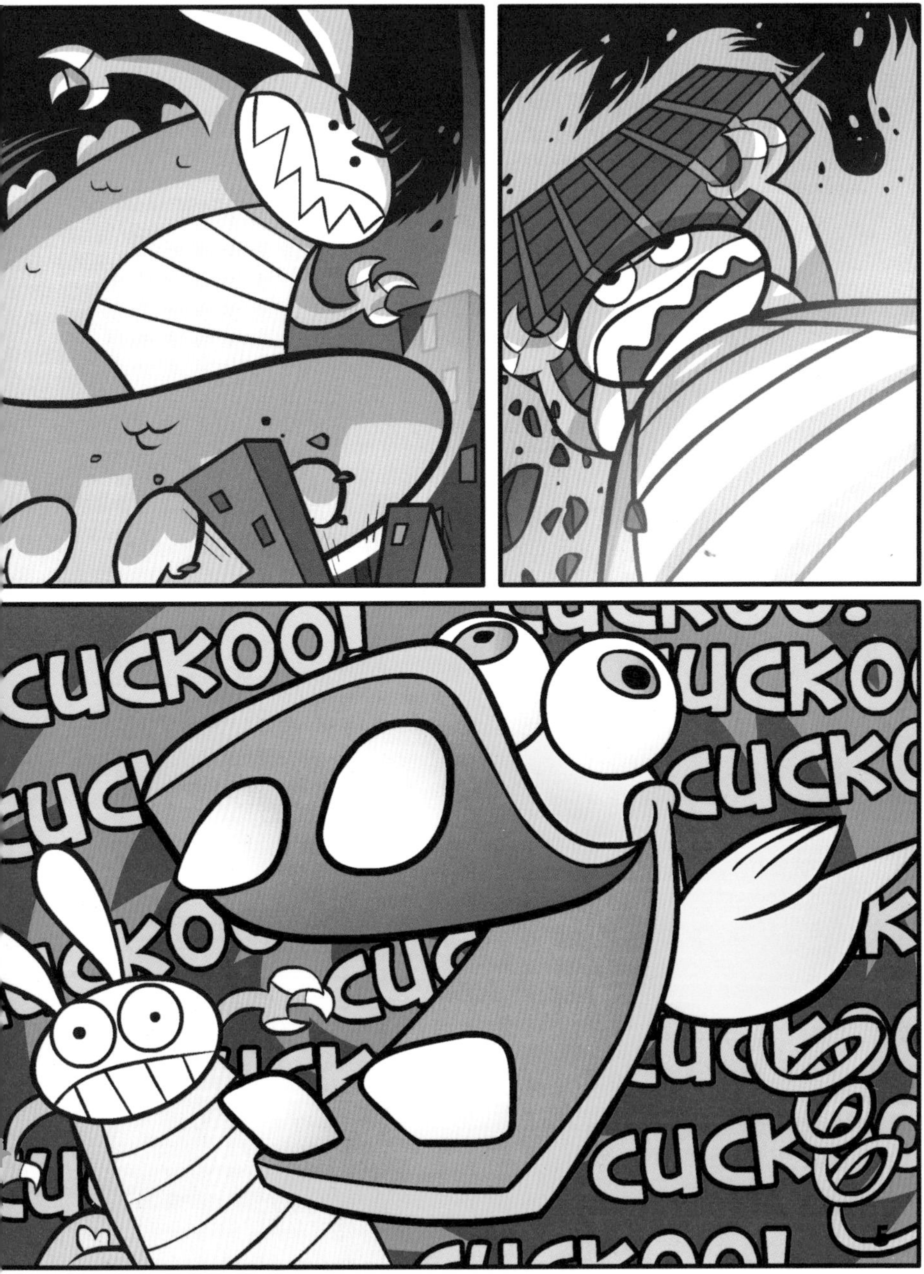
CUCKOO!

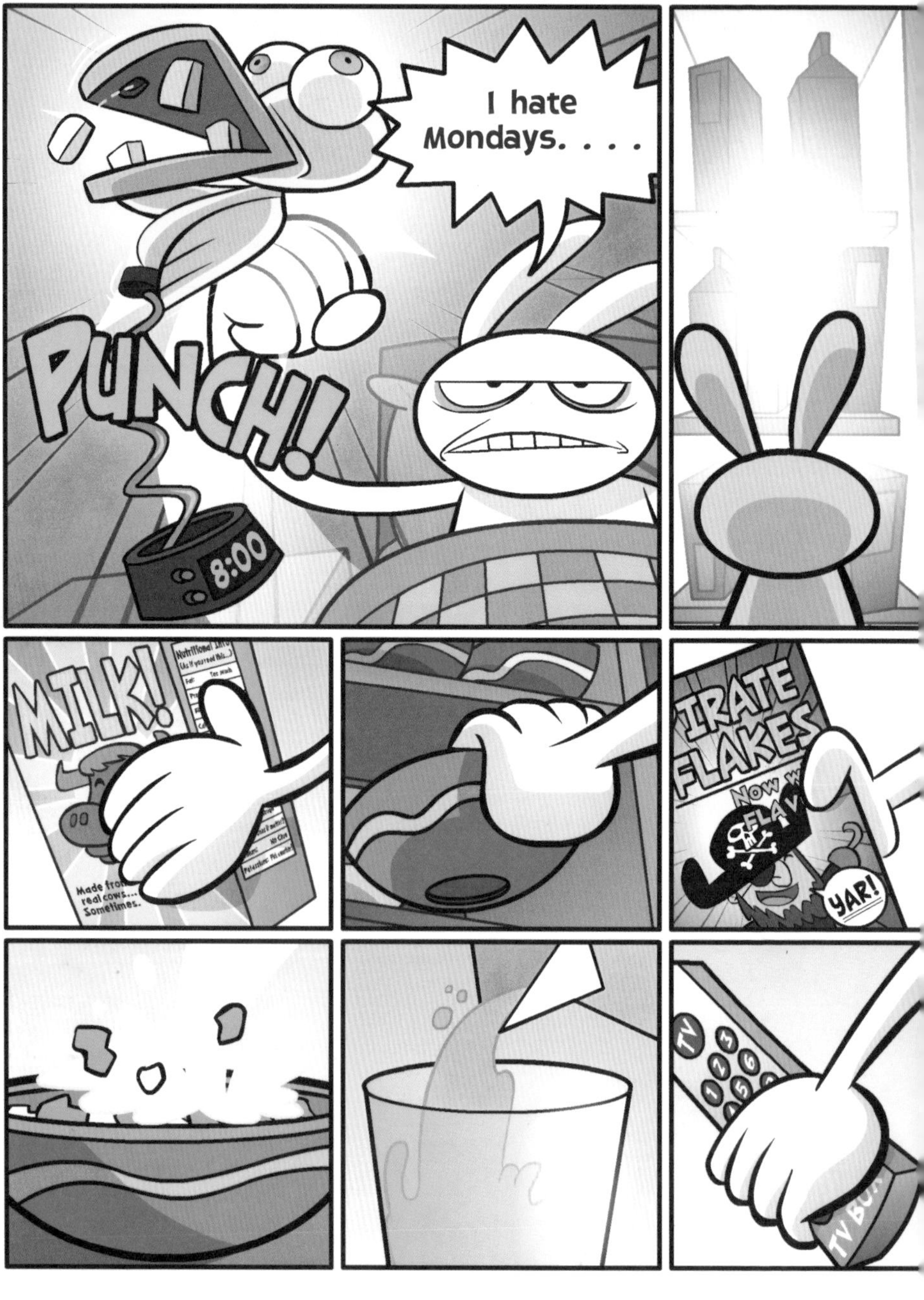
I hate Mondays. . . .
PUNCH!
8:00
MILK!
Made fro
real cows...
Sometimes.
IRATE
FLAKES
YAR!
TV
TV BU

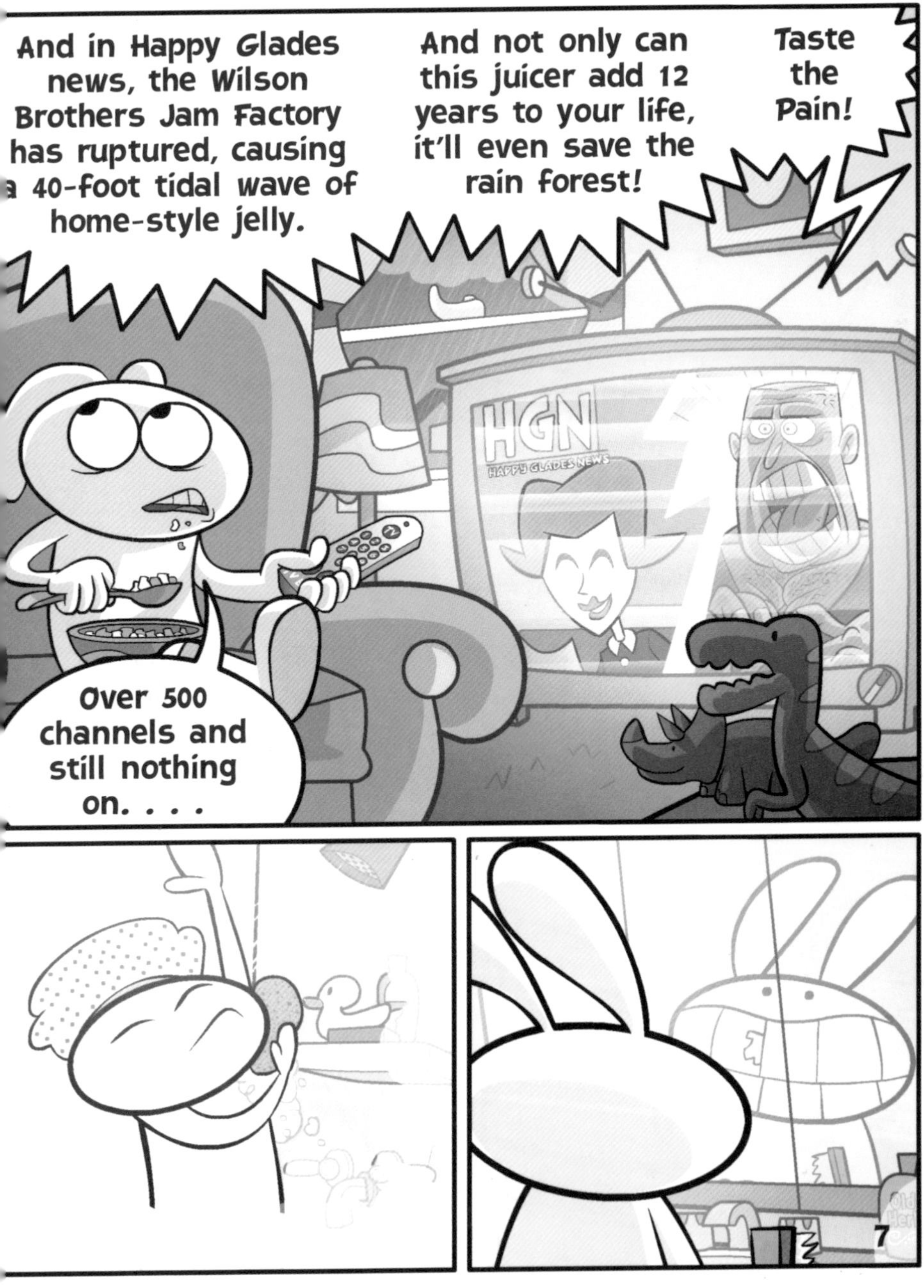
And in Happy Glades news, the Wilson Brothers Jam Factory has ruptured, causing a 40-foot tidal wave of home-style jelly.
And not only can this juicer add 12 years to your life, it'll even save the rain forest!
Taste the Pain!
HGN
HAPPY GLADES NEWS
Over 500 channels and still nothing on. . . .

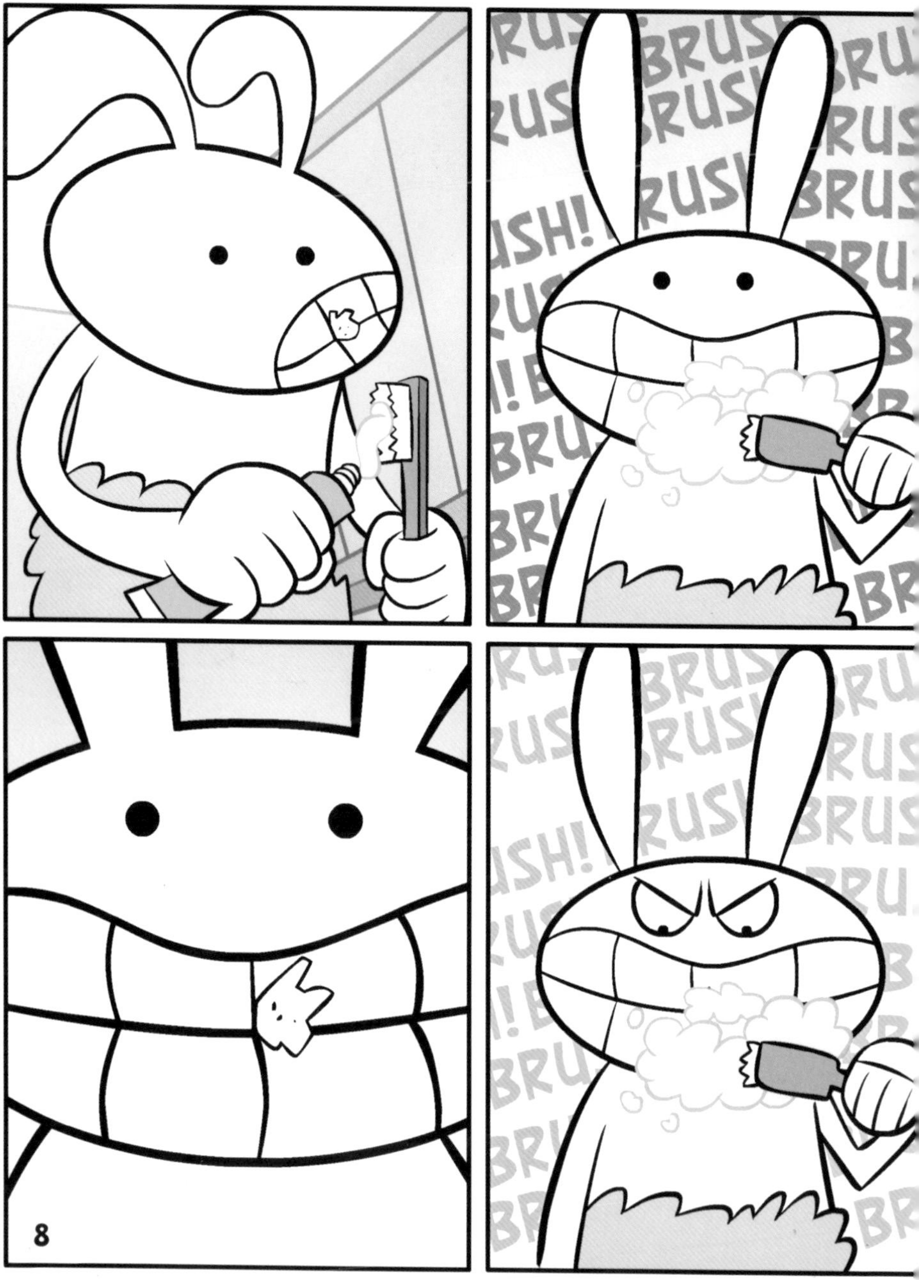
BRUSH!
BRUSH!

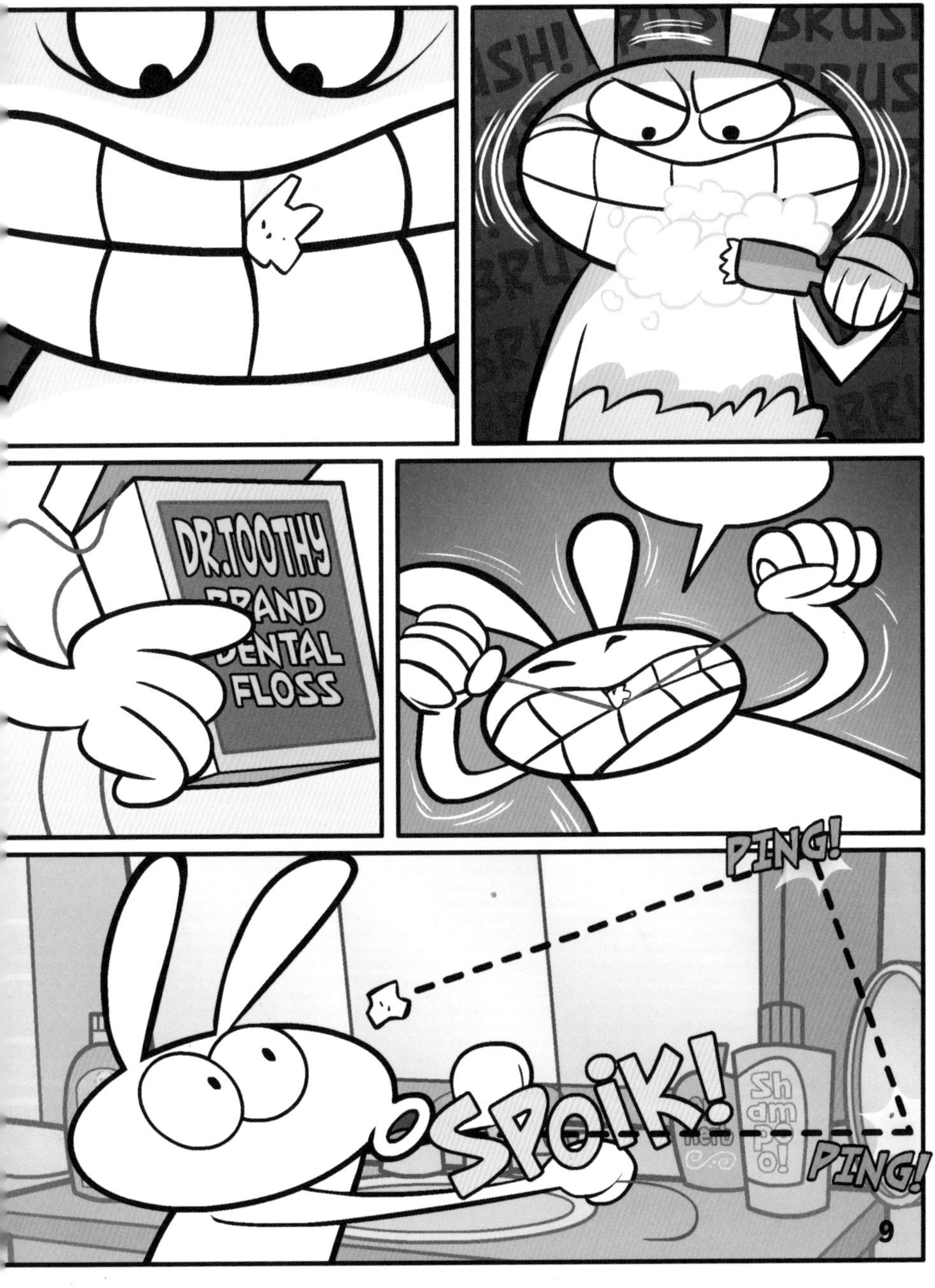
ASH!
BRUS
DR.TOOTHY
BRAND
DENTAL
FLOSS
PING!
SPOIK!
Sh
am
po
o!
PING!

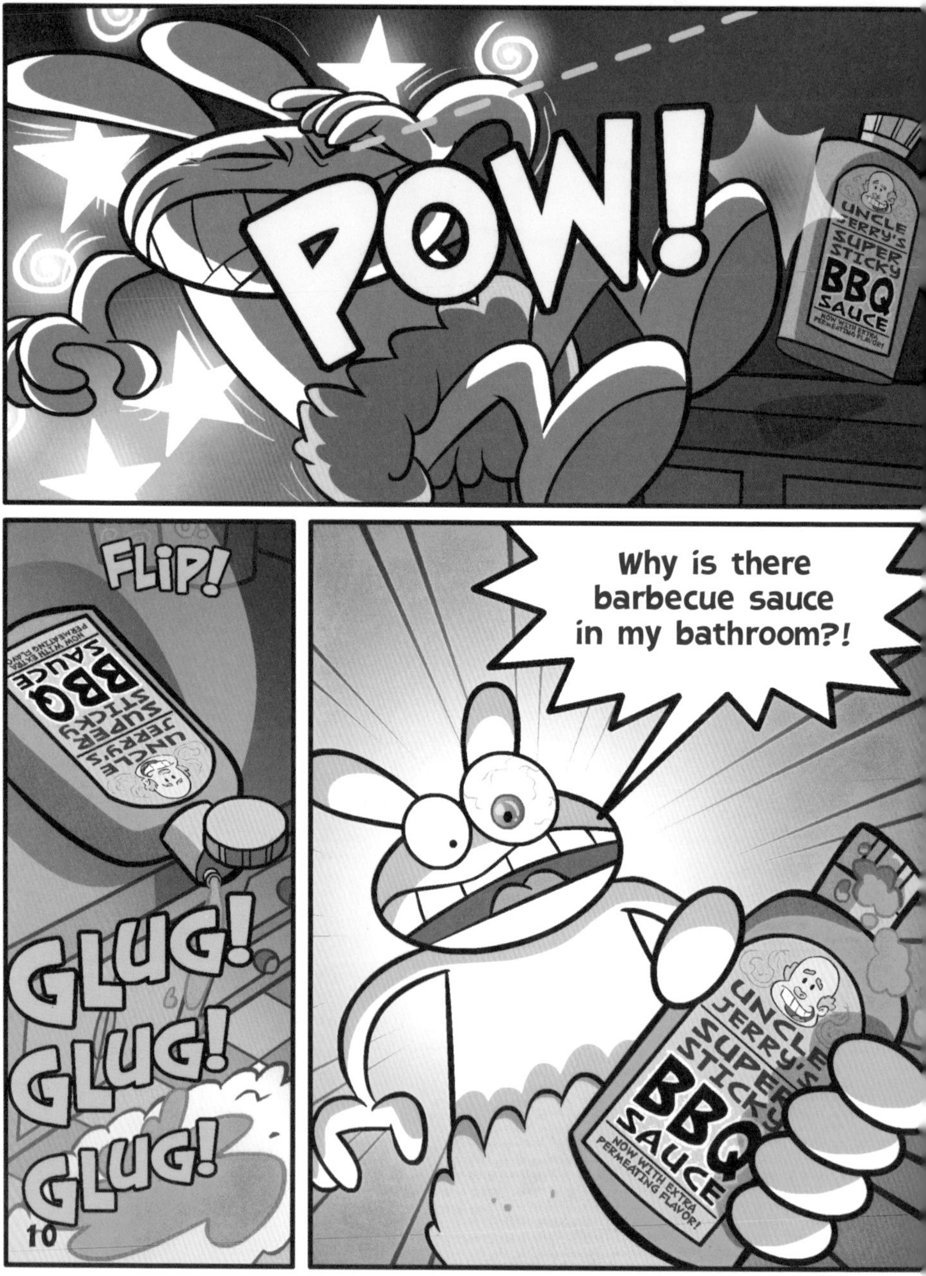
POW!
UNCLE JERRY'S SUPER STICKY BBQ SAUCE
NOW WITH EXTRA PERMEATING FLAVOR!
FLIP!
GLUG!
GLUG!
GLUG!
Why is there barbecue sauce in my bathroom?!
UNCLE JERRY'S SUPER STICKY BBQ SAUCE
NOW WITH EXTRA PERMEATING FLAVOR!

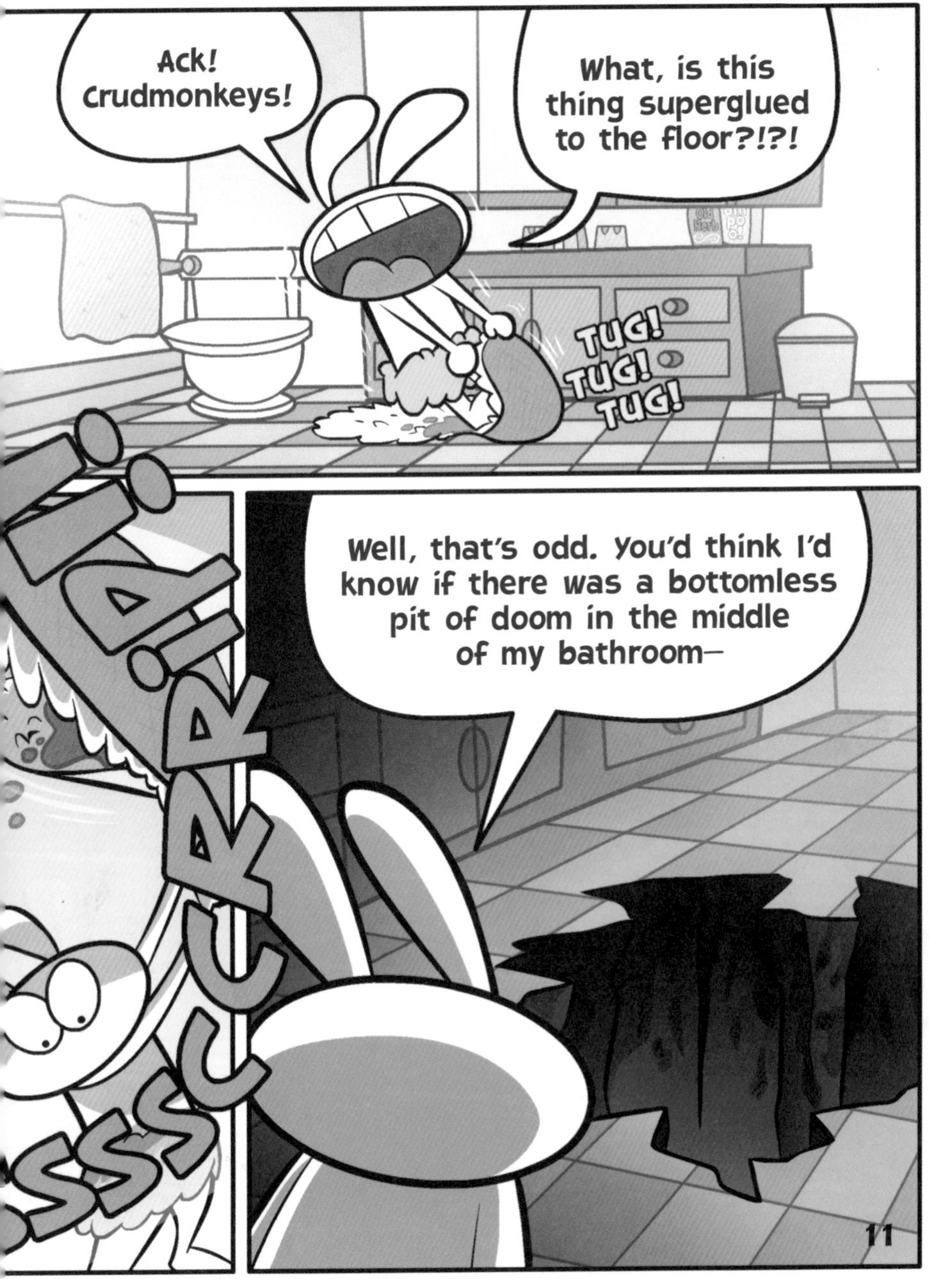
Ack! Crudmonkeys!
What, is this thing superglued to the floor?!?!
TUG! TUG! TUG!
Well, that's odd. You'd think I'd know if there was a bottomless pit of doom in the middle of my bathroom–

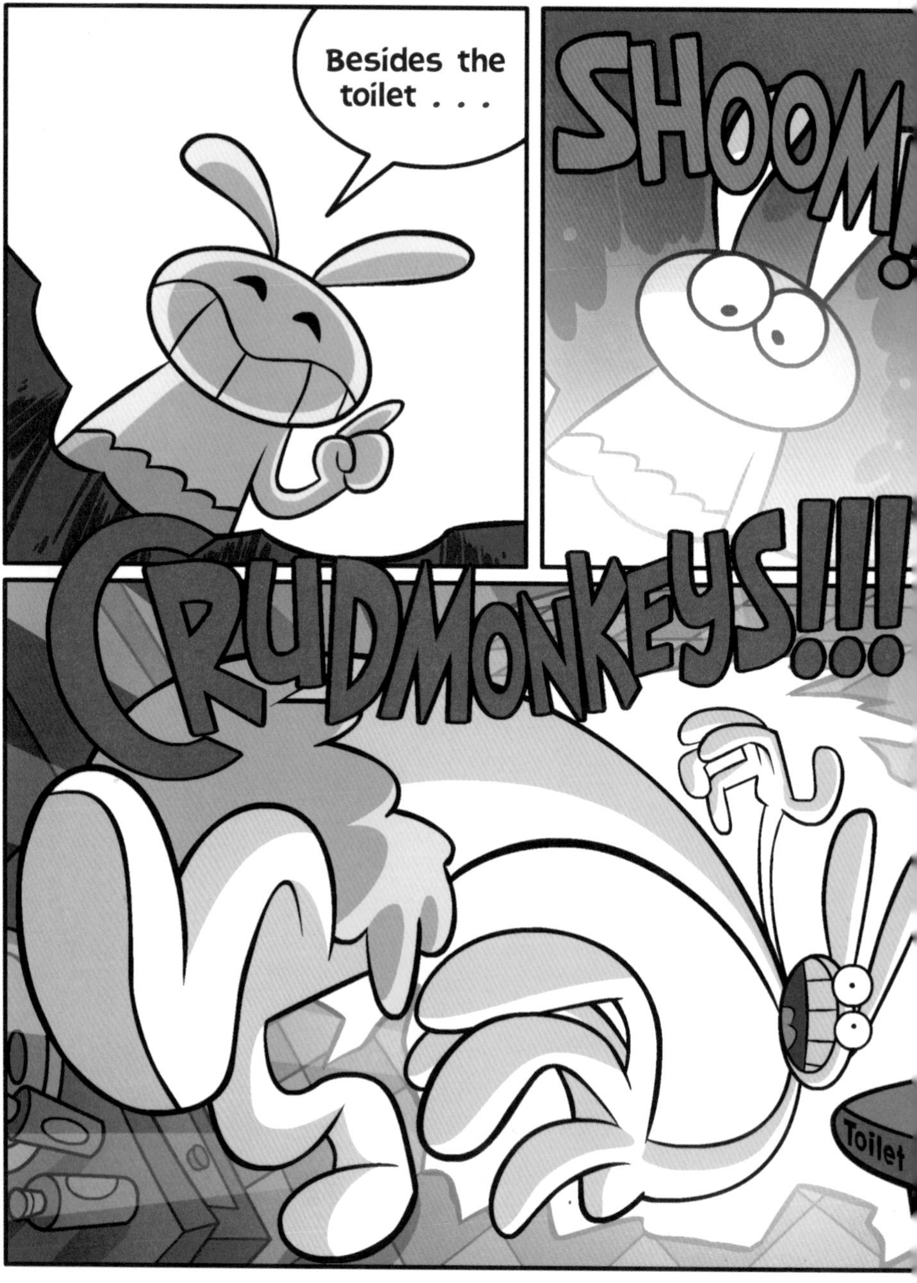
Besides the toilet . . .
SHOOM!
CRUDMONKEYS!!!!
Toilet

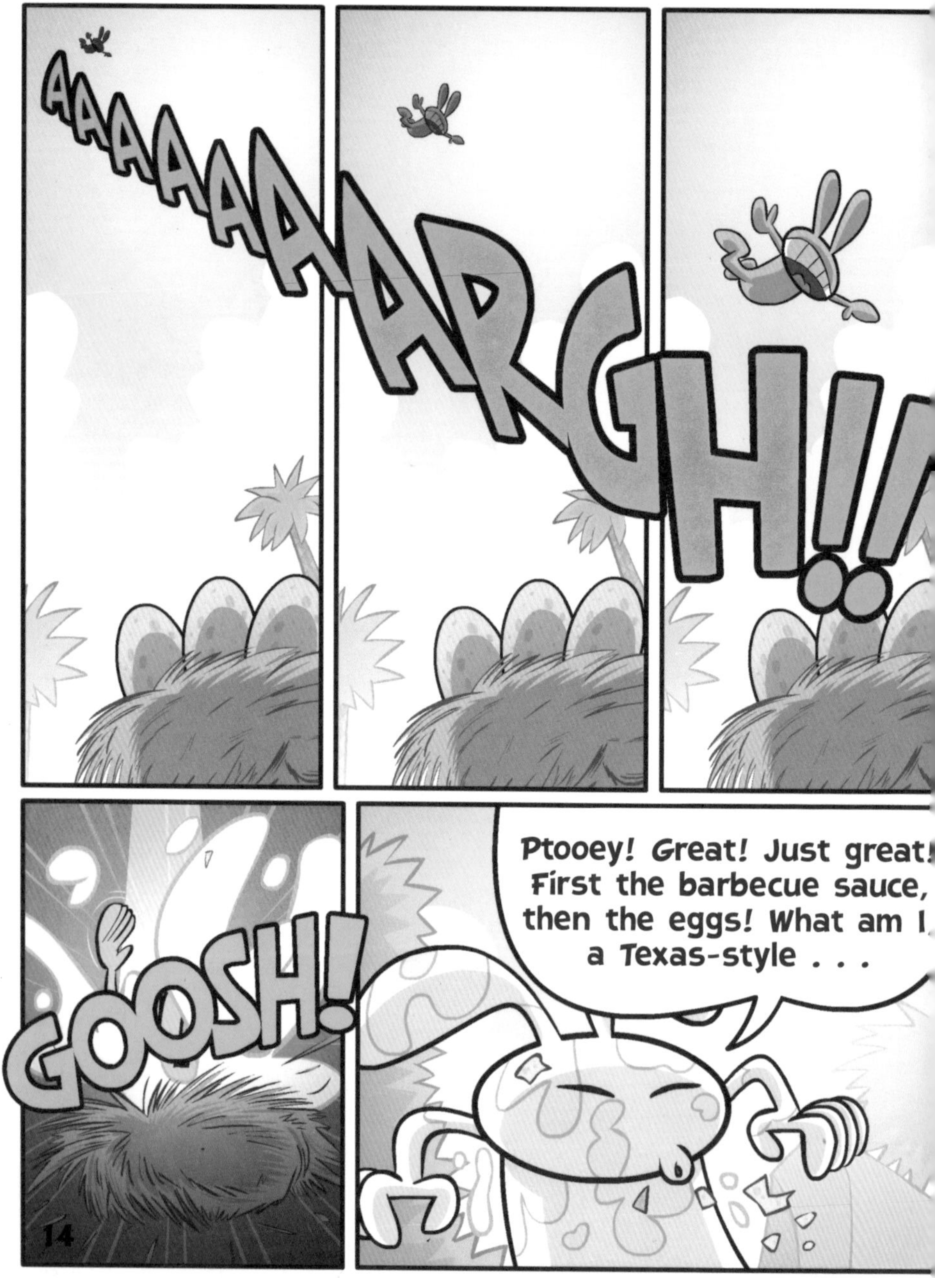
AAAAAAAAARGH!!!
GOOSH!
Ptooey! Great! Just great!
First the barbecue sauce,
then the eggs! What am I,
a Texas-style . . .

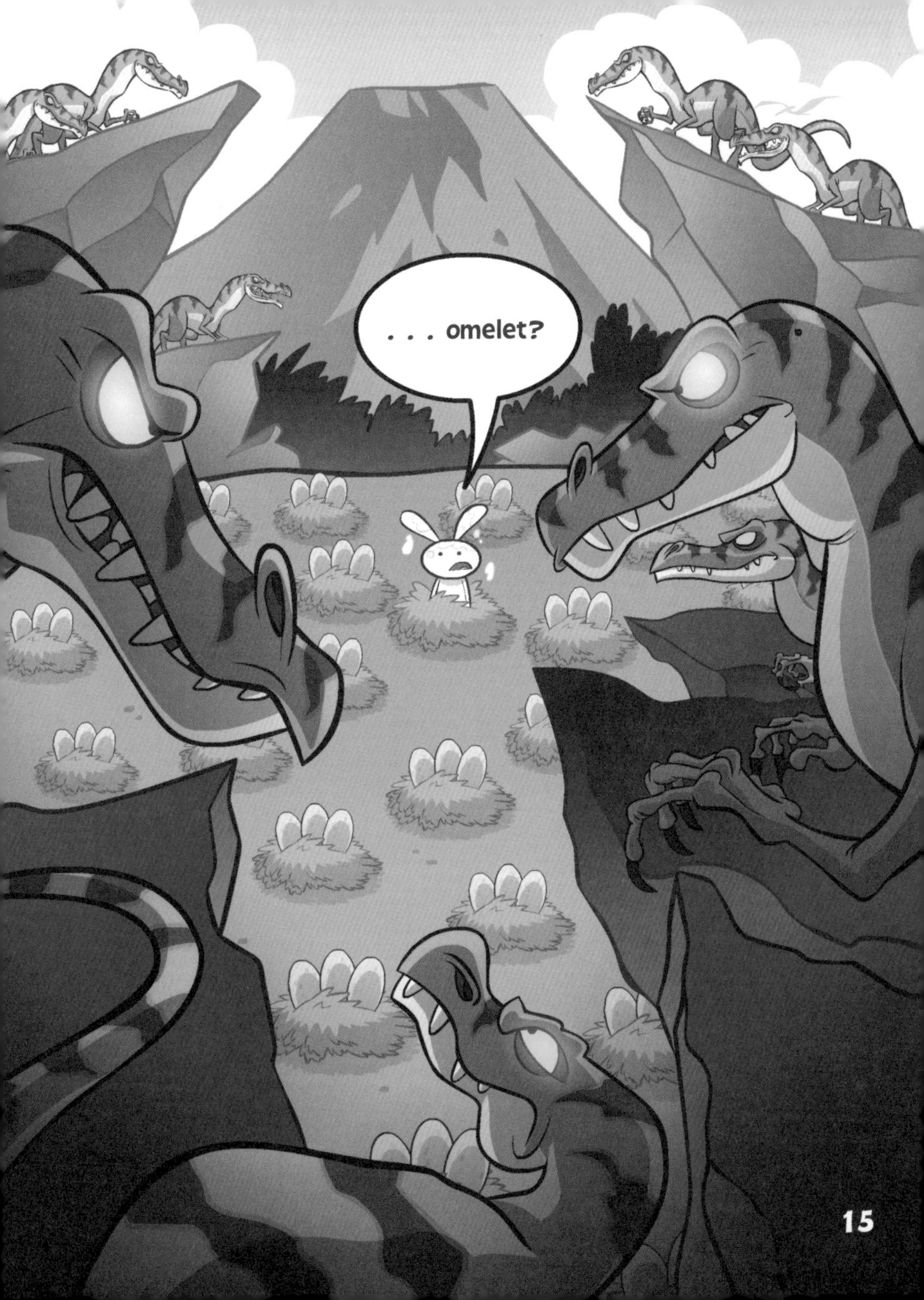
. . . omelet?

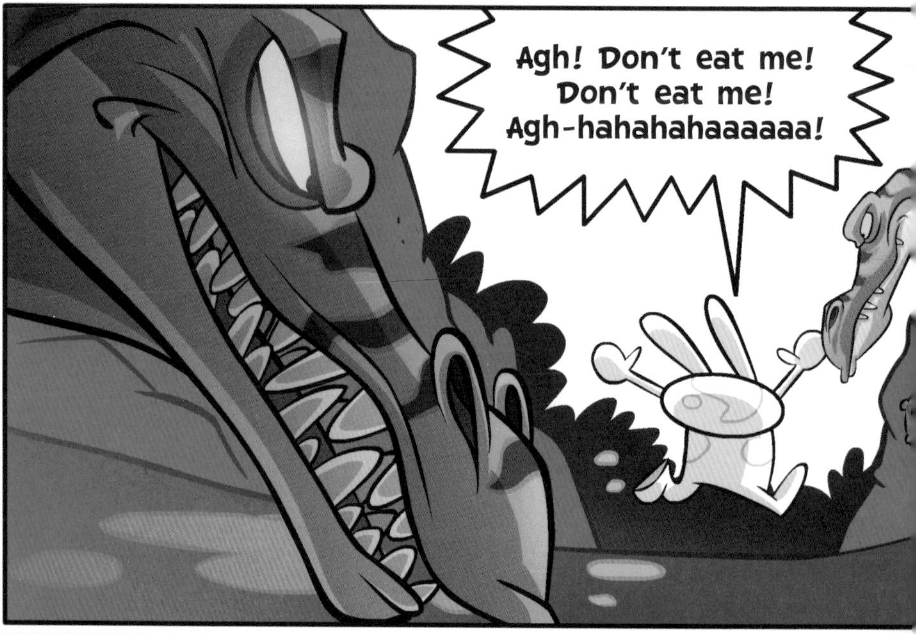
Agh! Don't eat me! Don't eat me! Agh-hahahahaaaaaa!

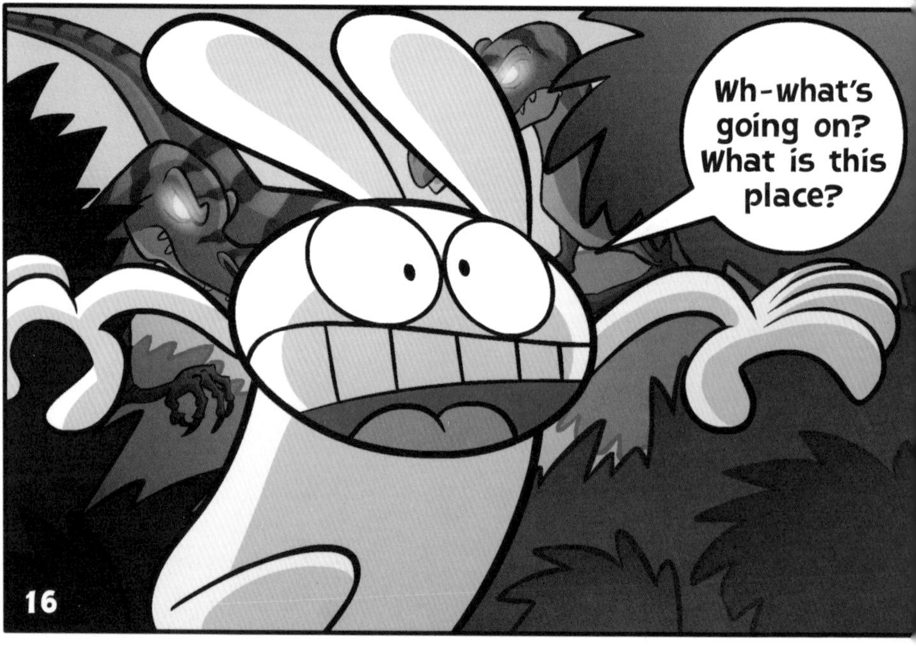
Wh-what's going on? What is this place?

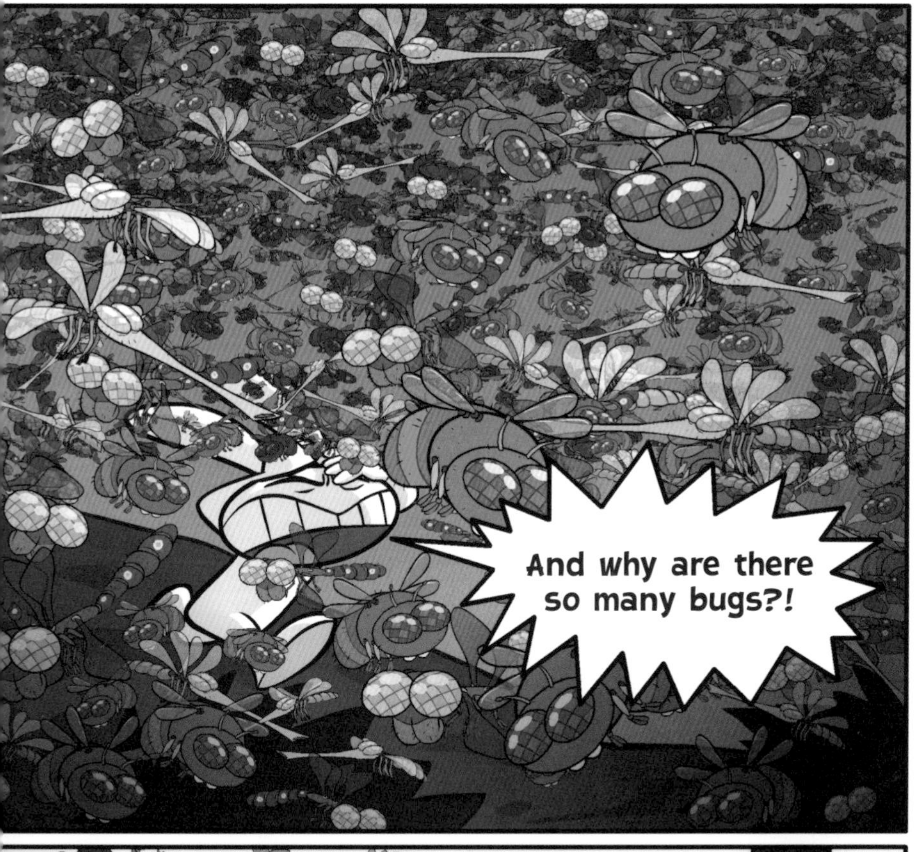
And why are there so many bugs?!
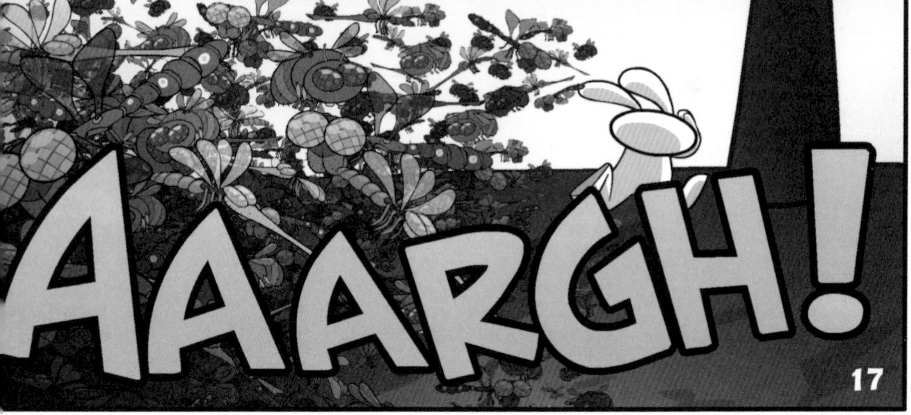
AAARGH!

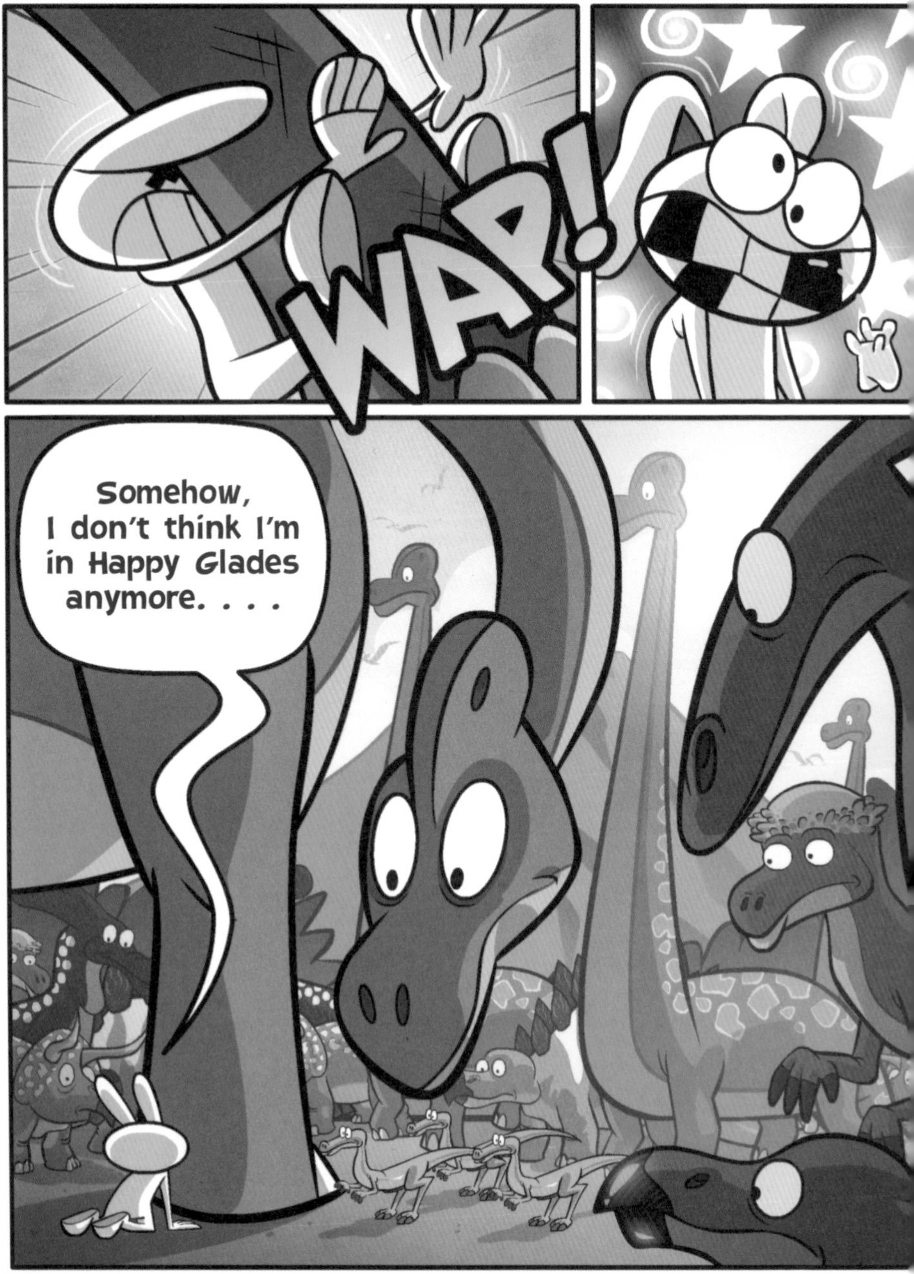
WAP!
Somehow, I don't think I'm in Happy Glades anymore. . . .

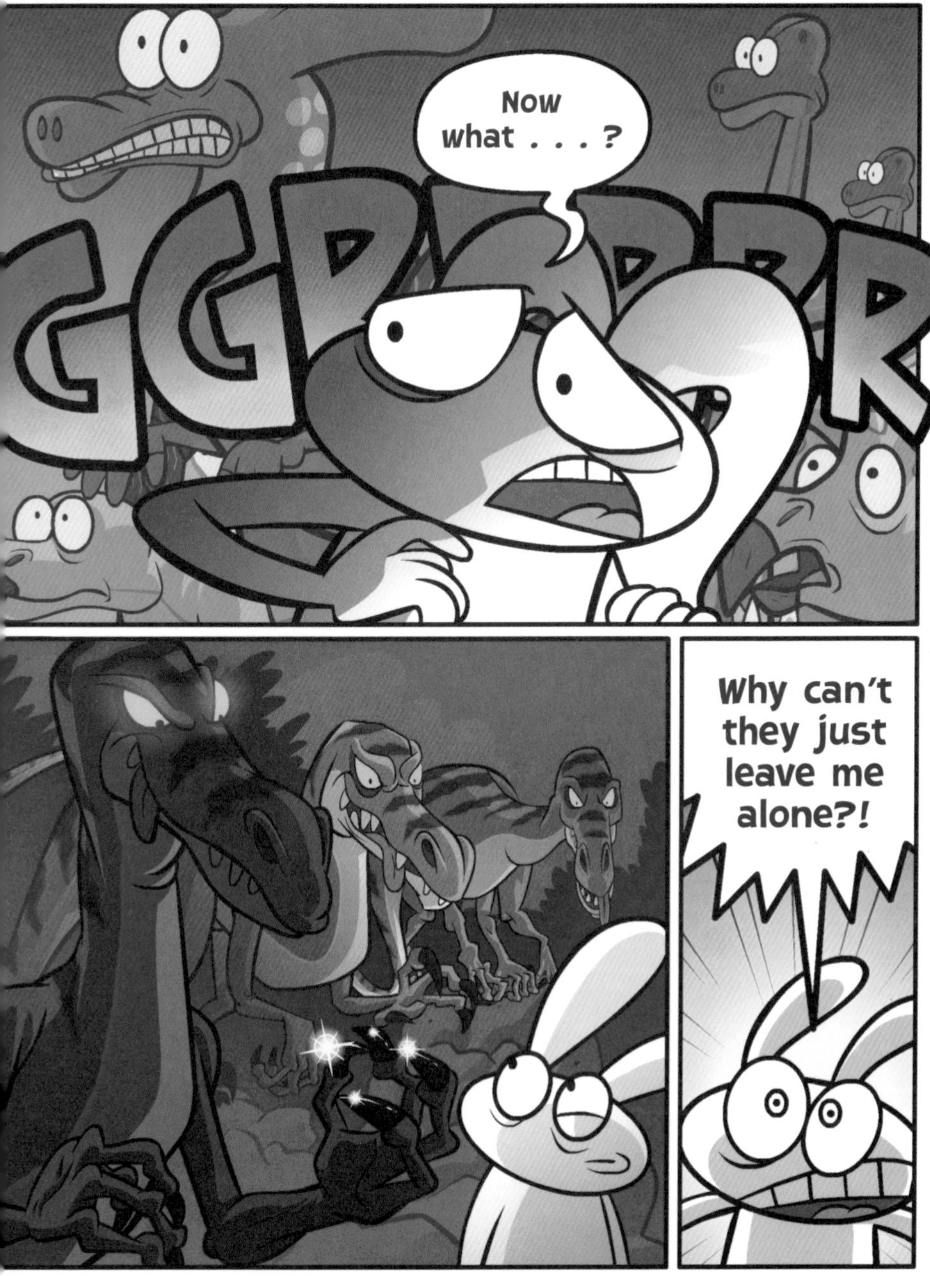
GGRRRR
Now what . . . ?
Why can't they just leave me alone?!

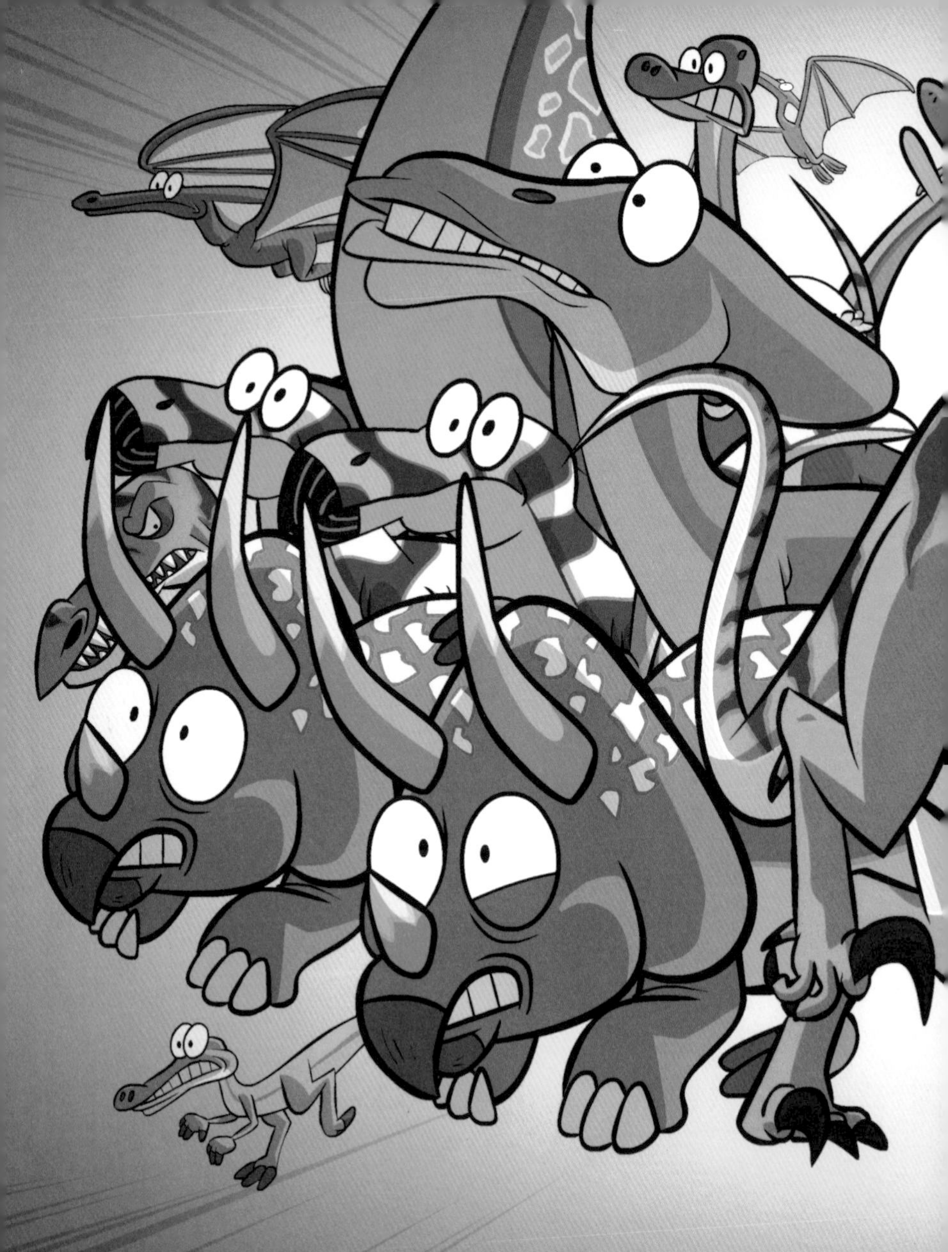

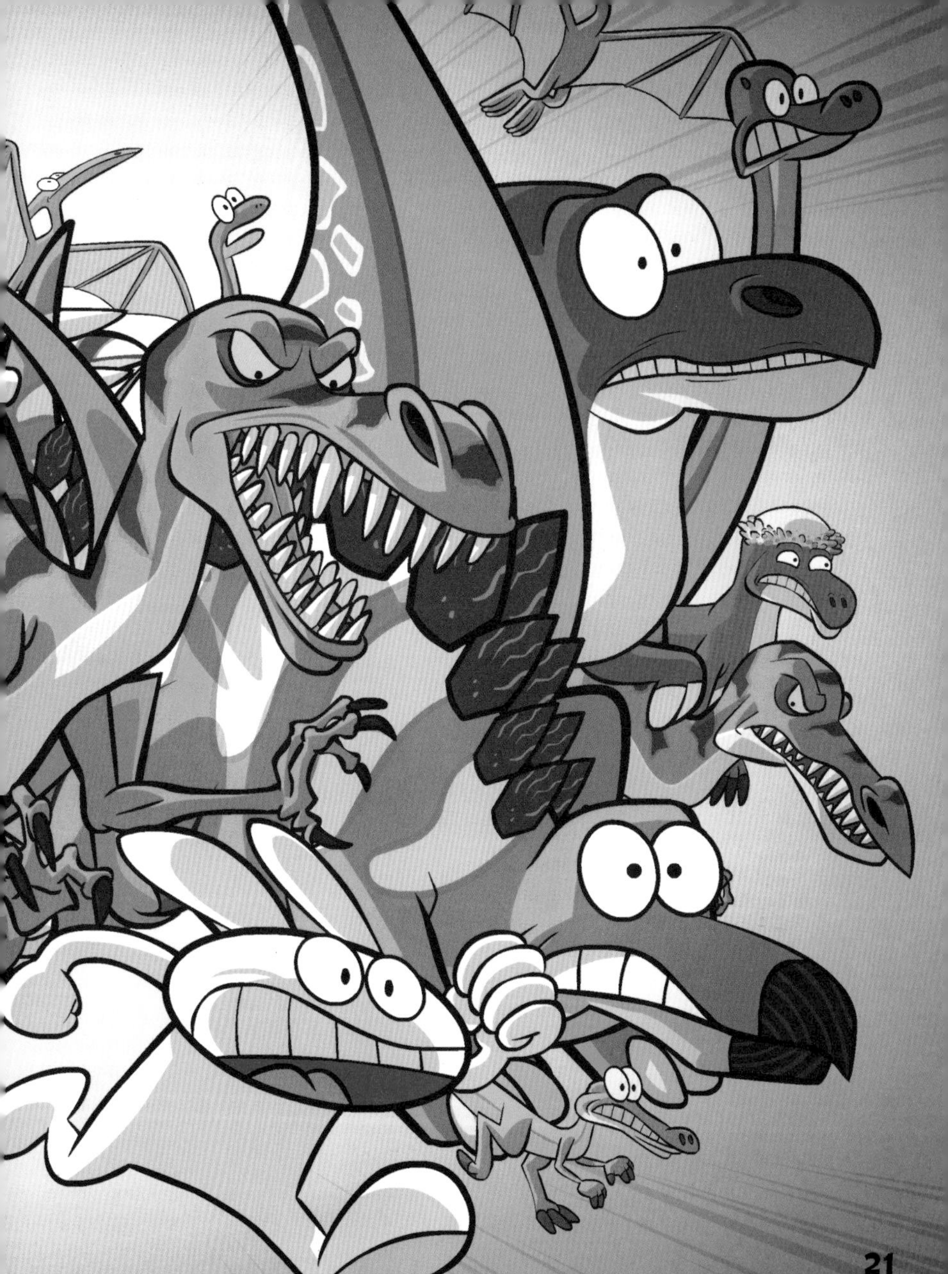

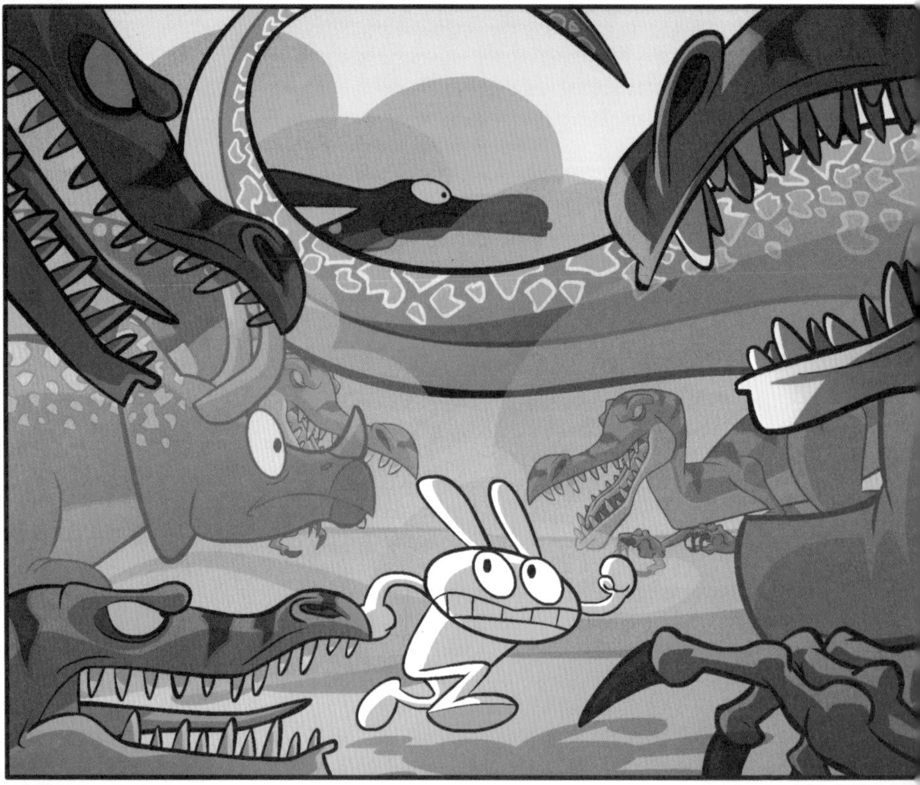

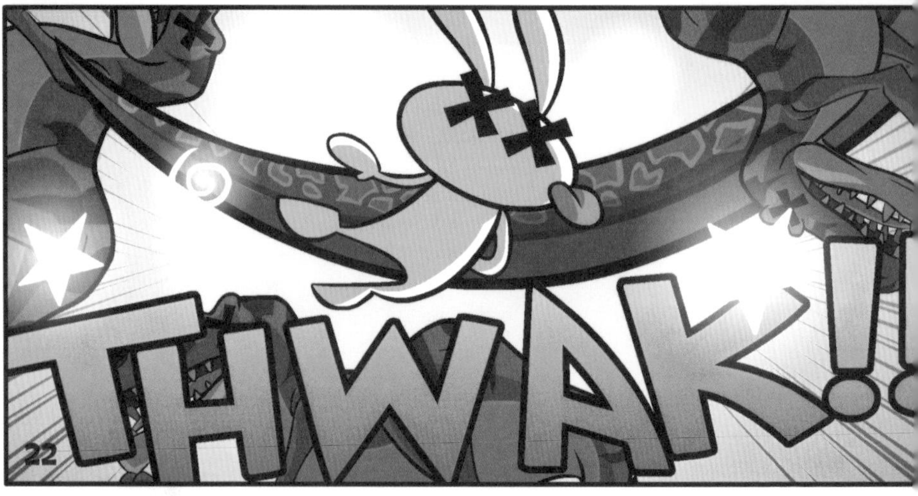
THWAK!!

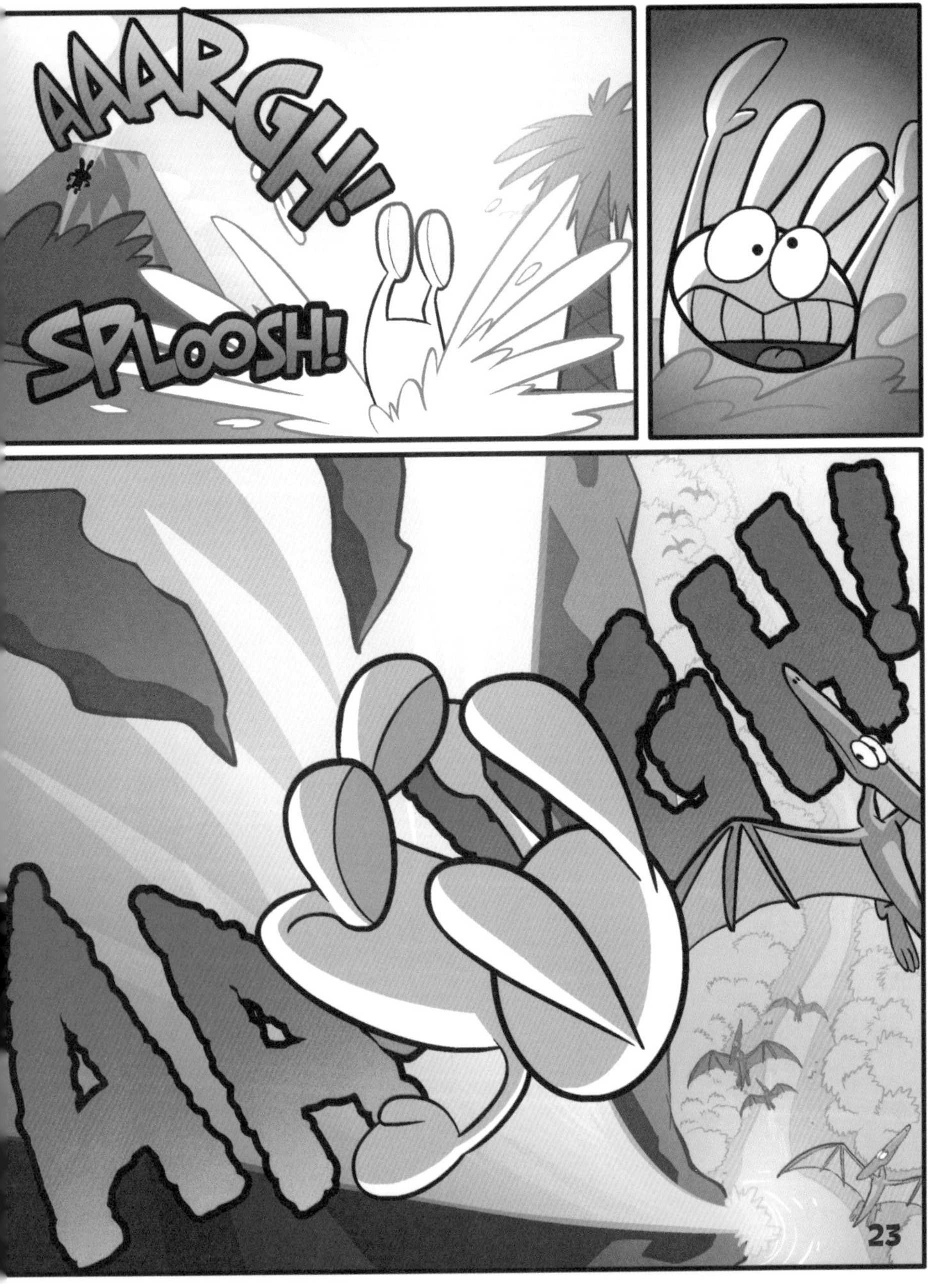
AAARGH!
SPLOOSH!
AAA
GH!

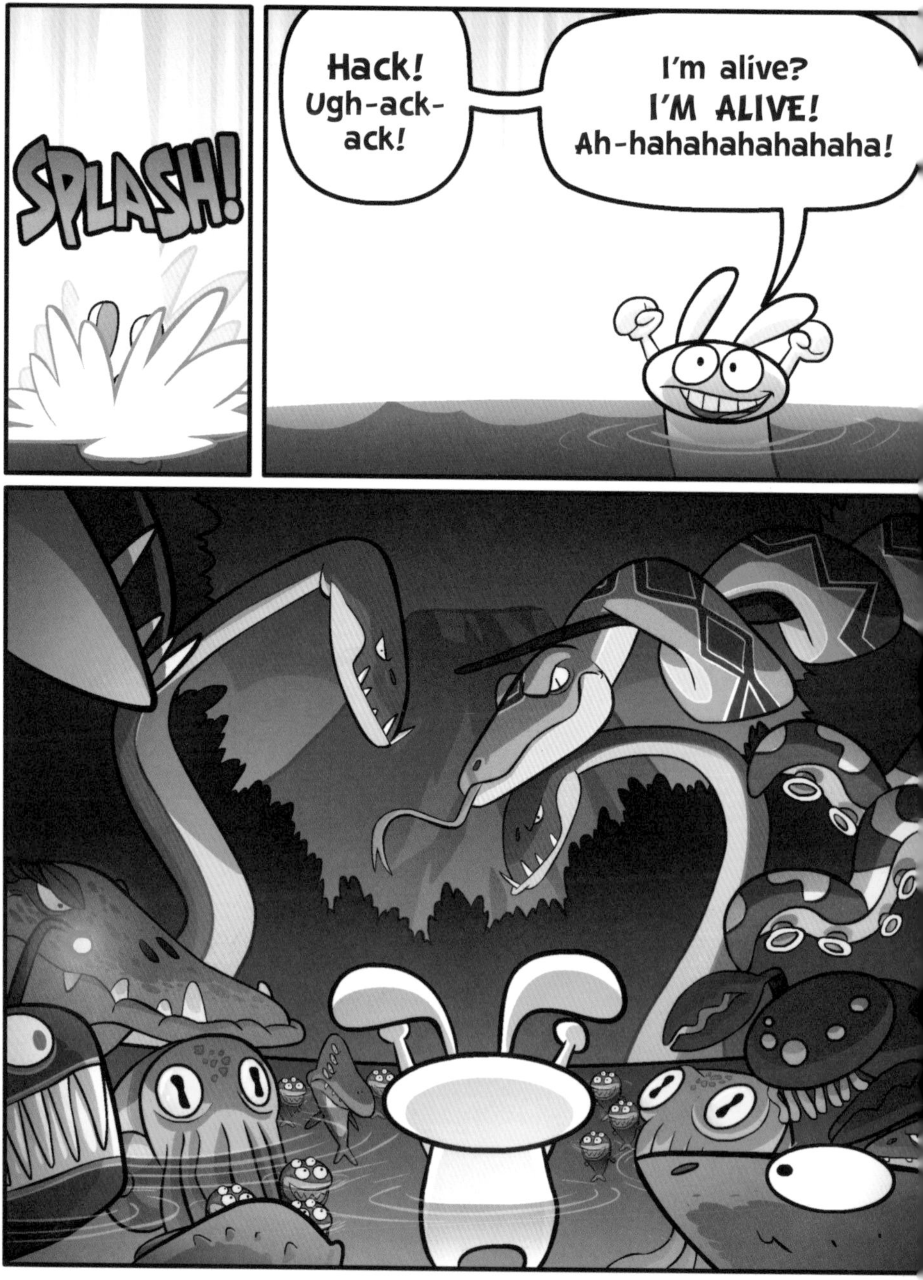
SPLASH!
Hack! Ugh-ack-ack!
I'm alive? I'M ALIVE! Ah-hahahahahahaha!

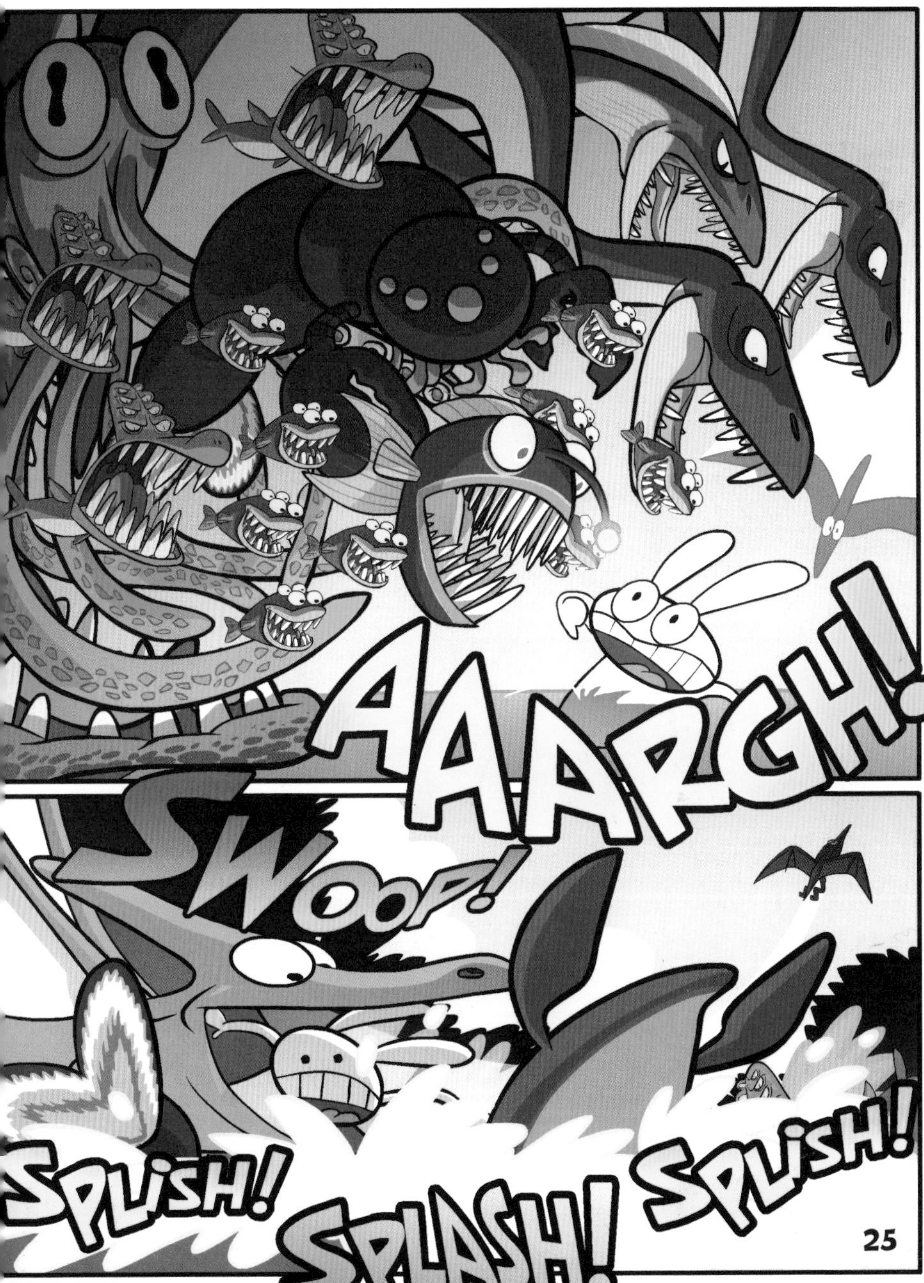
AAARGH!
SWOOP!
SPLISH!
SPLASH!
SPLISH!

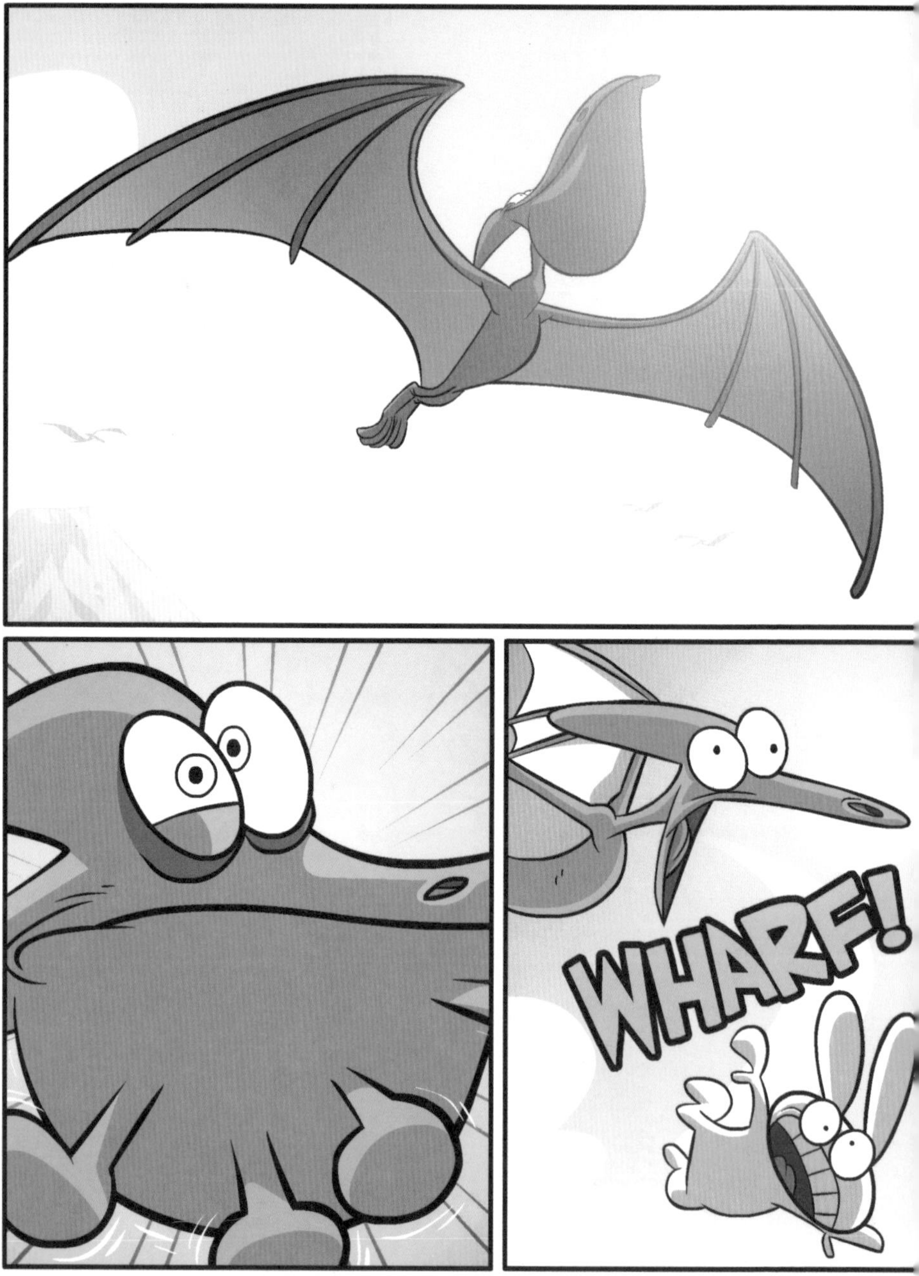
WHARF!

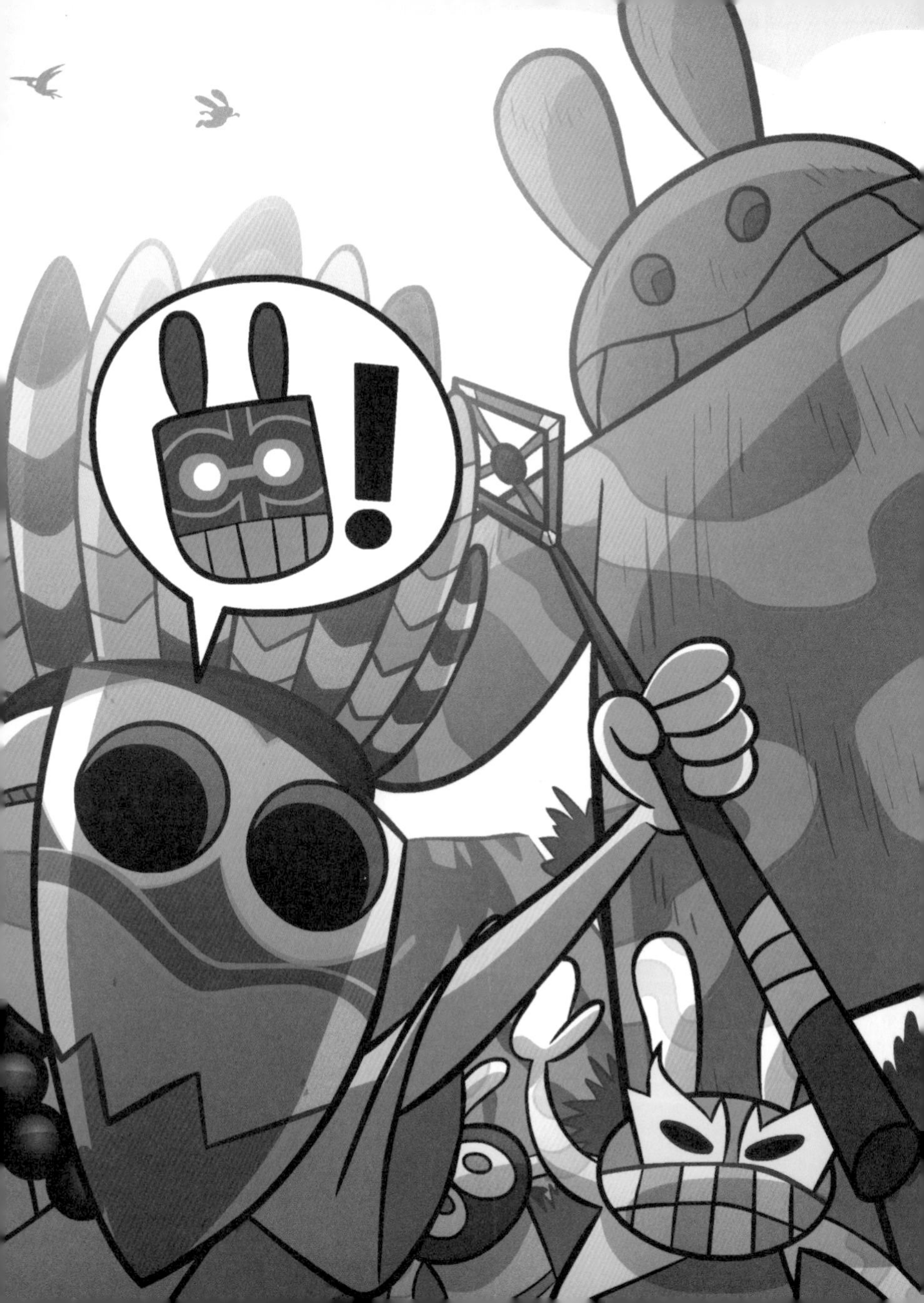
!

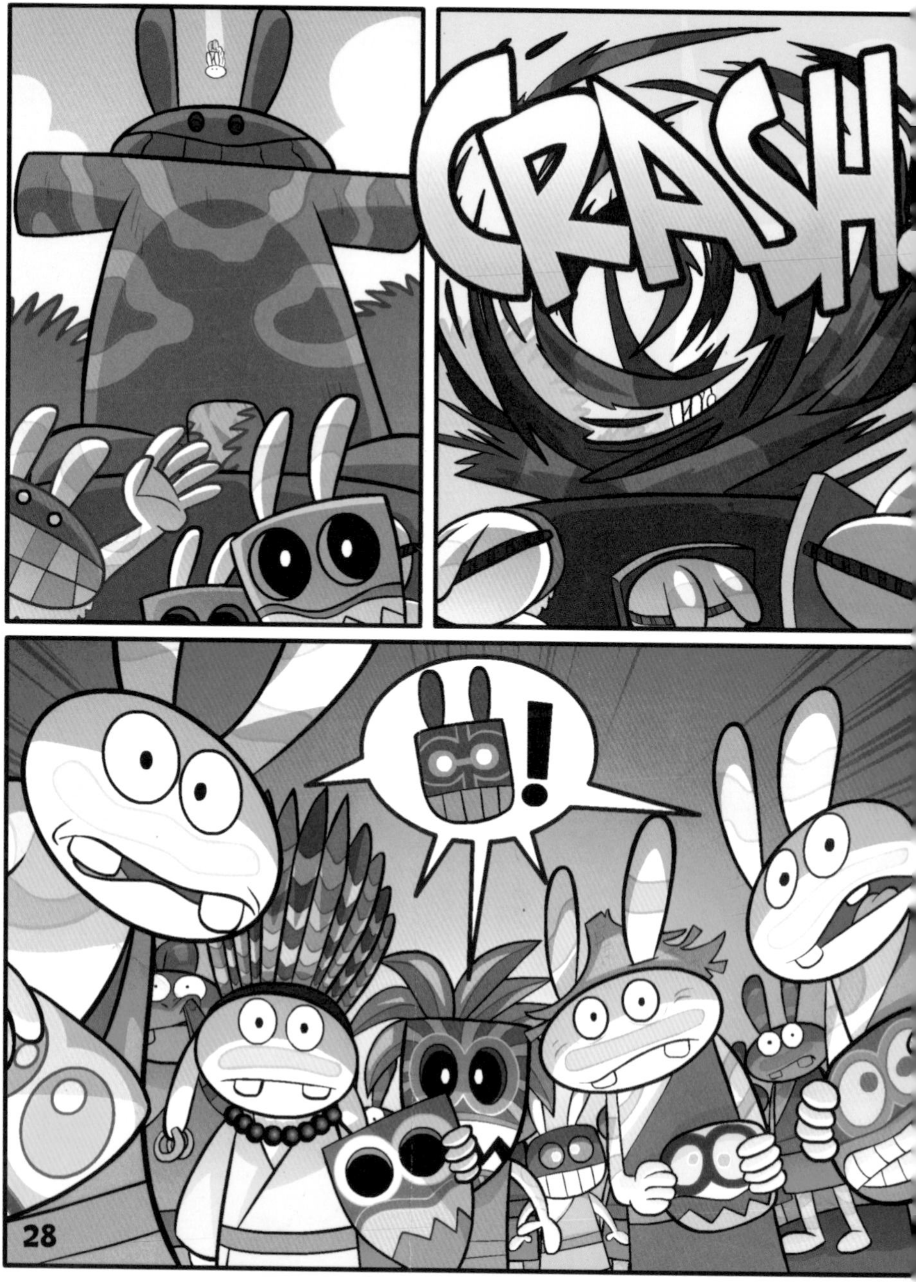
CRASH!
!

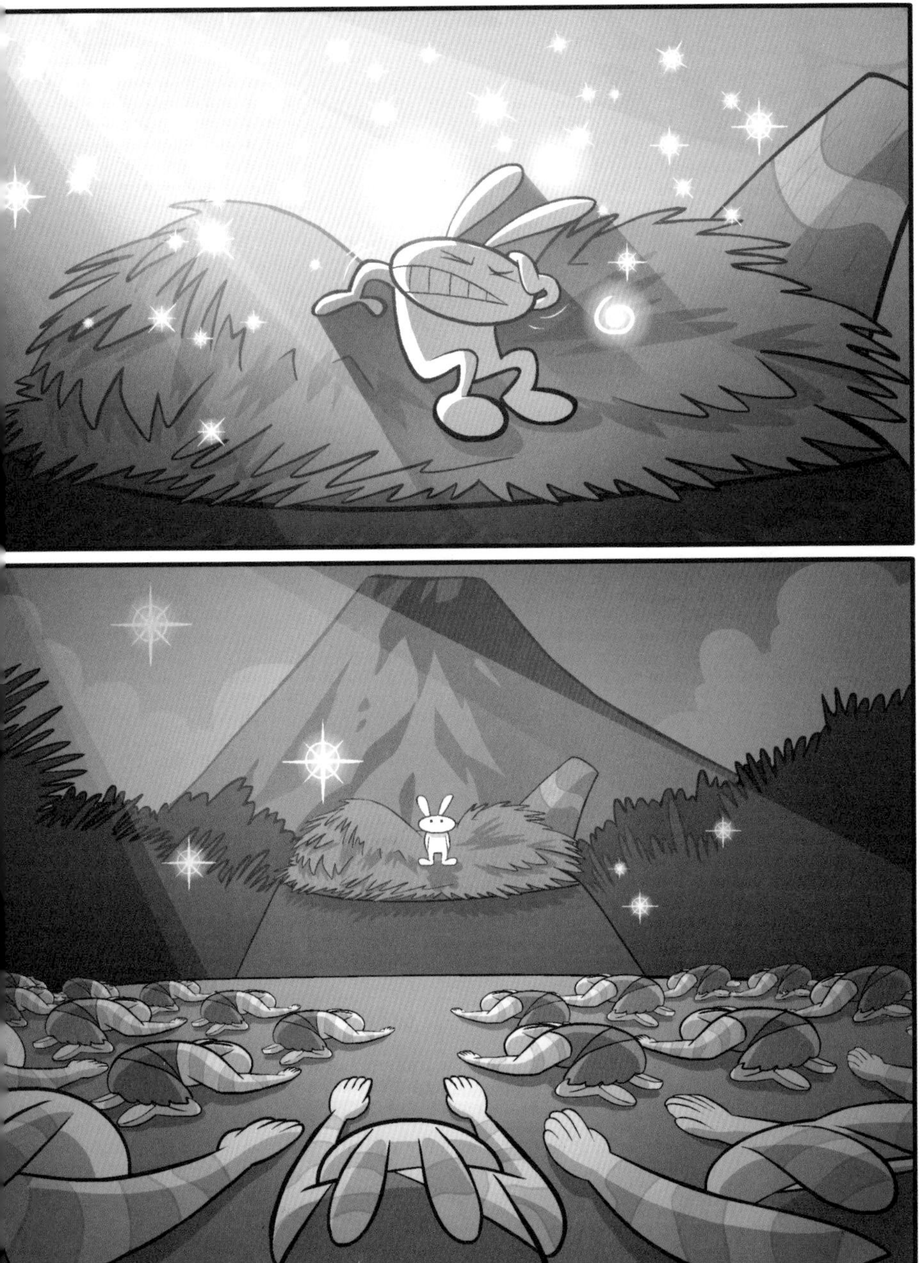

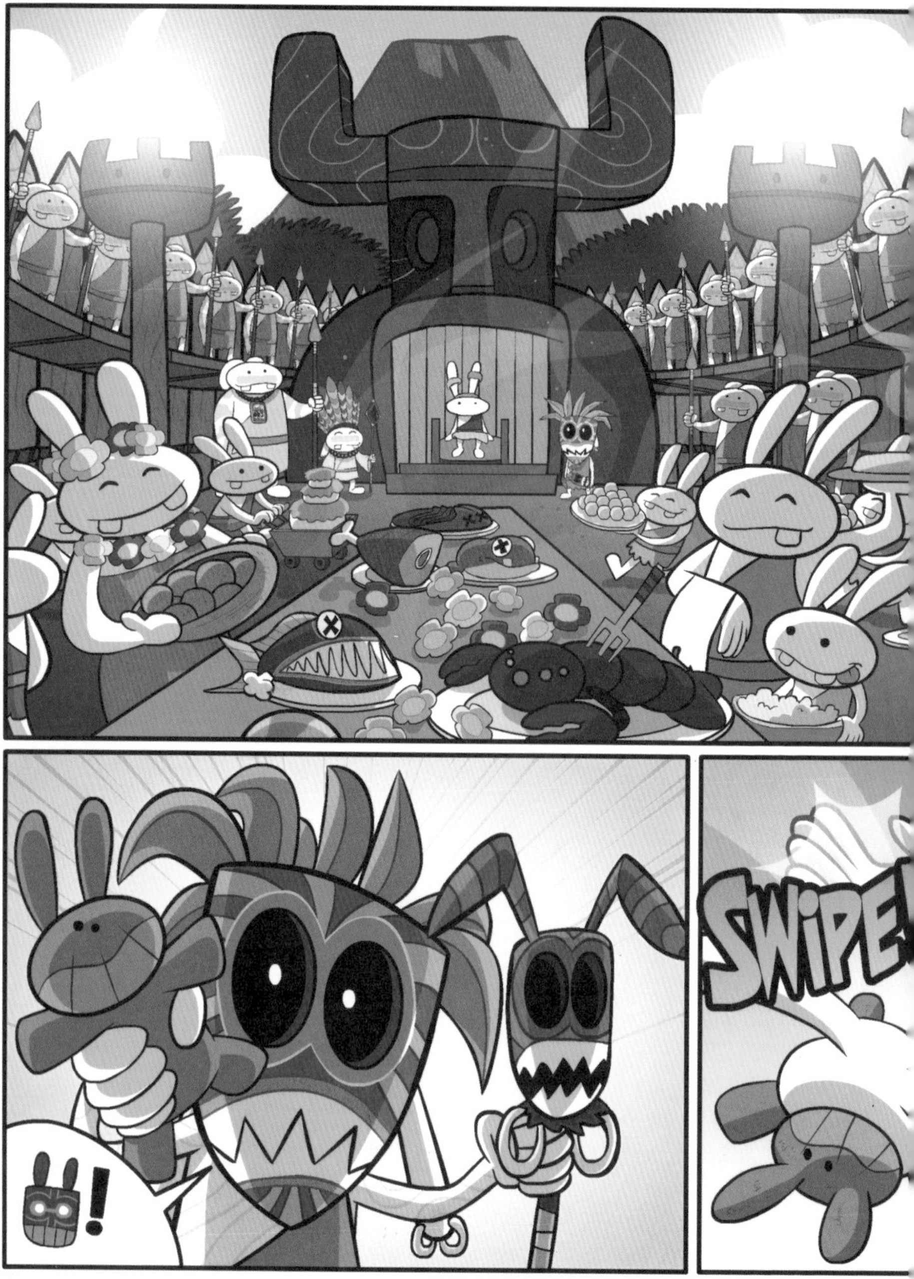
!
SWIPE

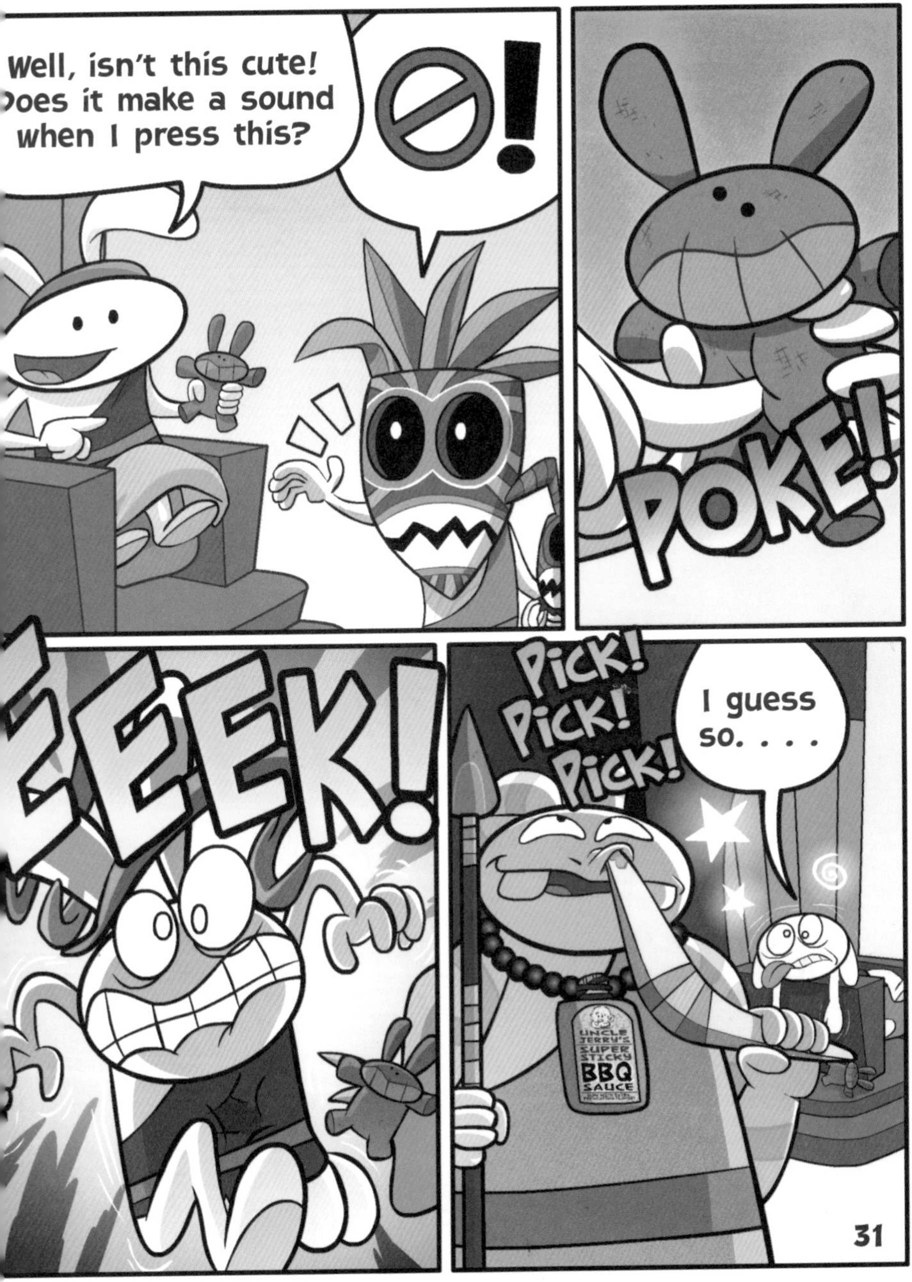

Well, isn't this cute!
Does it make a sound when I press this?
!
POKE!
EEK!
Pick! Pick! Pick!
I guess so. . . .
UNCLE JERRY'S SUPER STICKY BBQ SAUCE

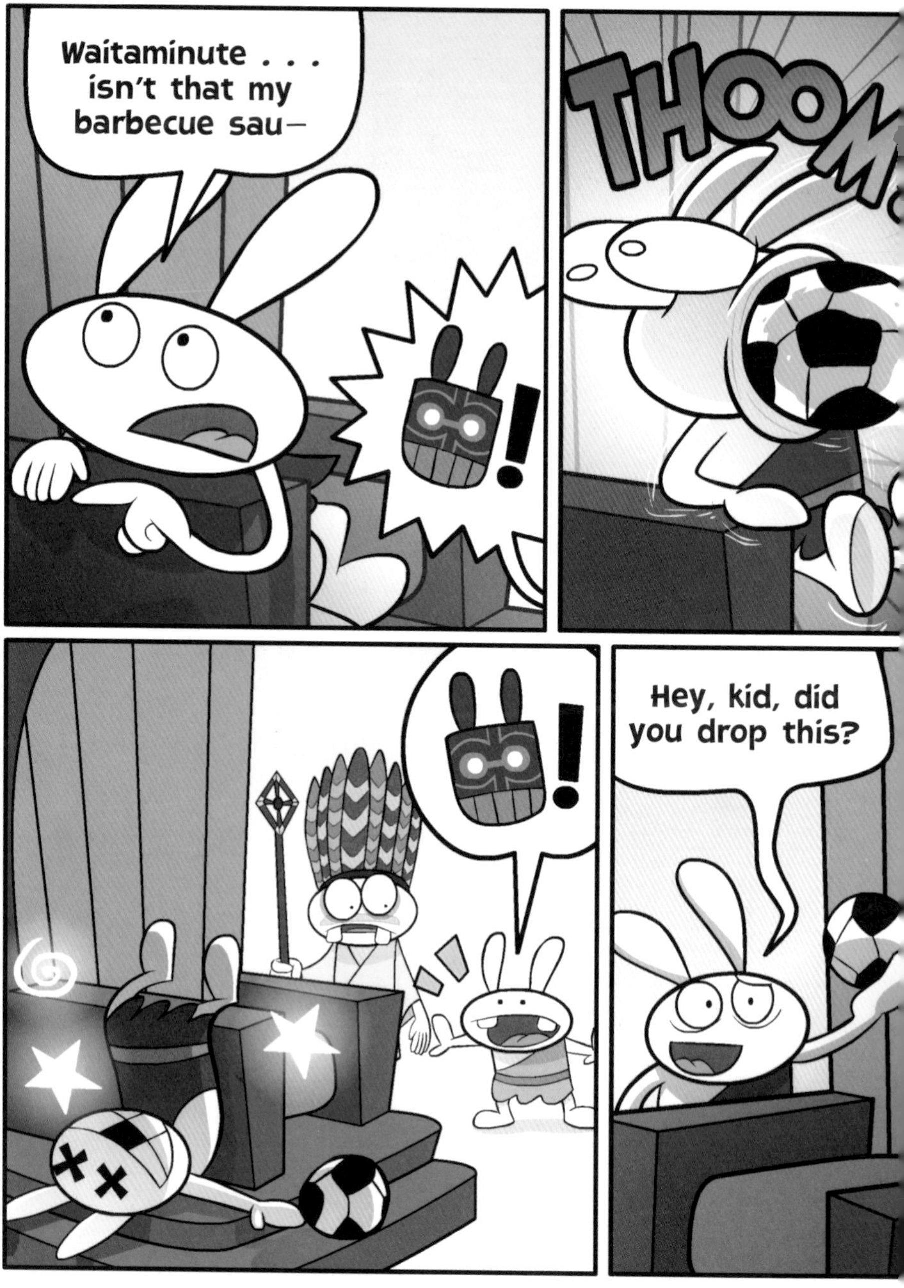
Waitaminute . . . isn't that my barbecue sau—
!
THOOM
!
Hey, kid, did you drop this?

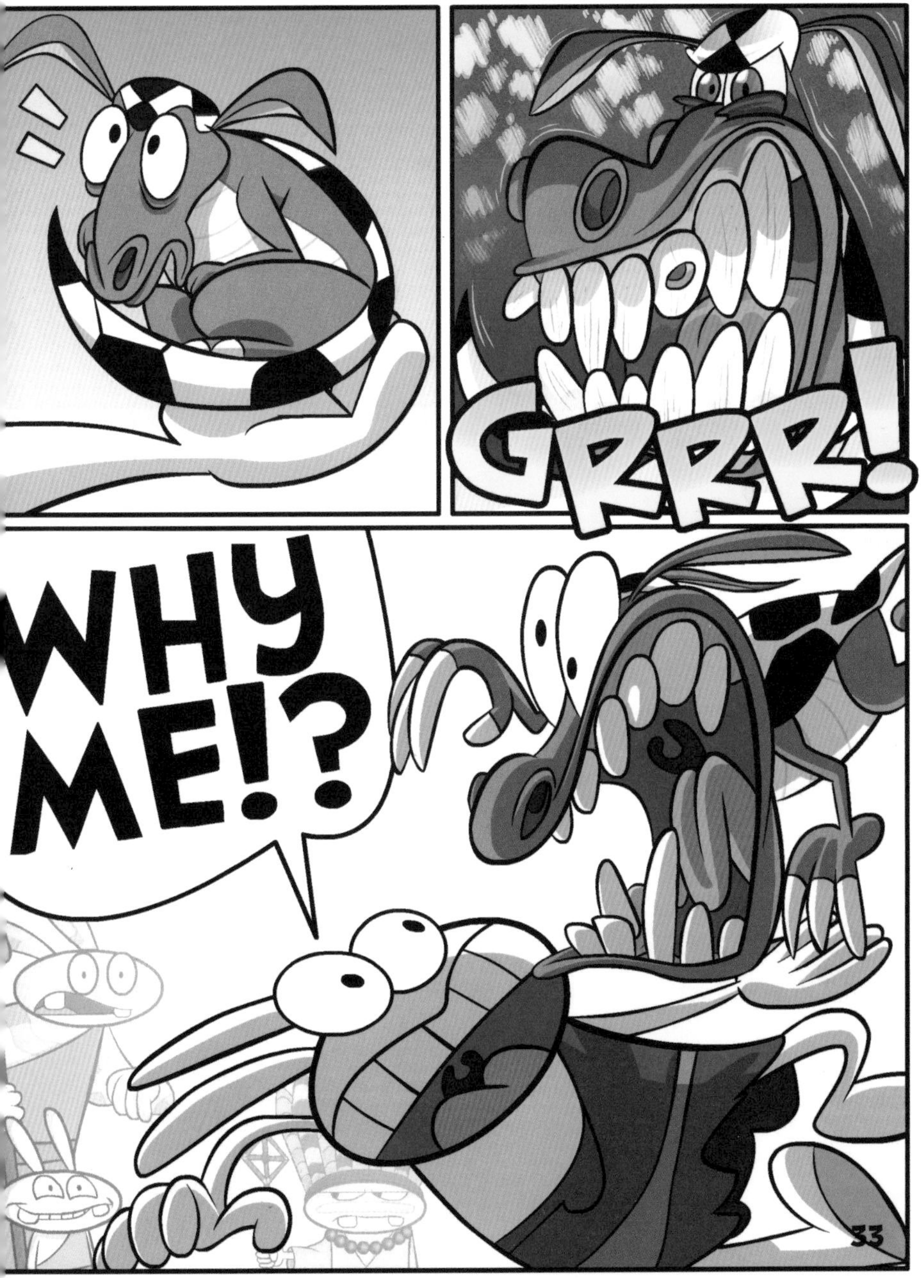
!
GRRR!
WHY ME!?

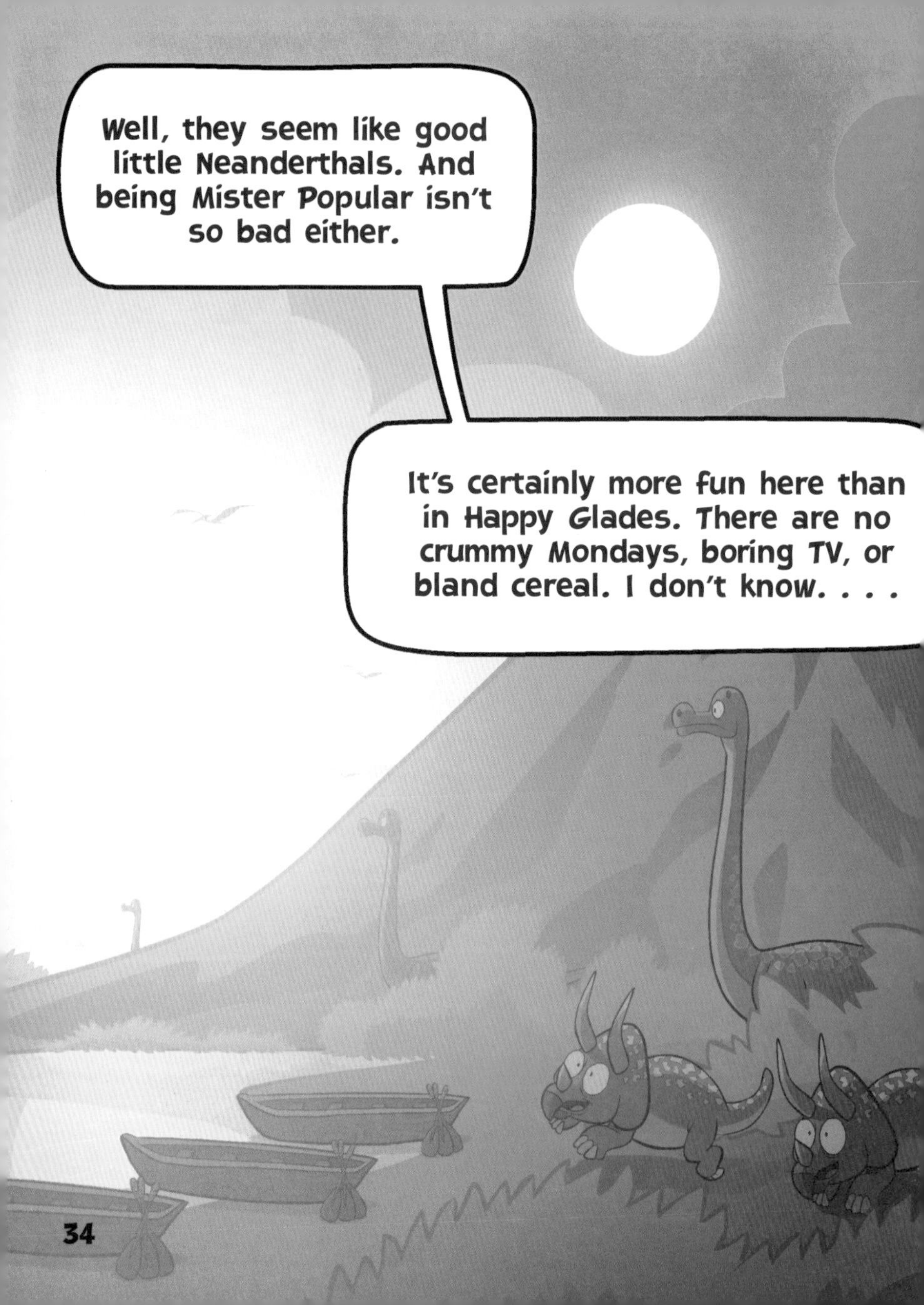
Well, they seem like good little Neanderthals. And being Mister Popular isn't so bad either.
It's certainly more fun here than in Happy Glades. There are no crummy Mondays, boring TV, or bland cereal. I don't know. . . .

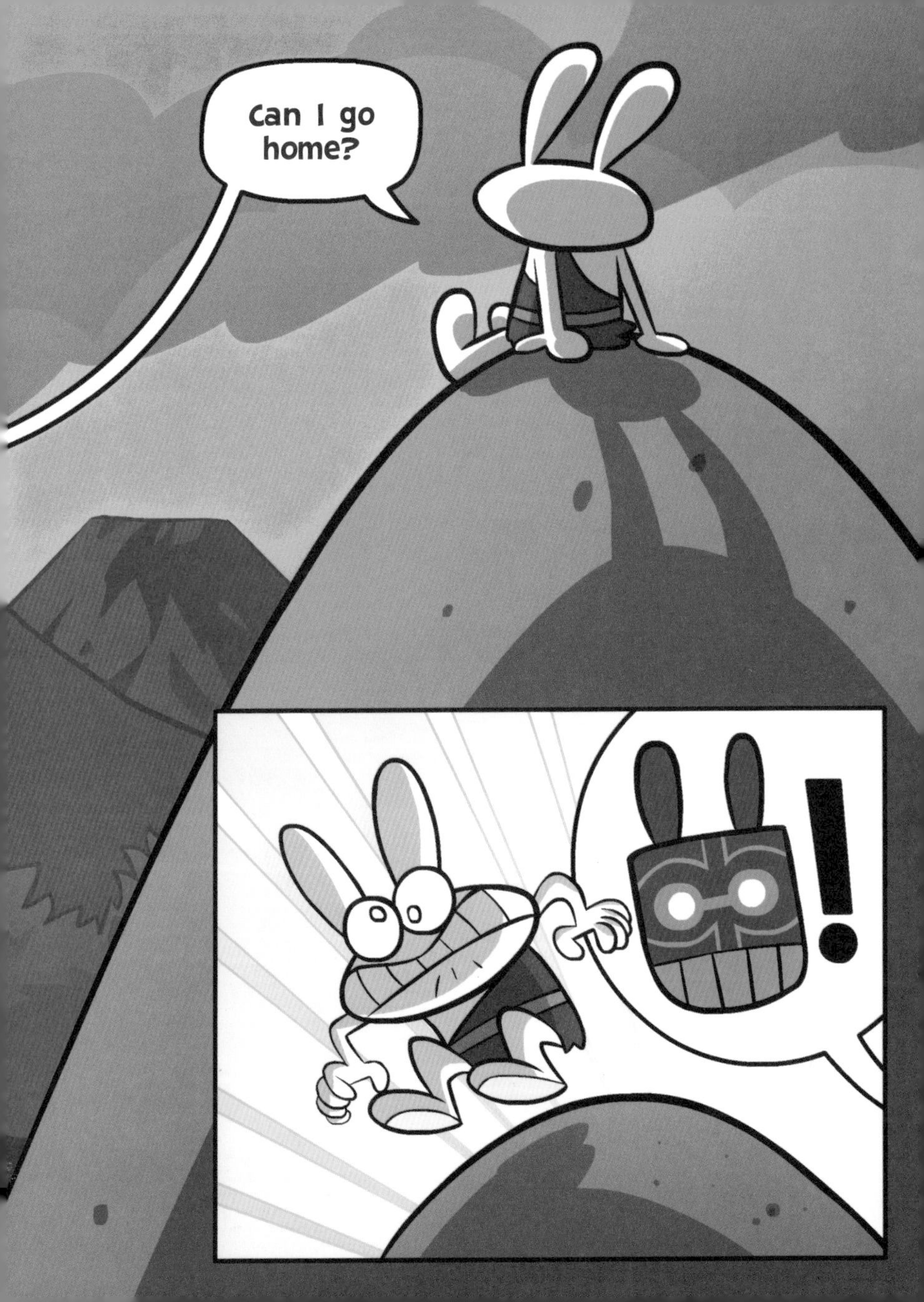
Can I go home?
!

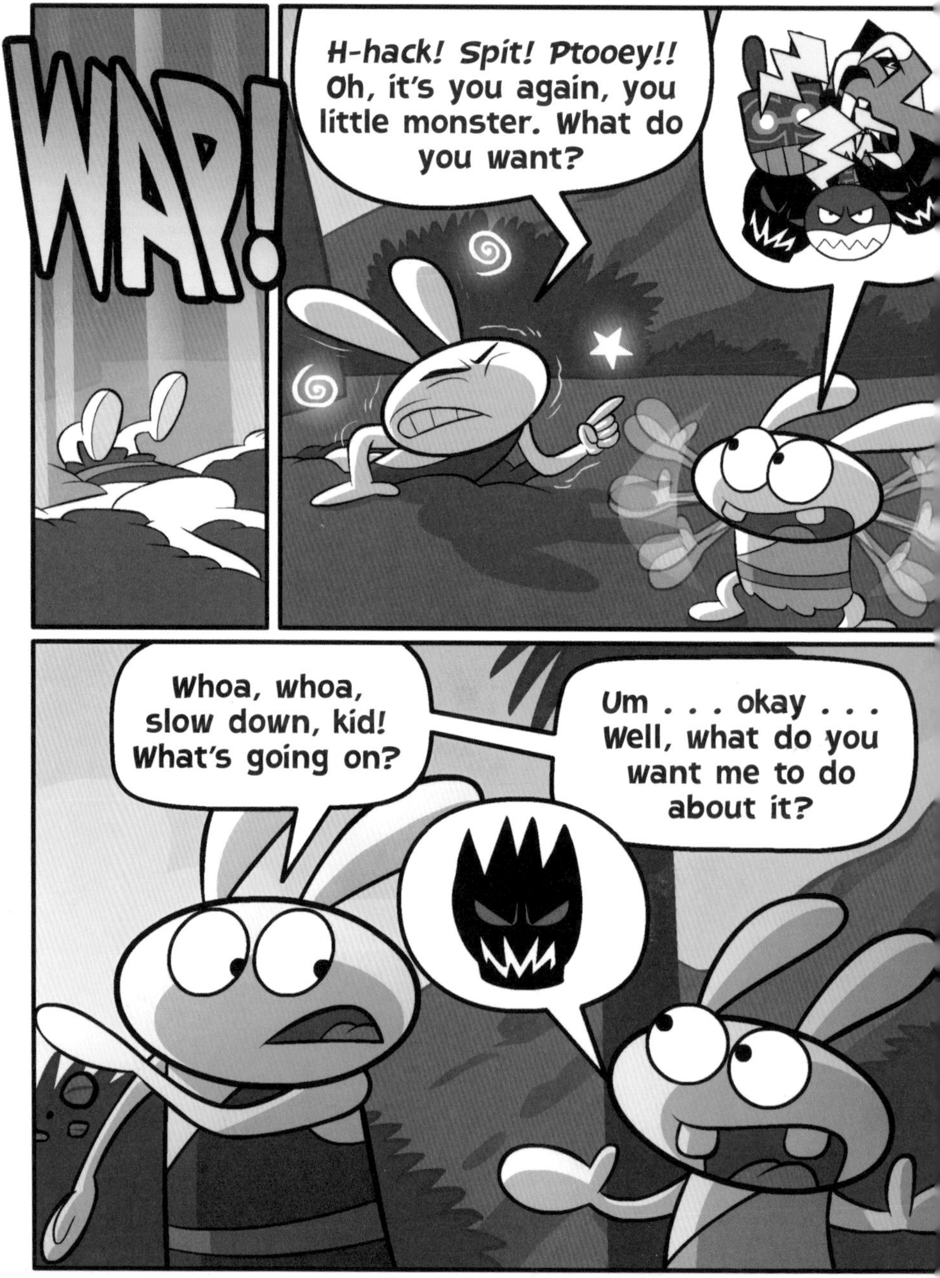
WAP!
H-hack! Spit! Ptooey!! Oh, it's you again, you little monster. What do you want?
Whoa, whoa, slow down, kid! What's going on?
Um . . . okay . . . Well, what do you want me to do about it?

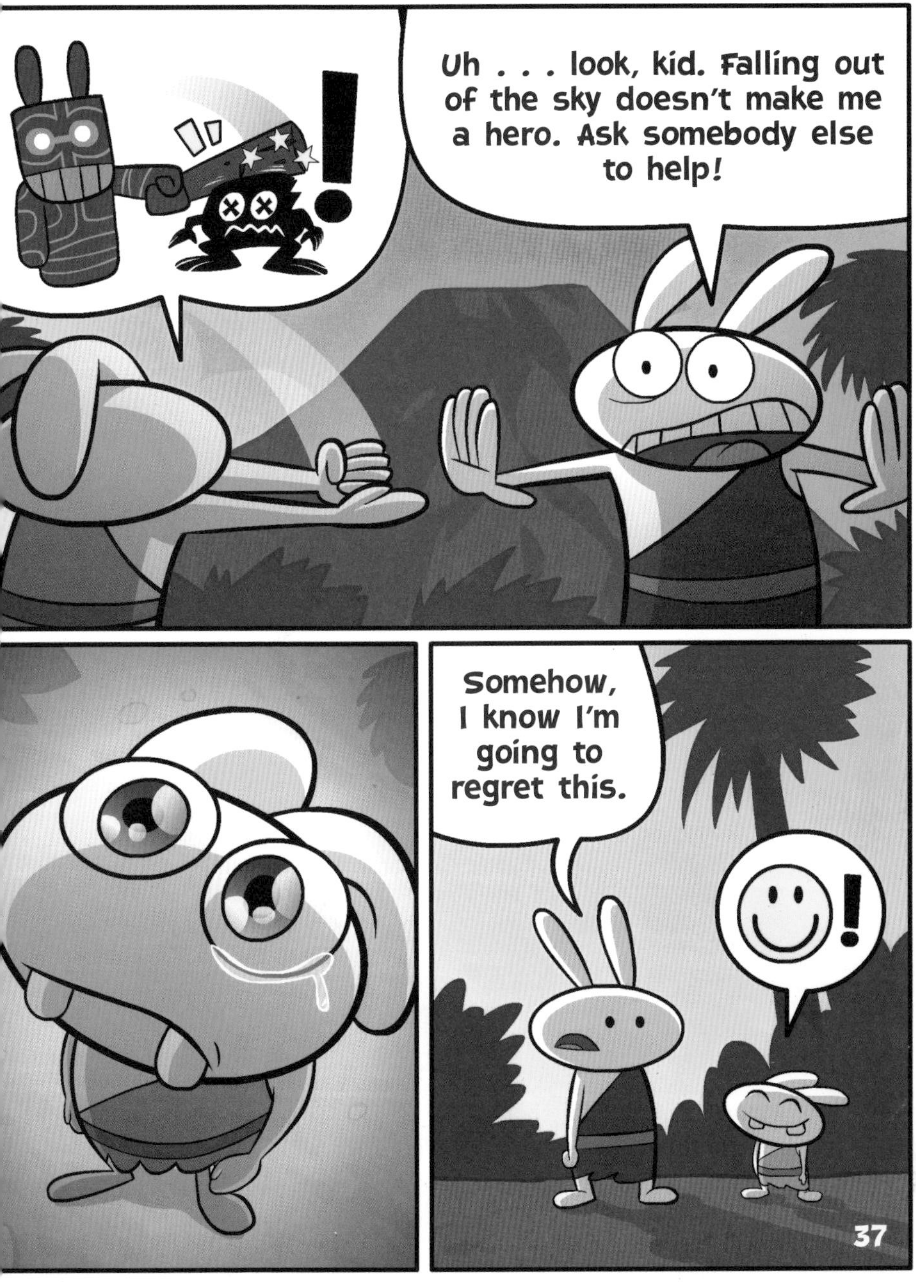
Uh . . . look, kid. Falling out of the sky doesn't make me a hero. Ask somebody else to help!
Somehow, I know I'm going to regret this.

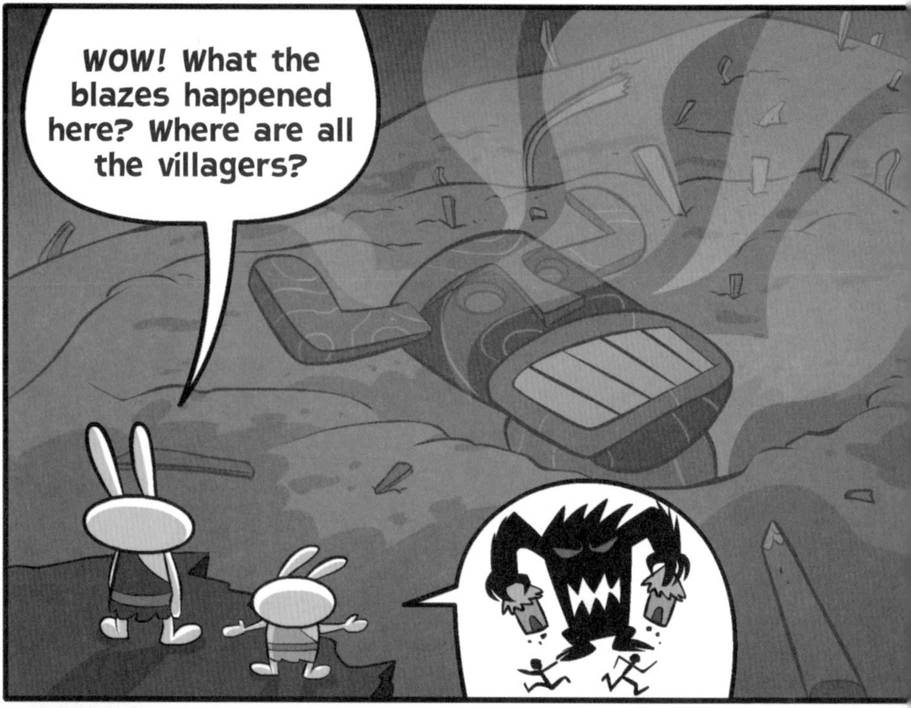
WOW! What the blazes happened here? Where are all the villagers?

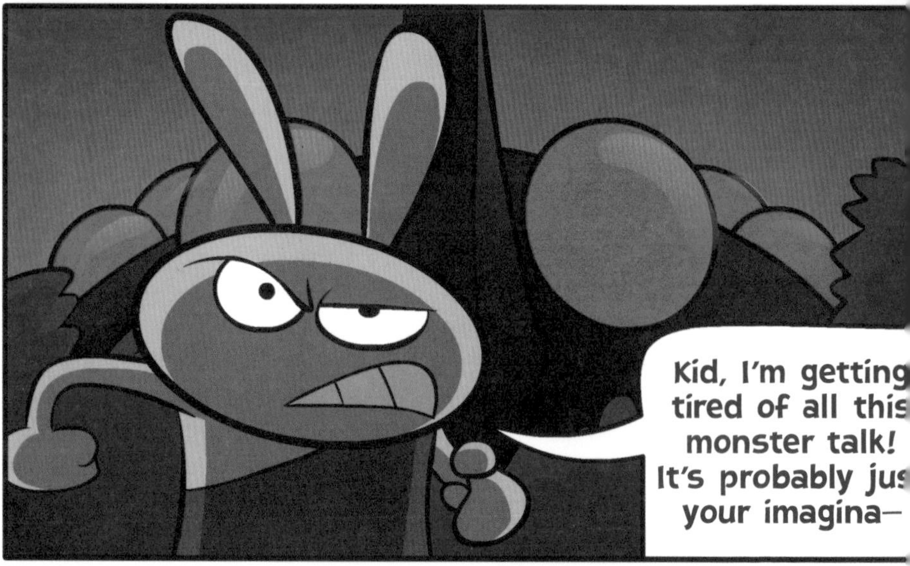
Kid, I'm getting tired of all this monster talk! It's probably jus your imagina—

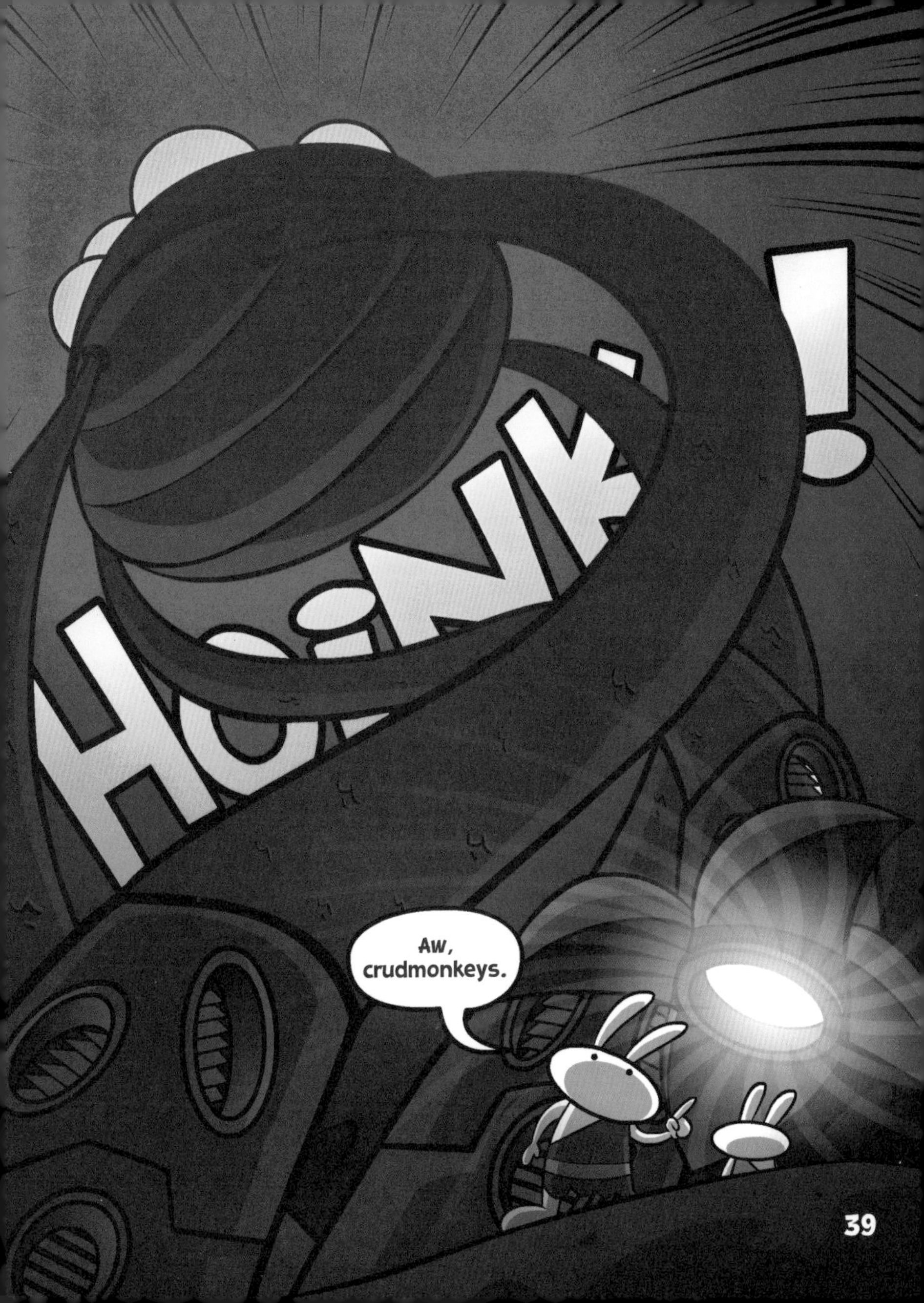
HONK!
Aw, crudmonkeys.

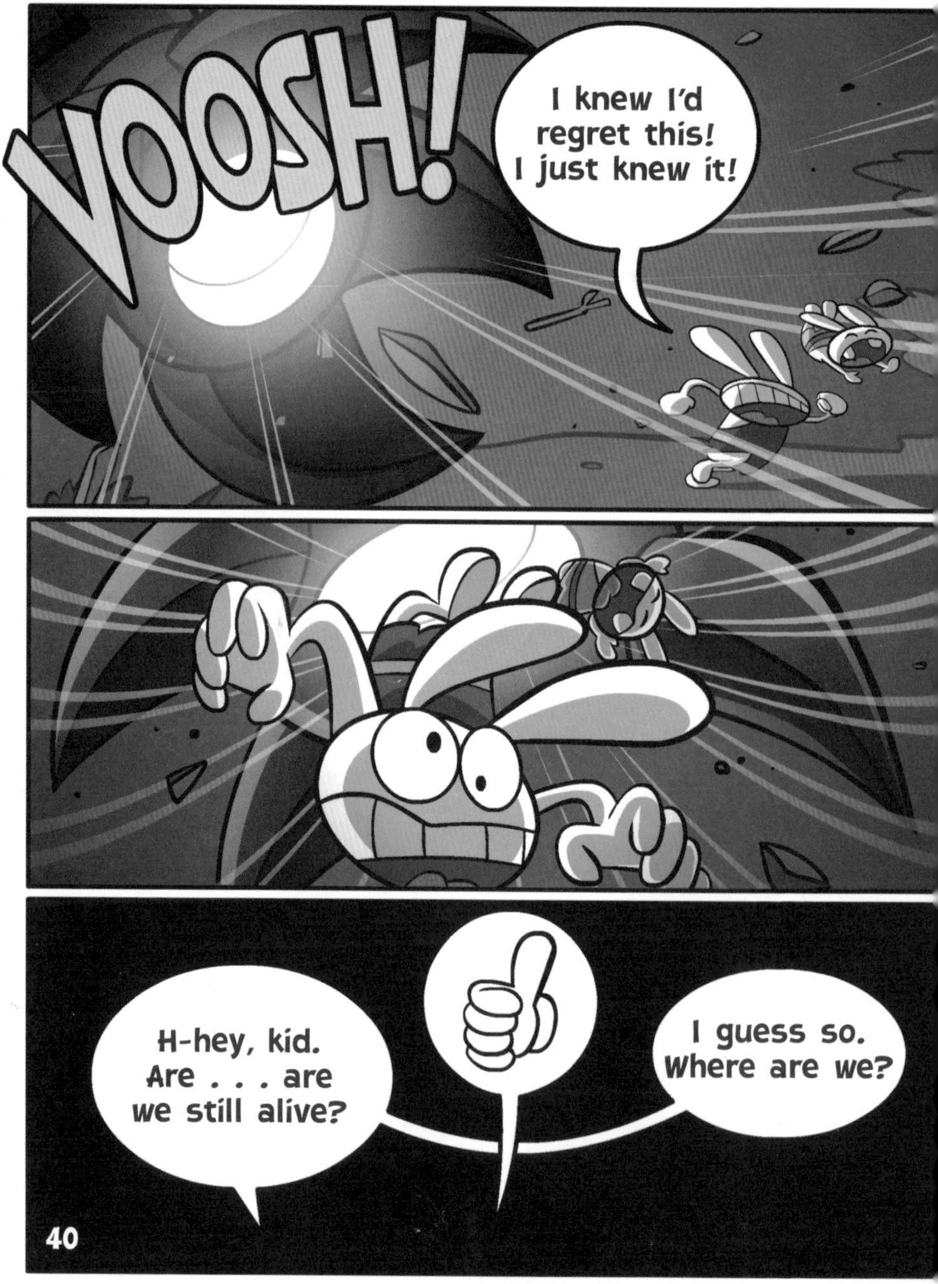
VOOSH!
I knew I'd regret this! I just knew it!
H-hey, kid. Are . . . are we still alive?
I guess so. Where are we?

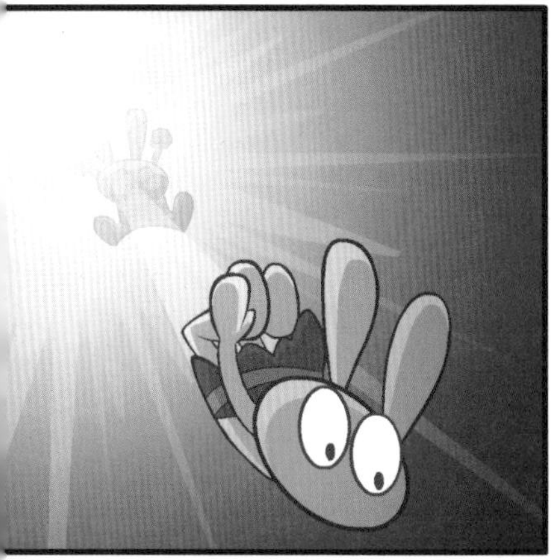

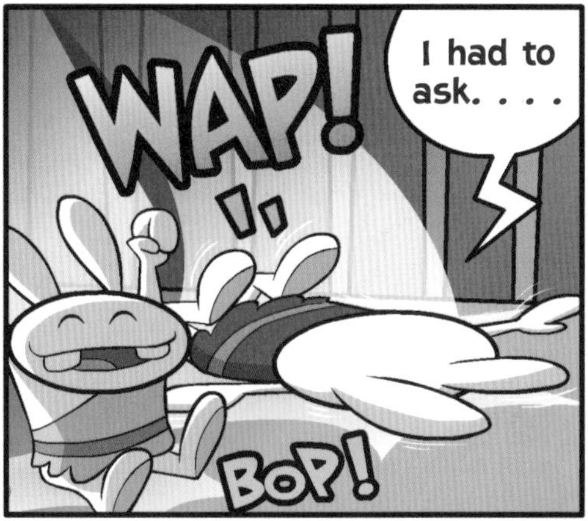
WAP!
I had to ask. . . .
BOP!

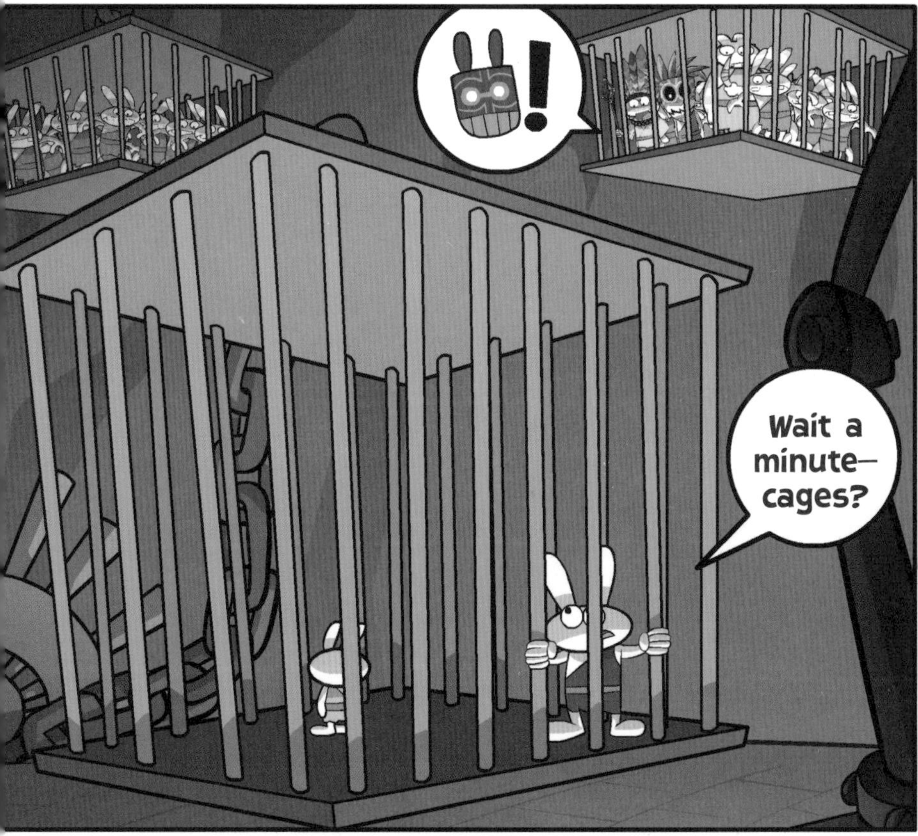
!
Wait a minute—cages?

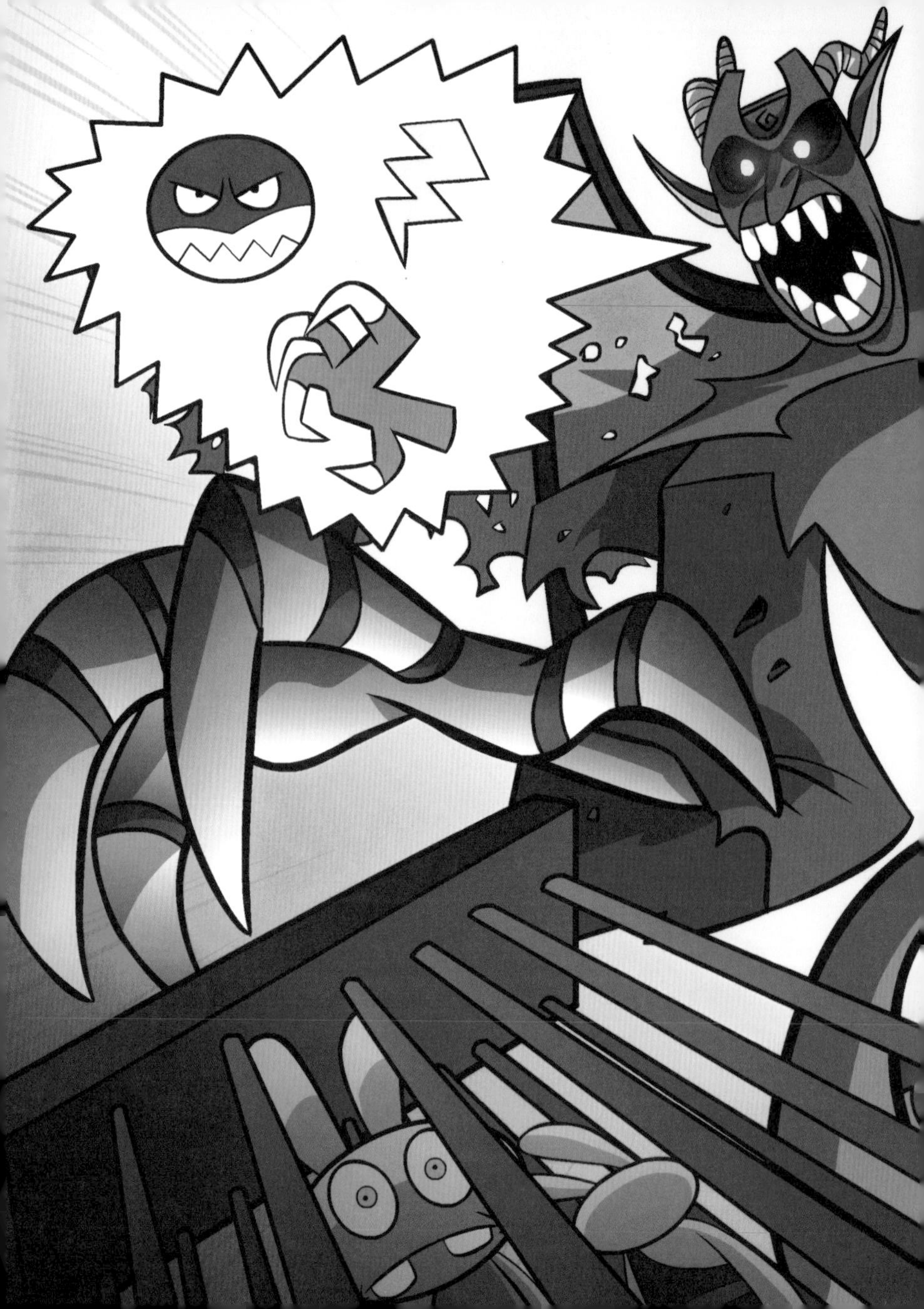

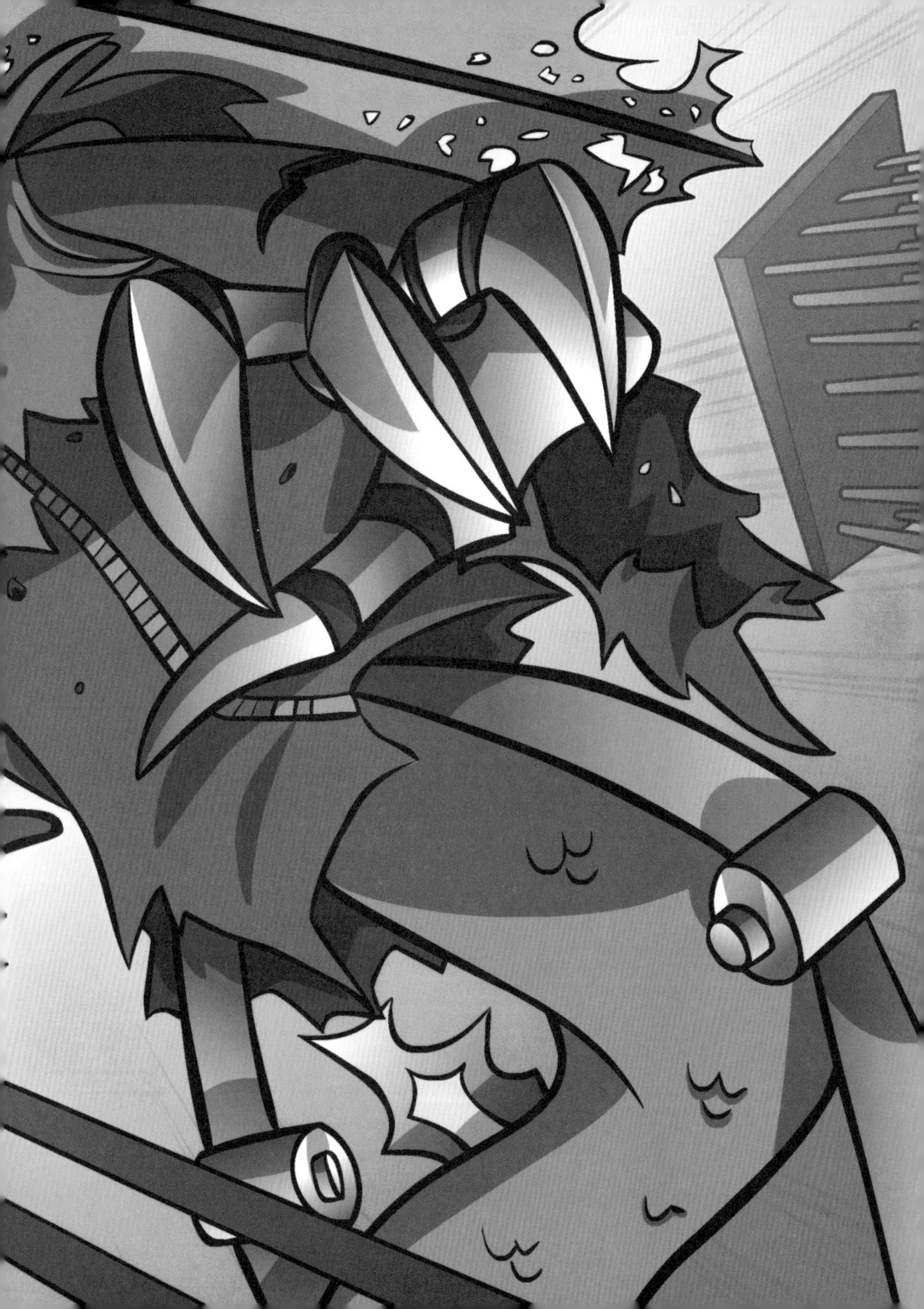

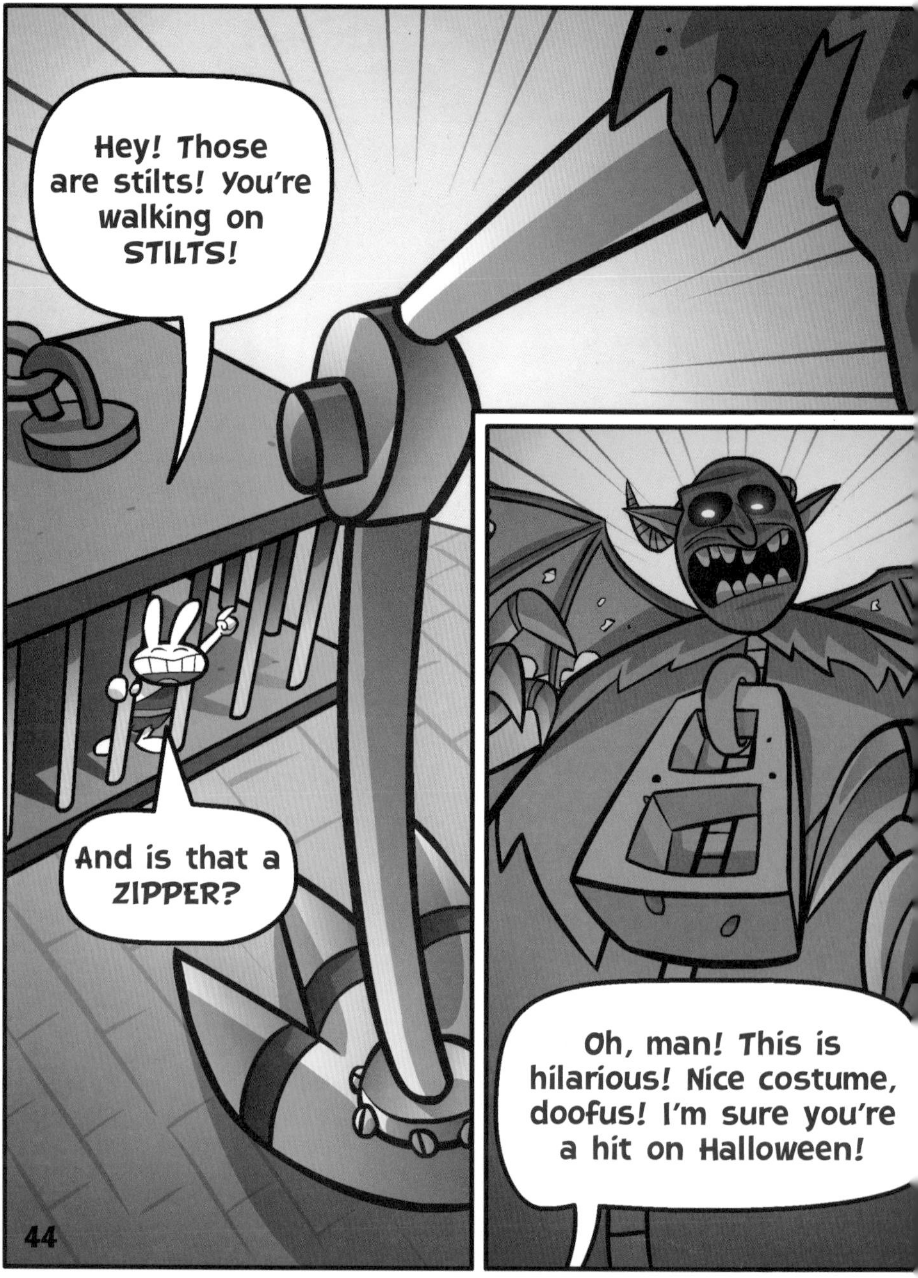
Hey! Those are stilts! You're walking on STILTS!
And is that a ZIPPER?
Oh, man! This is hilarious! Nice costume, doofus! I'm sure you're a hit on Halloween!

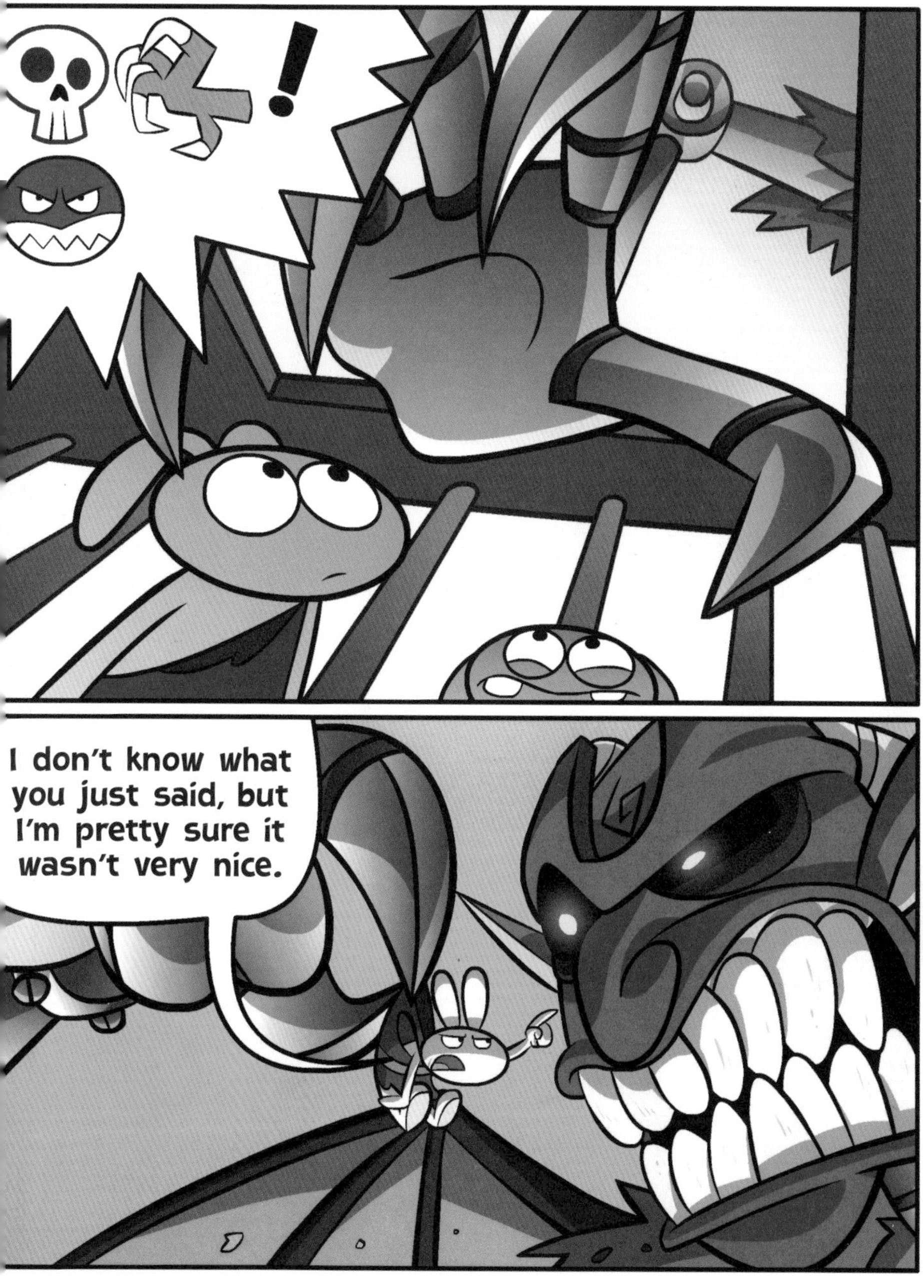
I don't know what you just said, but I'm pretty sure it wasn't very nice.

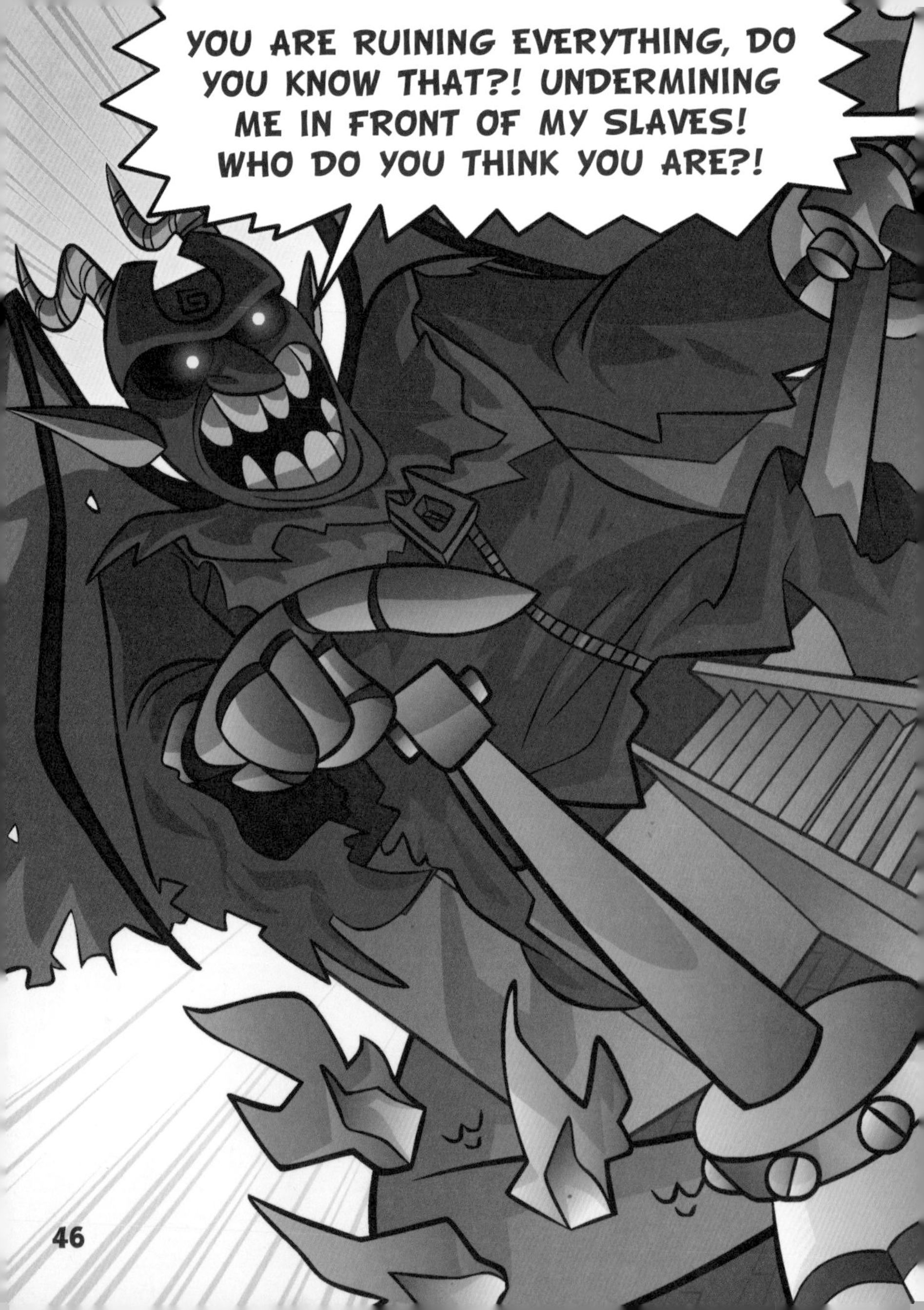
YOU ARE RUINING EVERYTHING, DO YOU KNOW THAT?! UNDERMINING ME IN FRONT OF MY SLAVES! WHO DO YOU THINK YOU ARE?!

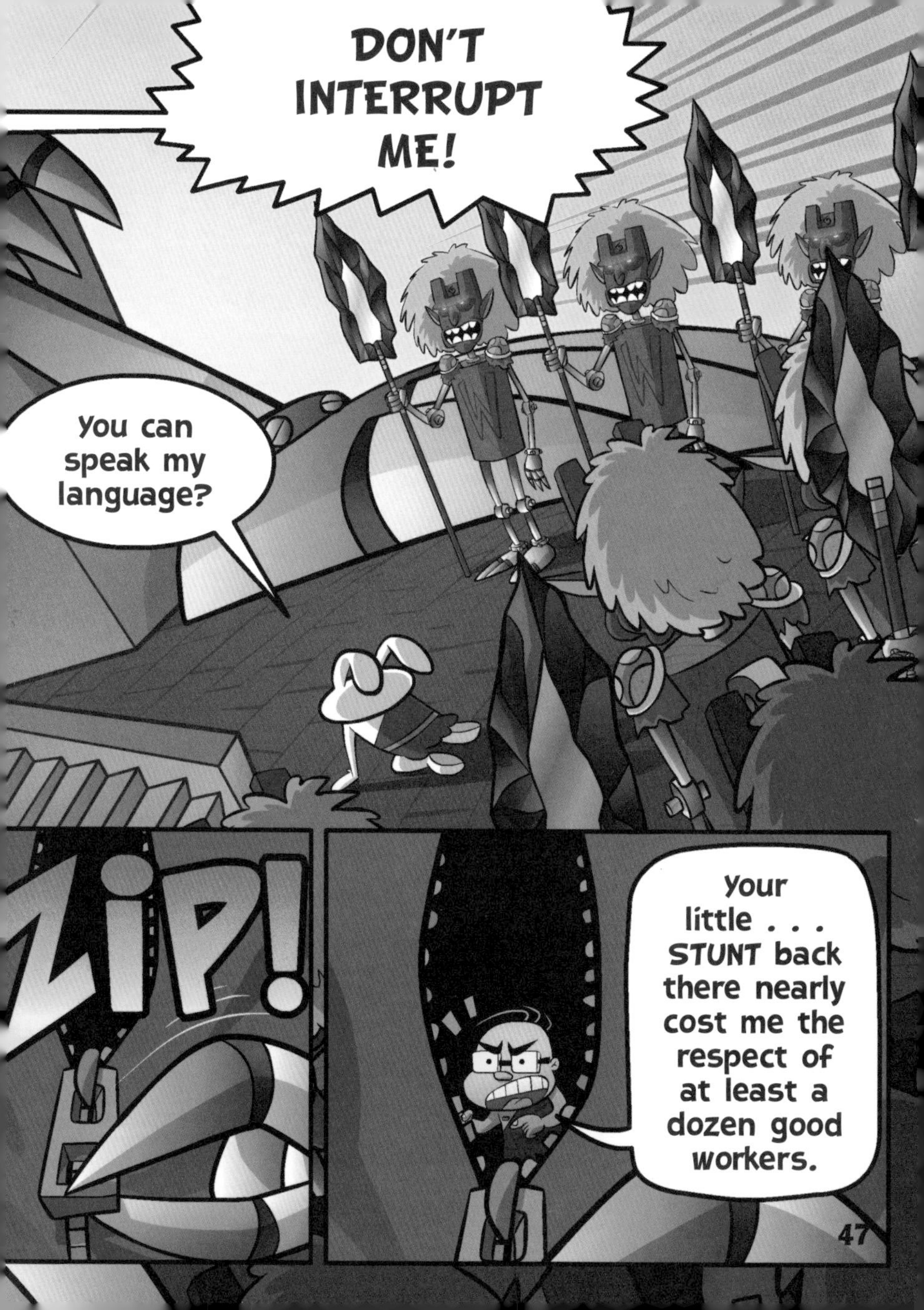
DON'T INTERRUPT ME!
You can speak my language?
ZIP!
Your little . . . STUNT back there nearly cost me the respect of at least a dozen good workers.

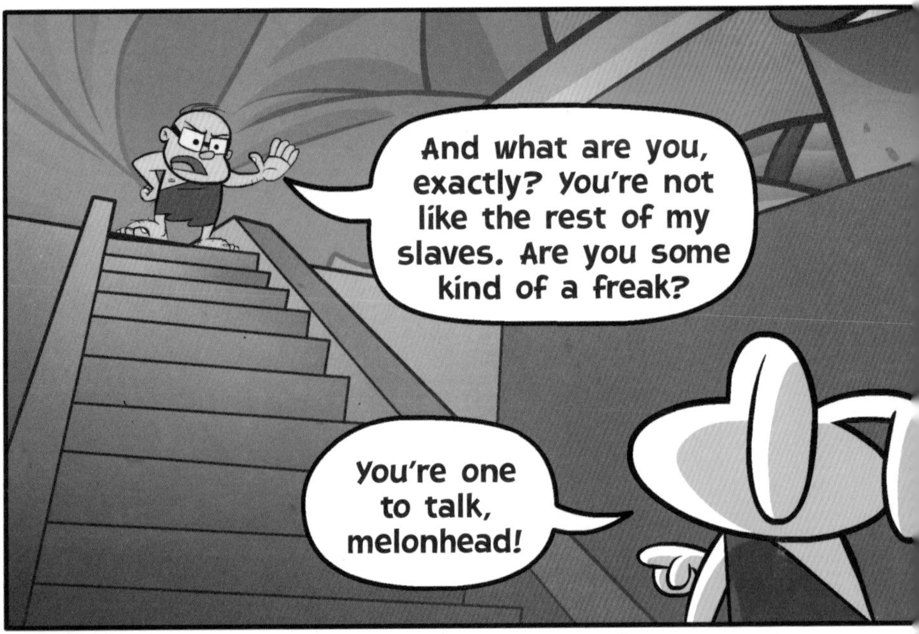
And what are you, exactly? You're not like the rest of my slaves. Are you some kind of a freak?
You're one to talk, melonhead!
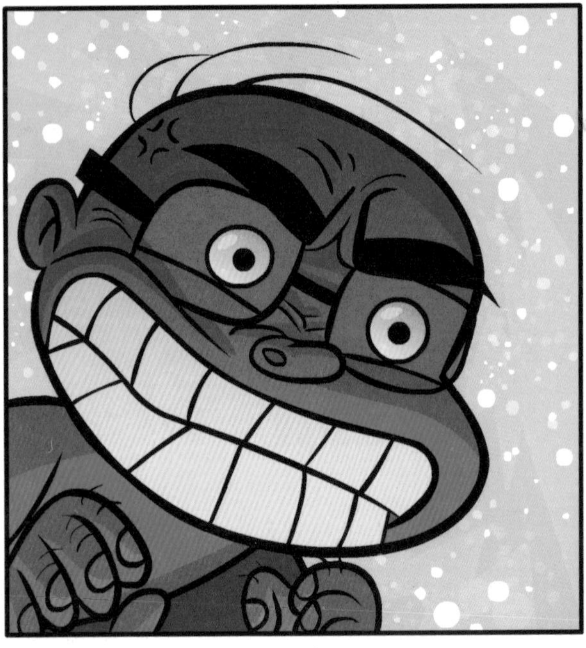
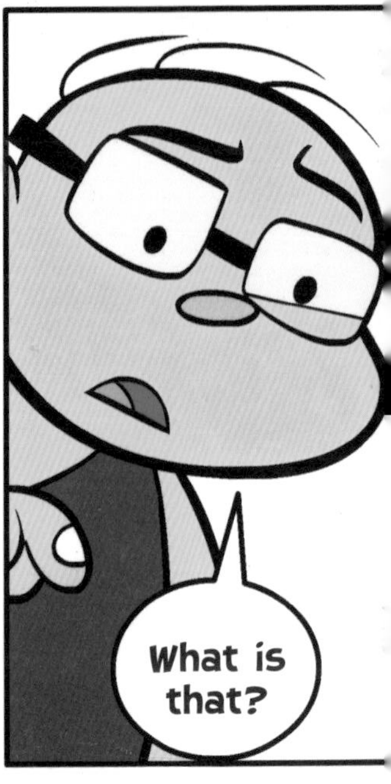
What is that?

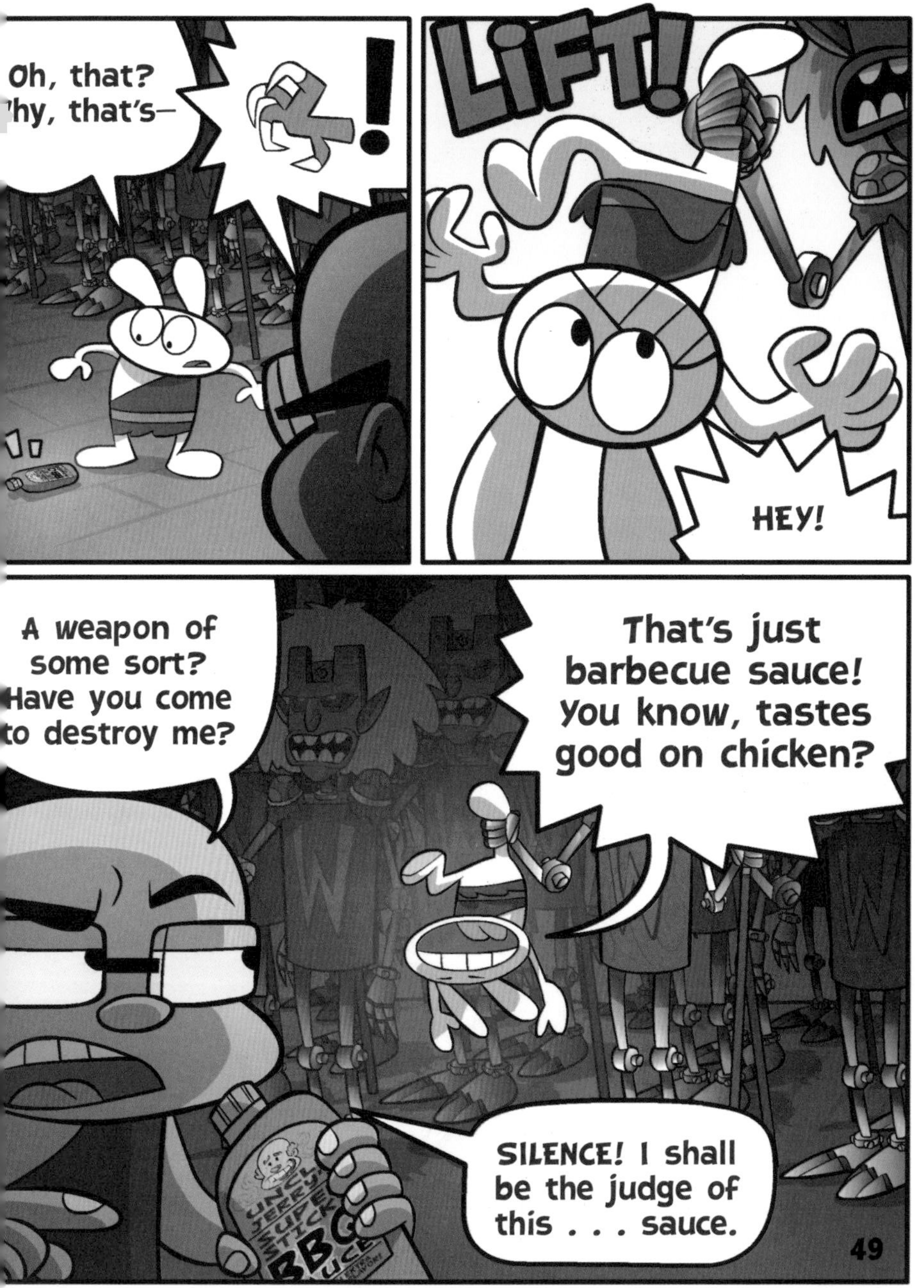
Oh, that?
'hy, that's—
!
LIFT!
HEY!
A weapon of some sort? Have you come to destroy me?
That's just barbecue sauce! You know, tastes good on chicken?
SILENCE! I shall be the judge of this . . . sauce.

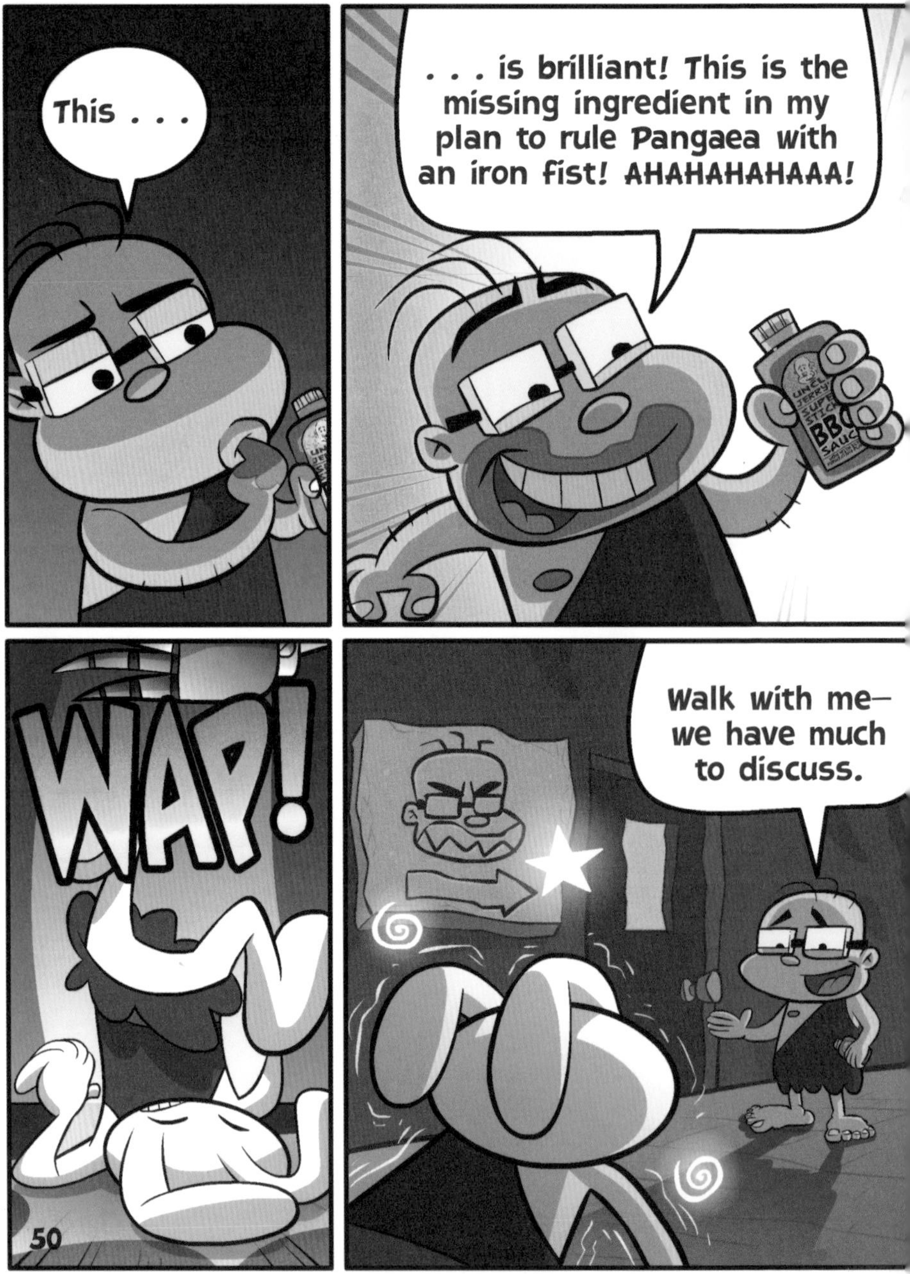
This . . .
. . . is brilliant! This is the missing ingredient in my plan to rule Pangaea with an iron fist! AHAHAHAHAAA!
WAP!
Walk with me—we have much to discuss.

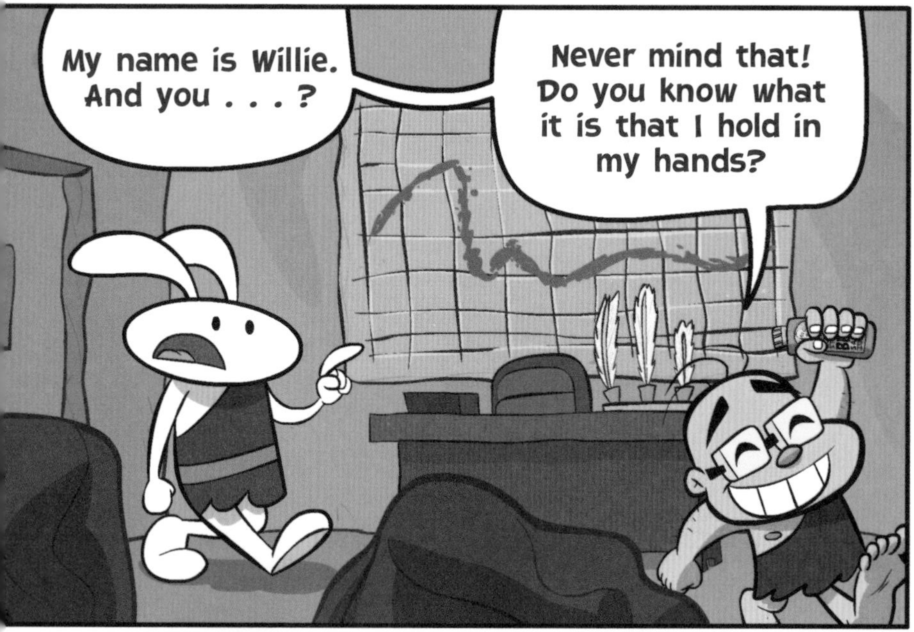
My name is Willie. And you . . . ?
Never mind that! Do you know what it is that I hold in my hands?

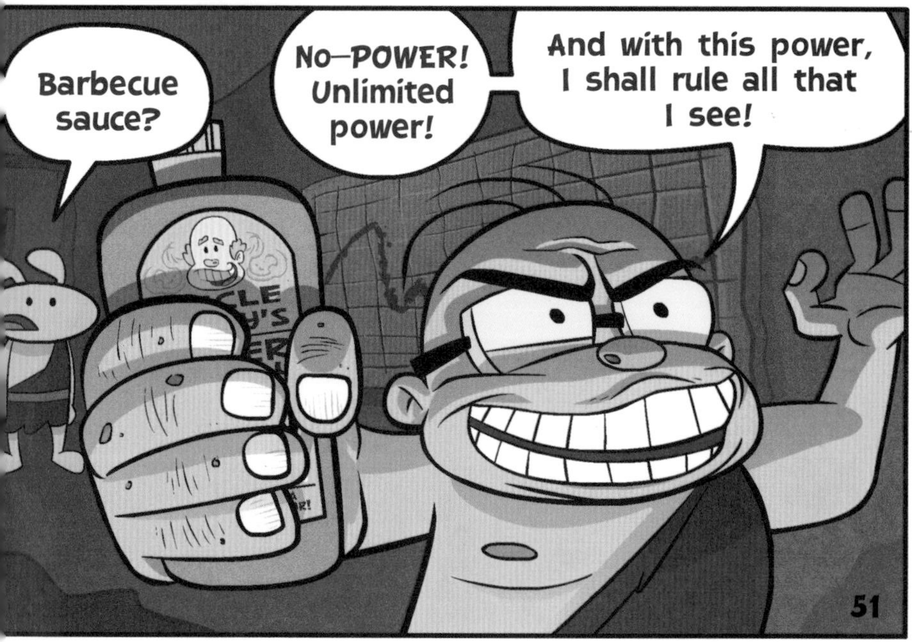
Barbecue sauce?
No—POWER! Unlimited power!
And with this power, I shall rule all that I see!

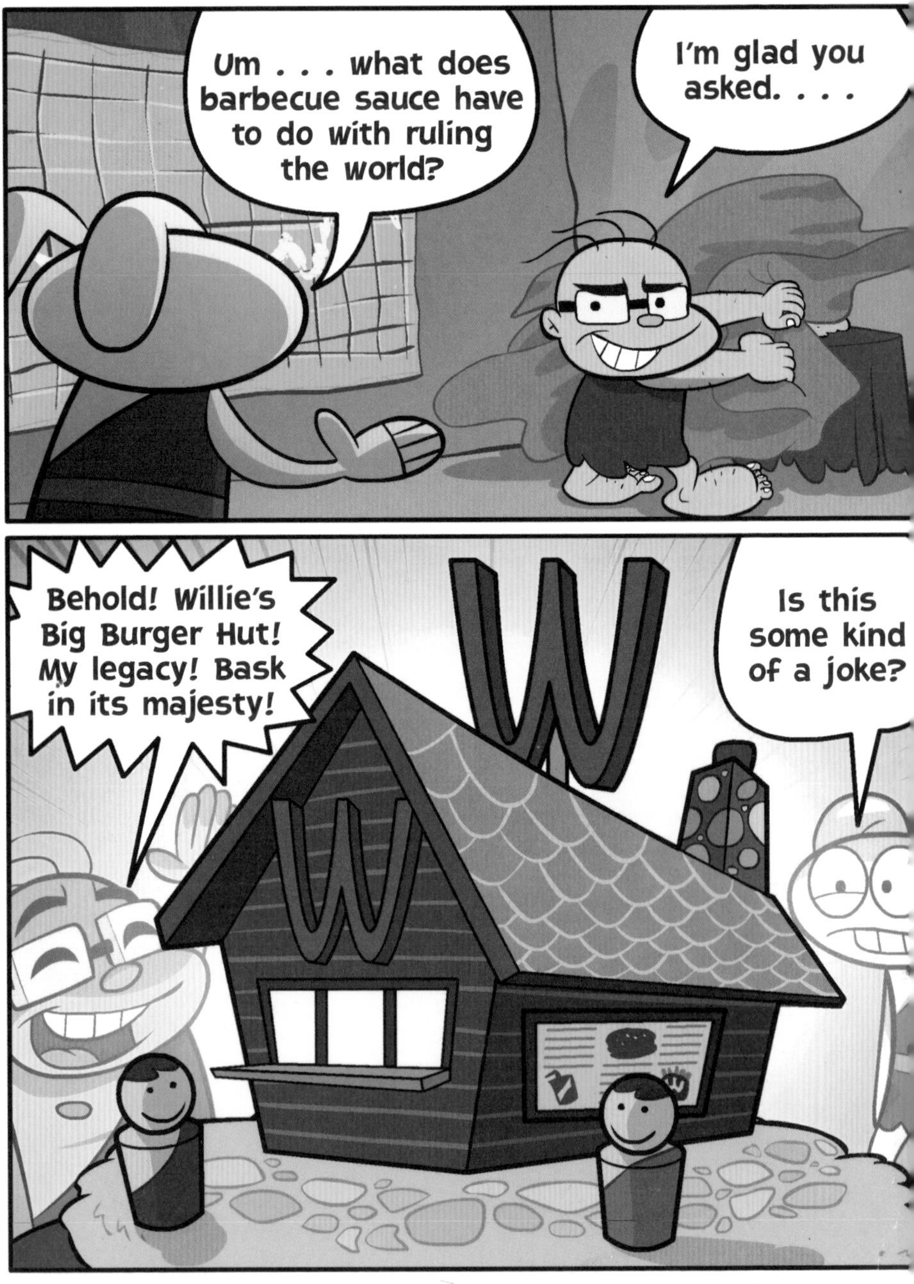
Um . . . what does barbecue sauce have to do with ruling the world?
I'm glad you asked. . . .
Behold! Willie's Big Burger Hut! My legacy! Bask in its majesty!
Is this some kind of a joke?

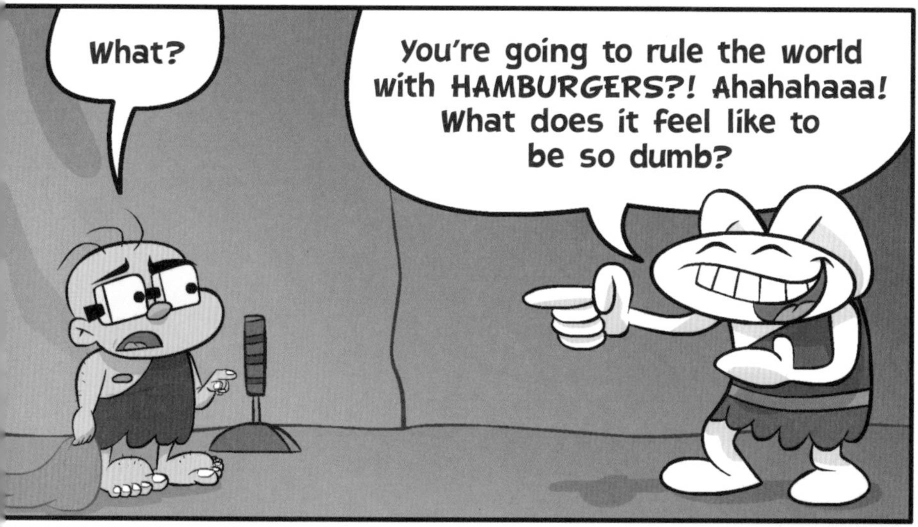
What?
You're going to rule the world with HAMBURGERS?! Ahahahaaa! What does it feel like to be so dumb?

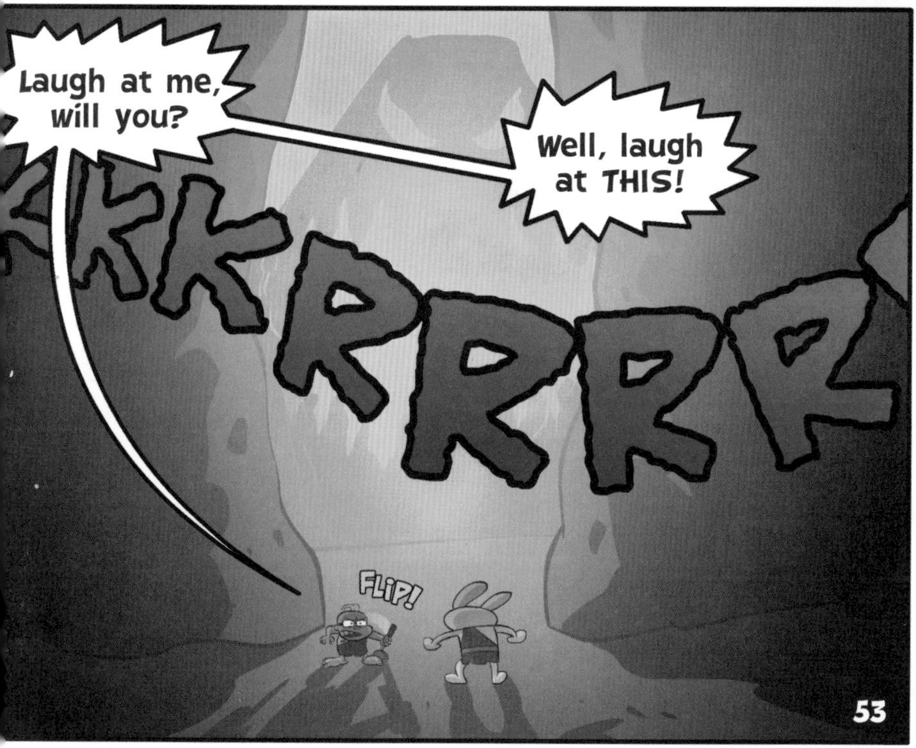
Laugh at me, will you?
Well, laugh at THIS!
KKRRRR
FLIP!

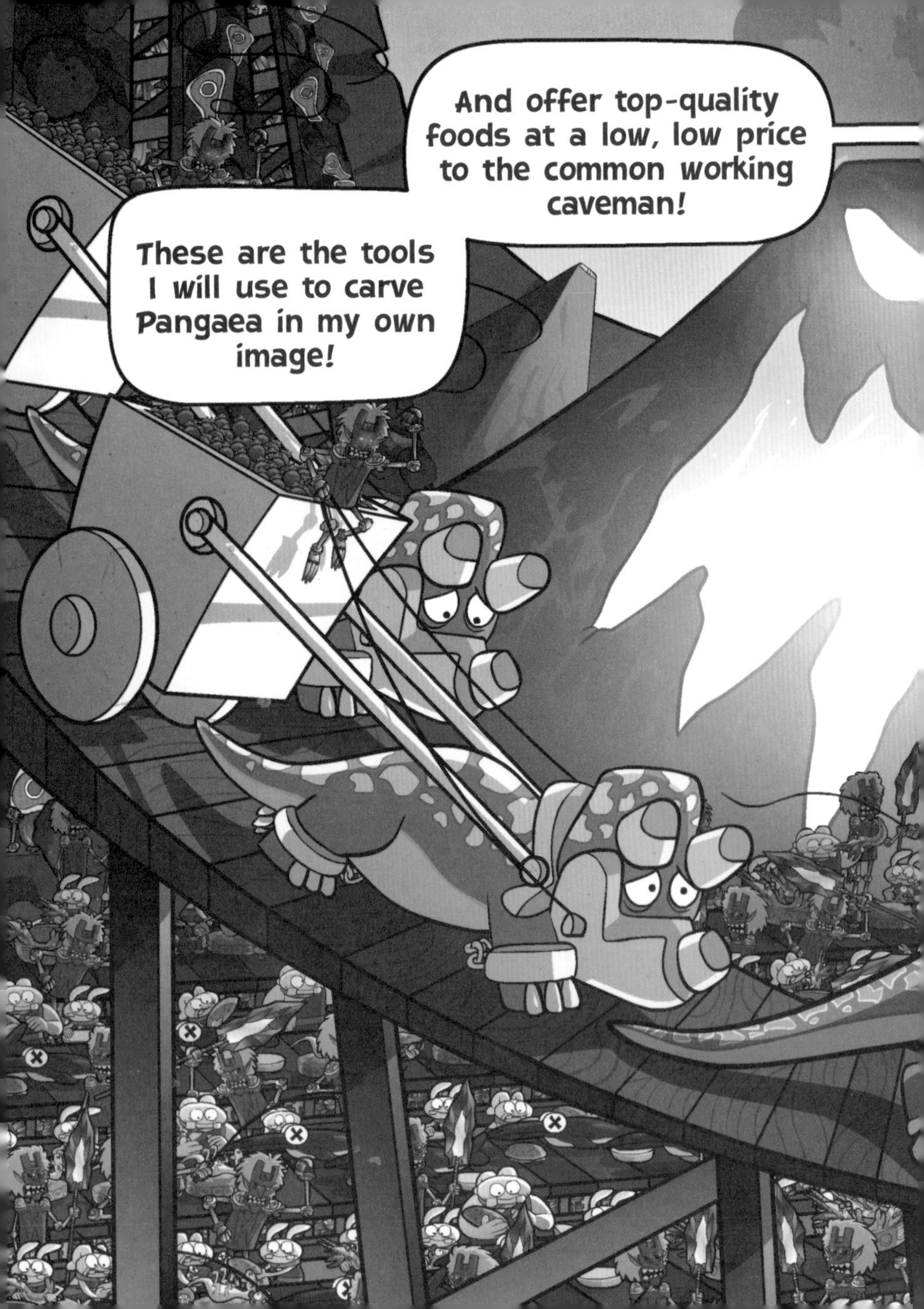
These are the tools I will use to carve Pangaea in my own image!
And offer top-quality foods at a low, low price to the common working caveman!

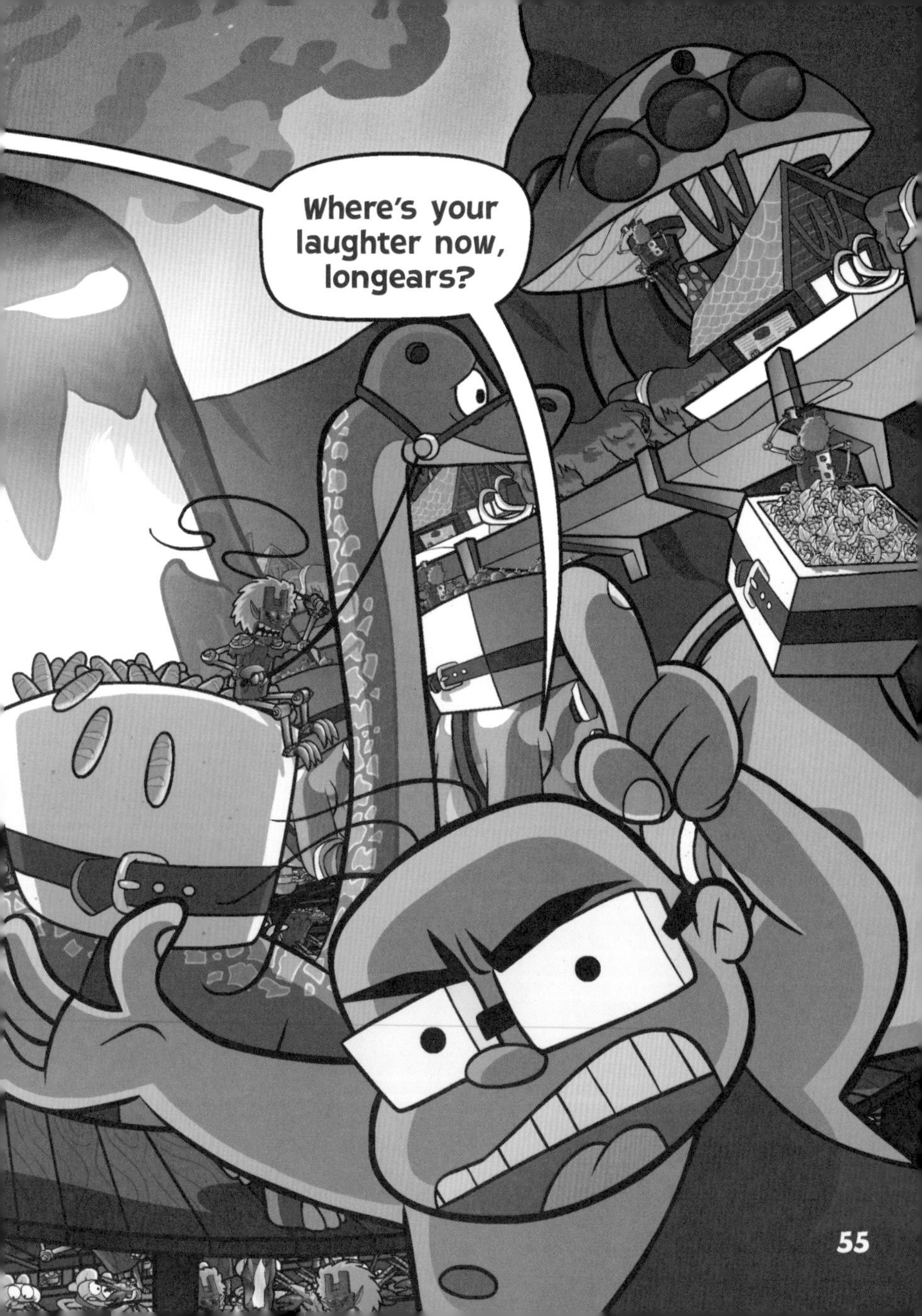
Where's your laughter now, longears?

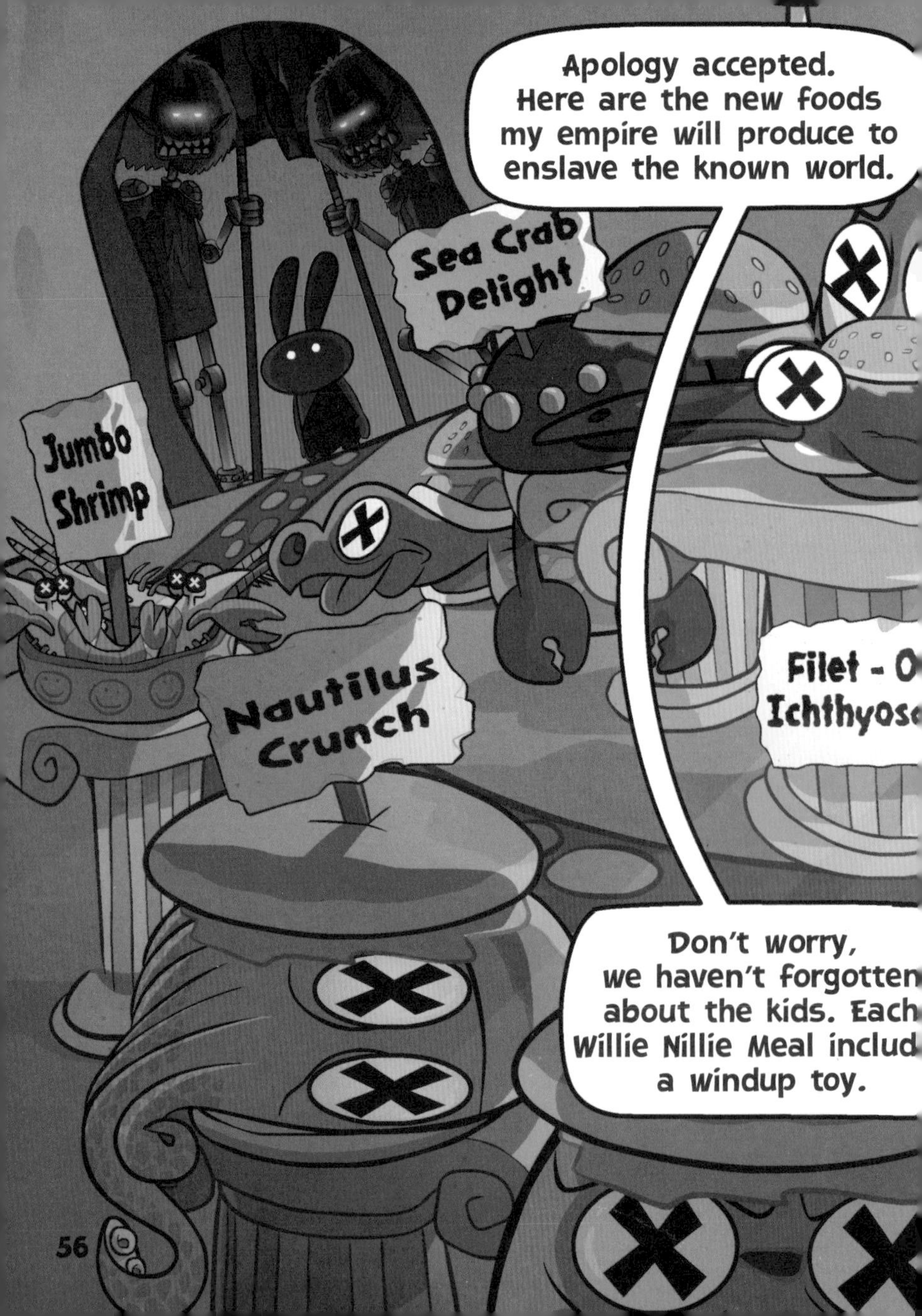
Apology accepted. Here are the new foods my empire will produce to enslave the known world.
Sea Crab Delight
Jumbo Shrimp
Nautilus Crunch
Filet - O
Ichthyos
Don't worry, we haven't forgotten about the kids. Each Willie Nillie Meal includ a windup toy.

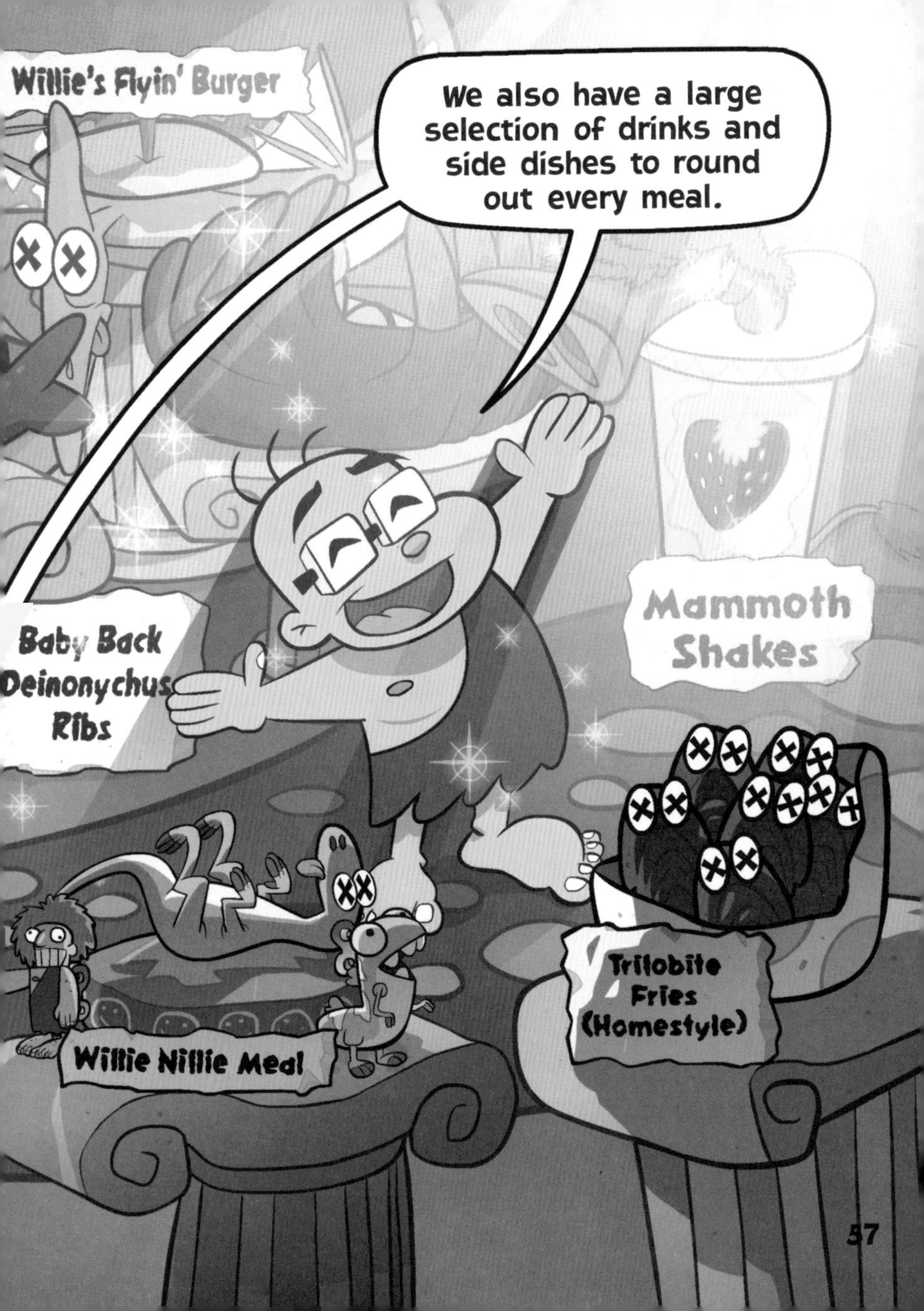
Willie's Flyin' Burger
We also have a large selection of drinks and side dishes to round out every meal.
Baby Back Deinonychus Ribs
Mammoth Shakes
Trilobite Fries (Homestyle)
Willie Nillie Meal

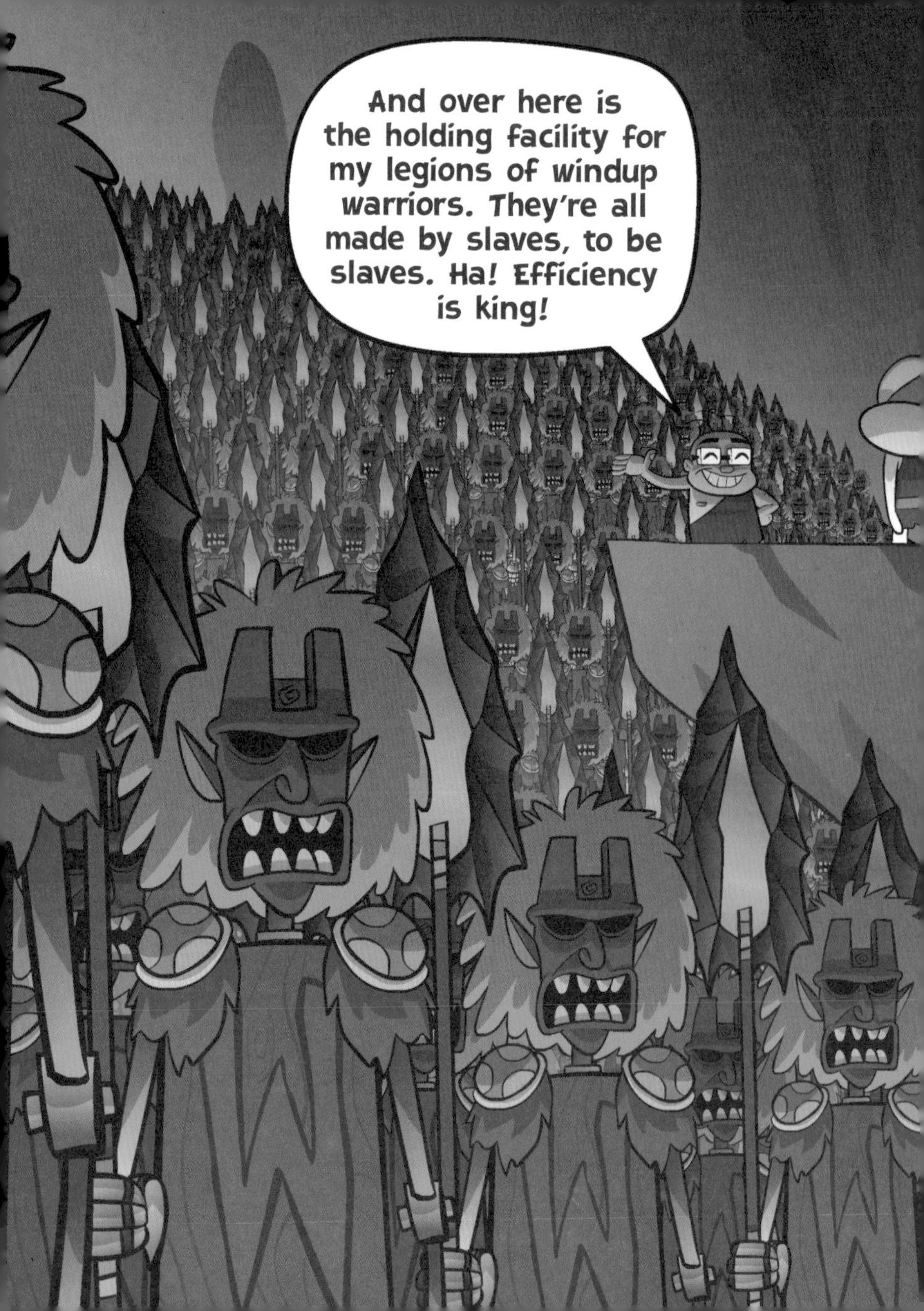
And over here is the holding facility for my legions of windup warriors. They're all made by slaves, to be slaves. Ha! Efficiency is king!

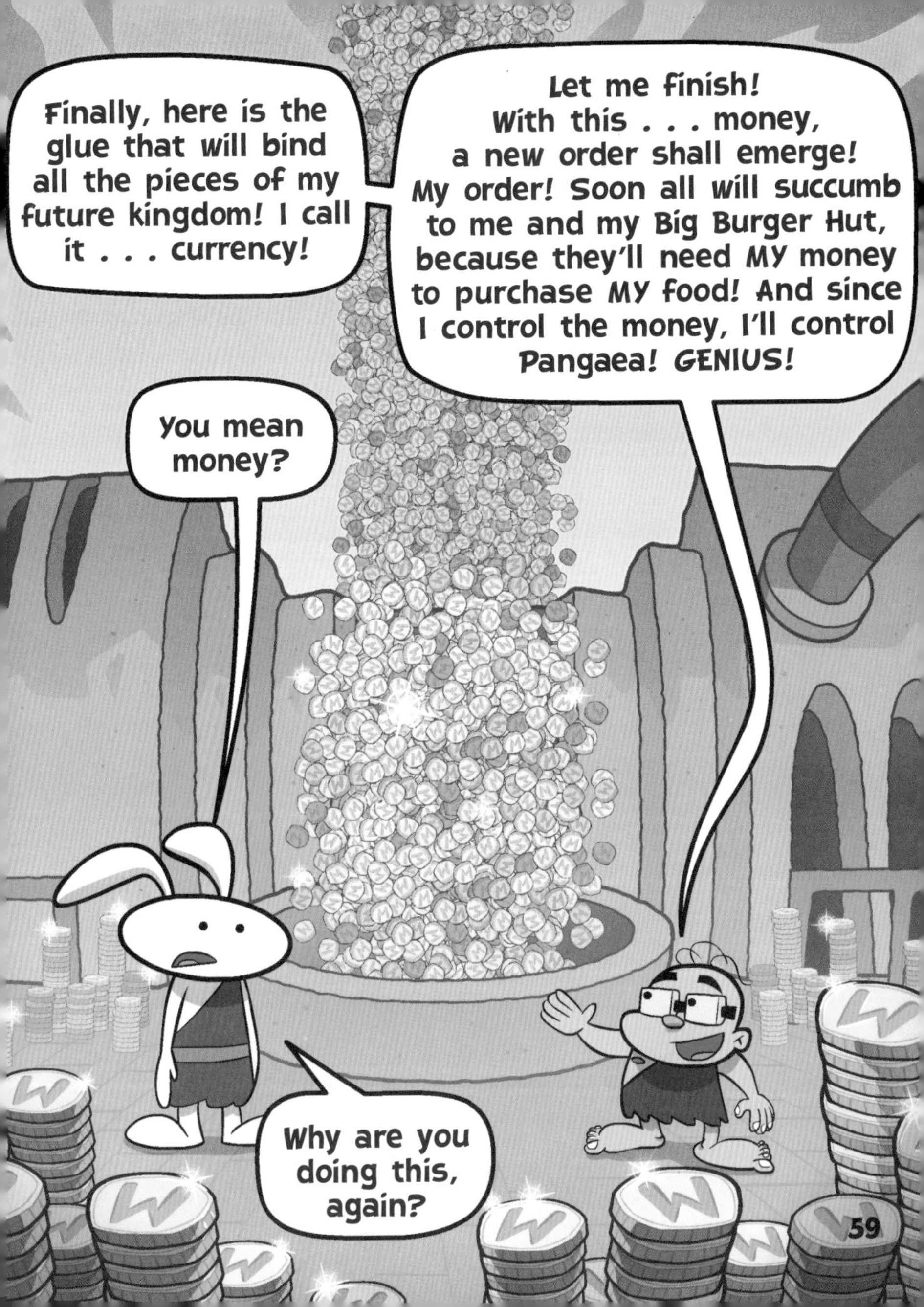
Finally, here is the glue that will bind all the pieces of my future kingdom! I call it . . . currency!
Let me finish! With this . . . money, a new order shall emerge! My order! Soon all will succumb to me and my Big Burger Hut, because they'll need MY money to purchase MY food! And since I control the money, I'll control Pangaea! GENIUS!
You mean money?
Why are you doing this, again?

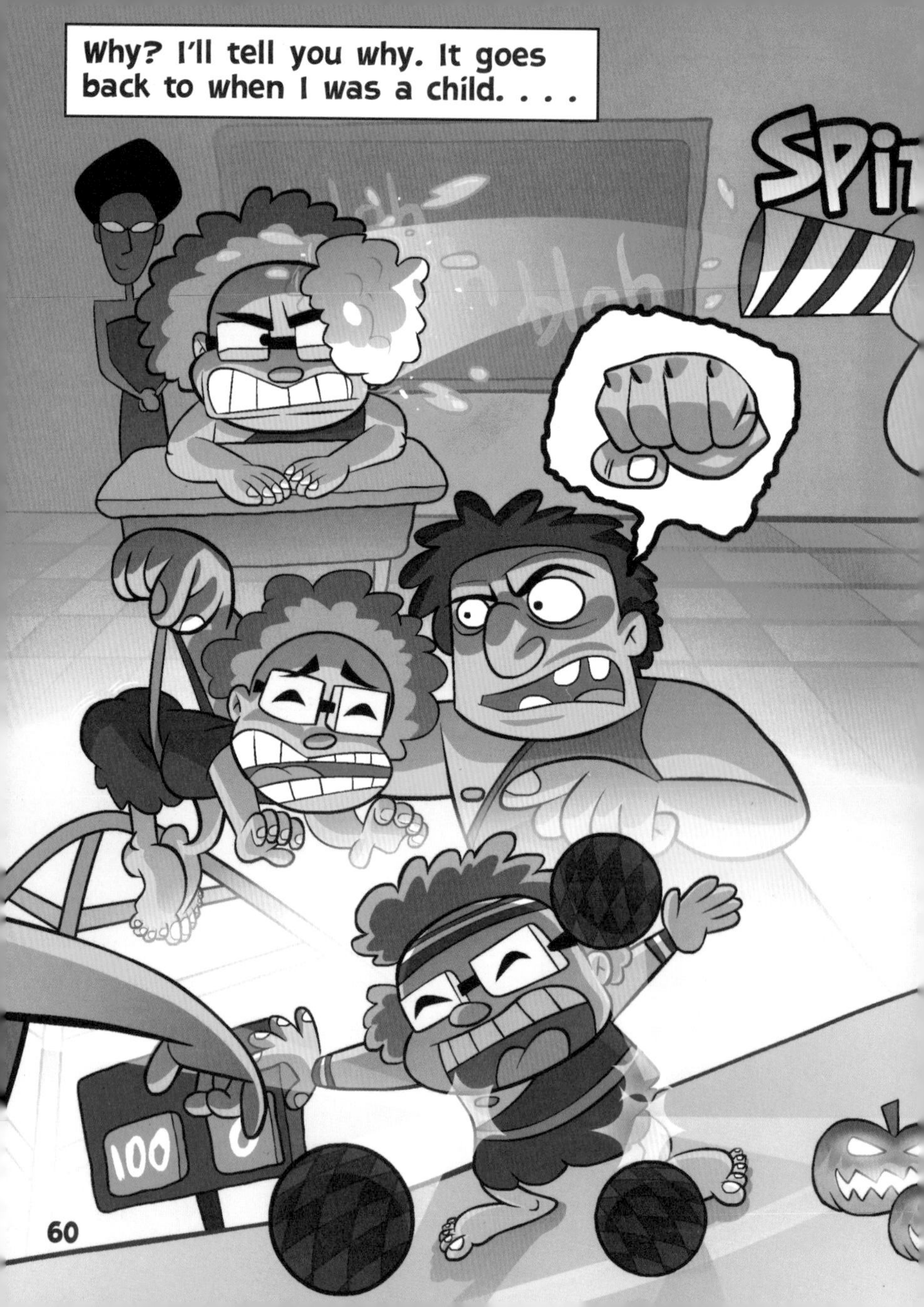
Why? I'll tell you why. It goes back to when I was a child. . . .
100

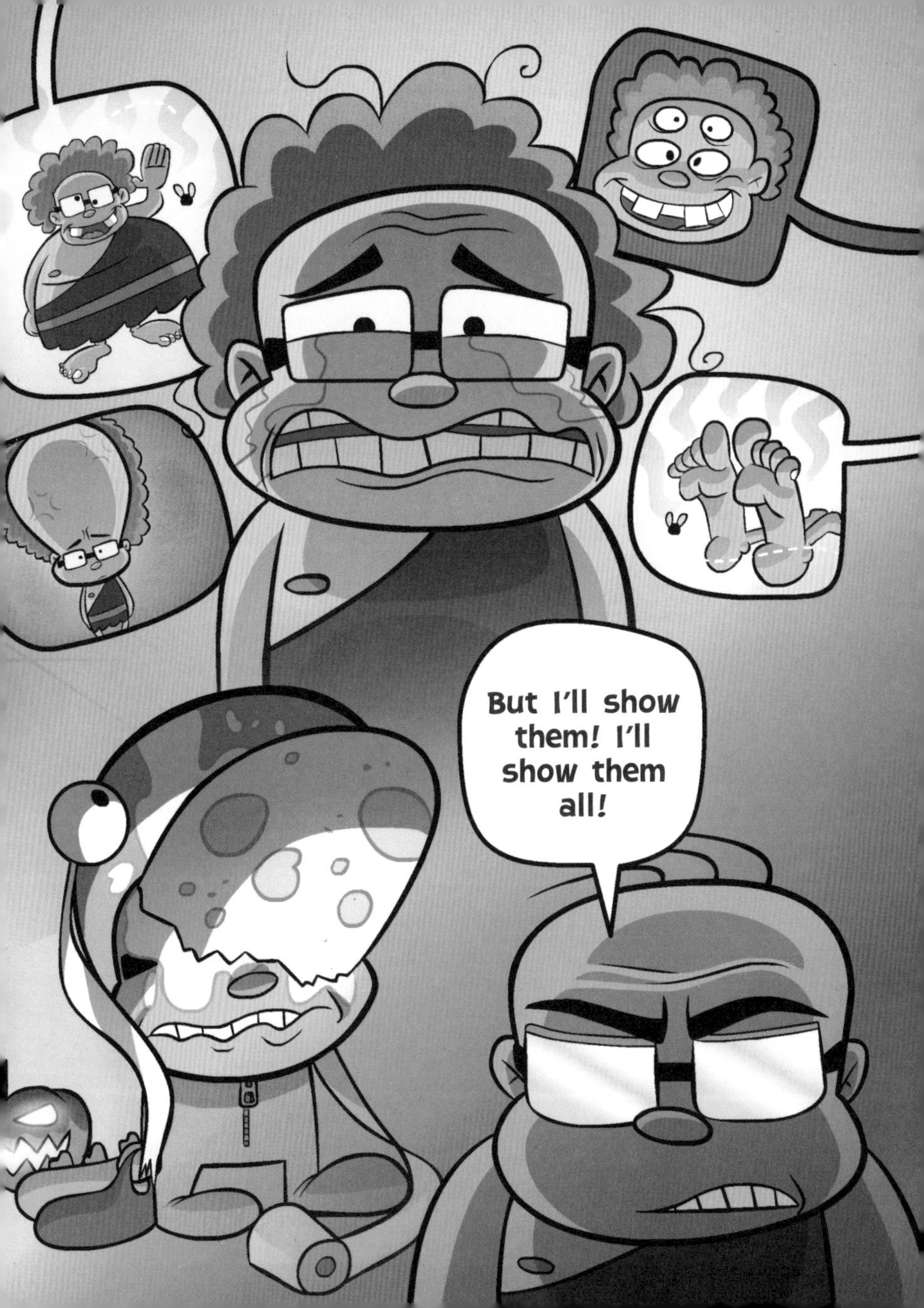
But I'll show them! I'll show them all!

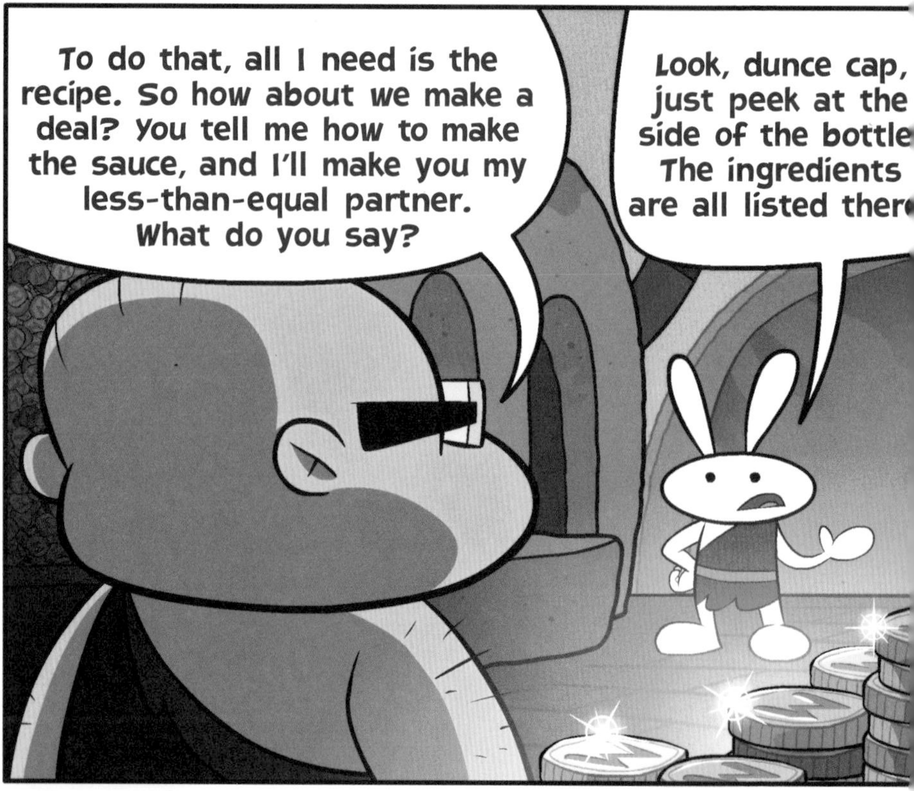
To do that, all I need is the recipe. So how about we make a deal? You tell me how to make the sauce, and I'll make you my less-than-equal partner. What do you say?
Look, dunce cap, just peek at the side of the bottle The ingredients are all listed ther

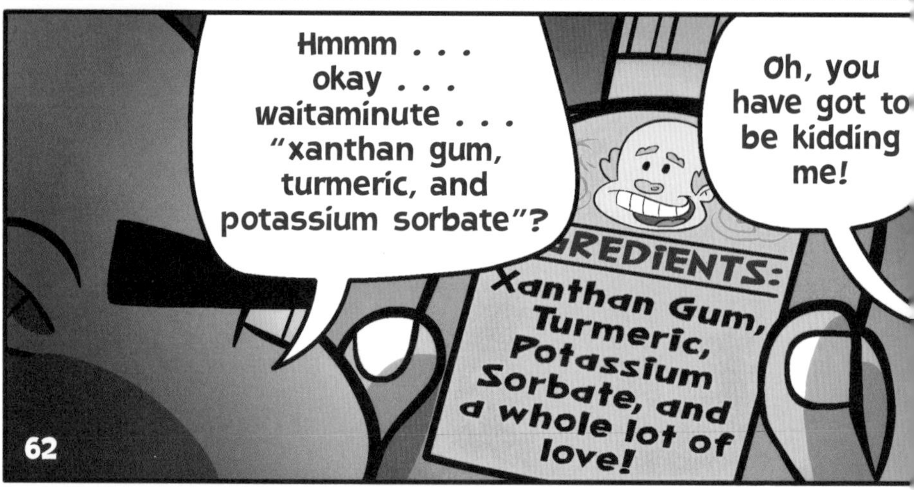
Hmmm . . . okay . . . waitaminute . . . "xanthan gum, turmeric, and potassium sorbate"?
GREDIENTS:
Xanthan Gum, Turmeric, Potassium Sorbate, and a whole lot of love!
Oh, you have got to be kidding me!

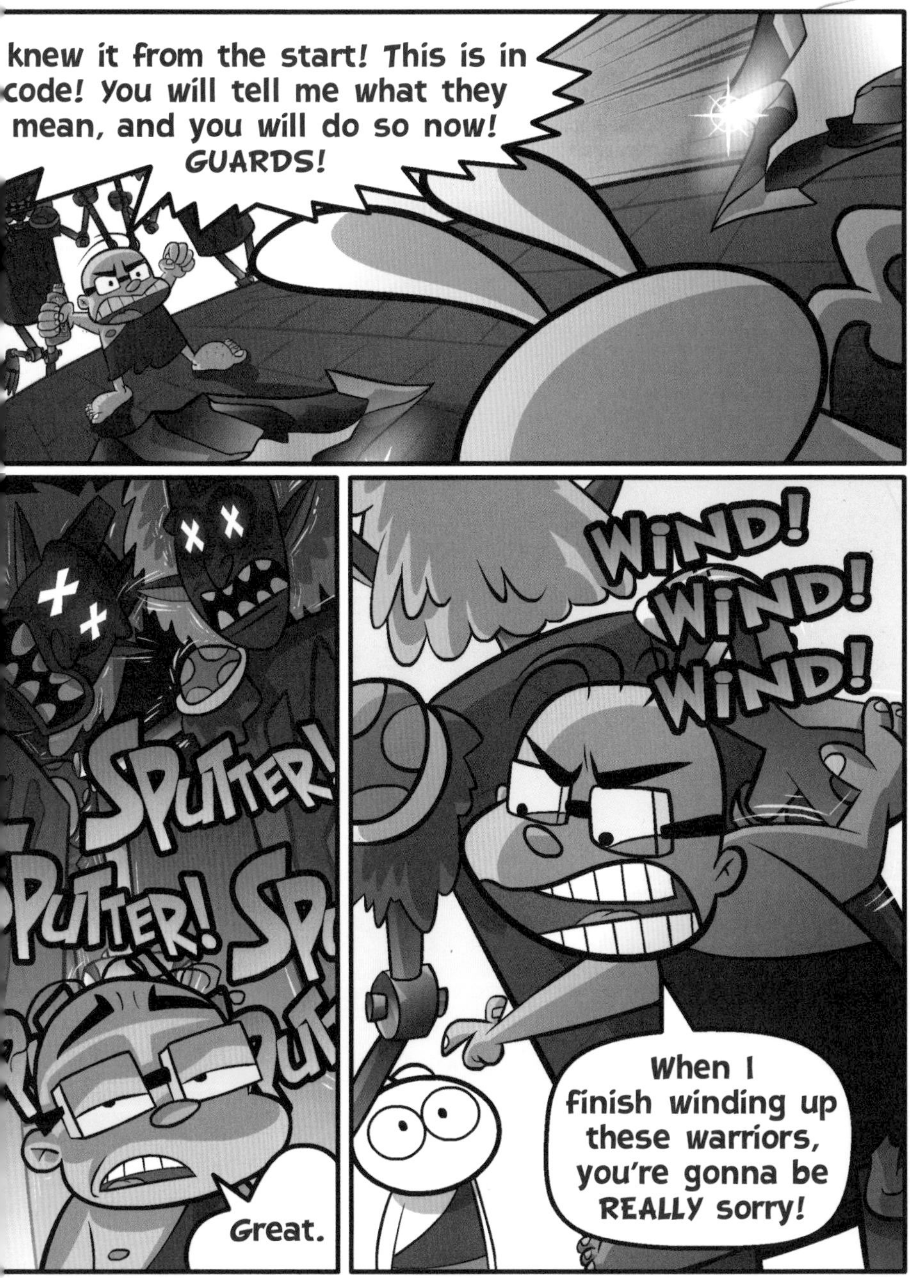
knew it from the start! This is in code! You will tell me what they mean, and you will do so now! GUARDS!
SPUTTER! SPUTTER! SP
Great.
WIND! WIND! WIND!
When I finish winding up these warriors, you're gonna be REALLY sorry!

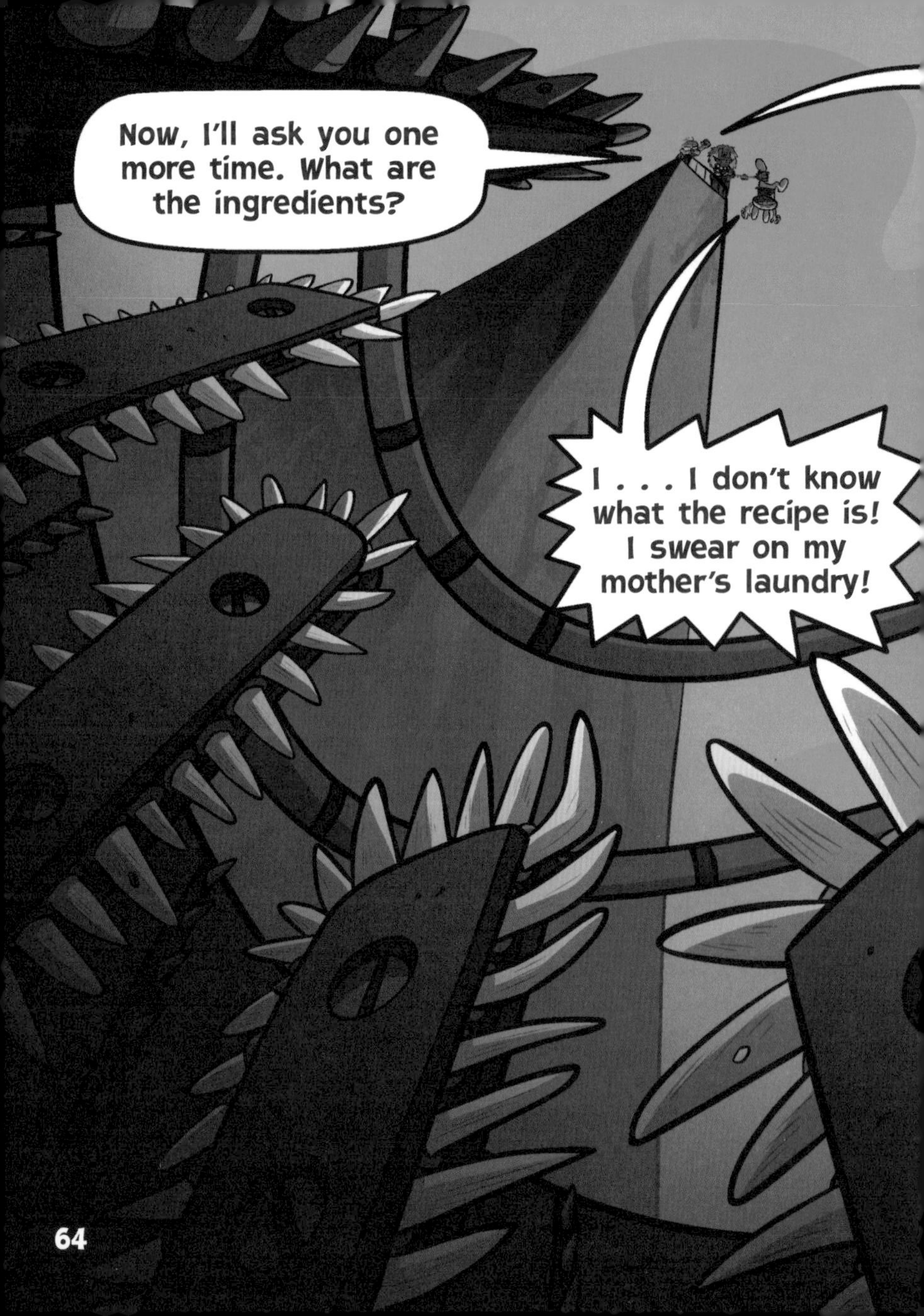
Now, I'll ask you one more time. What are the ingredients?
I . . . I don't know what the recipe is! I swear on my mother's laundry!

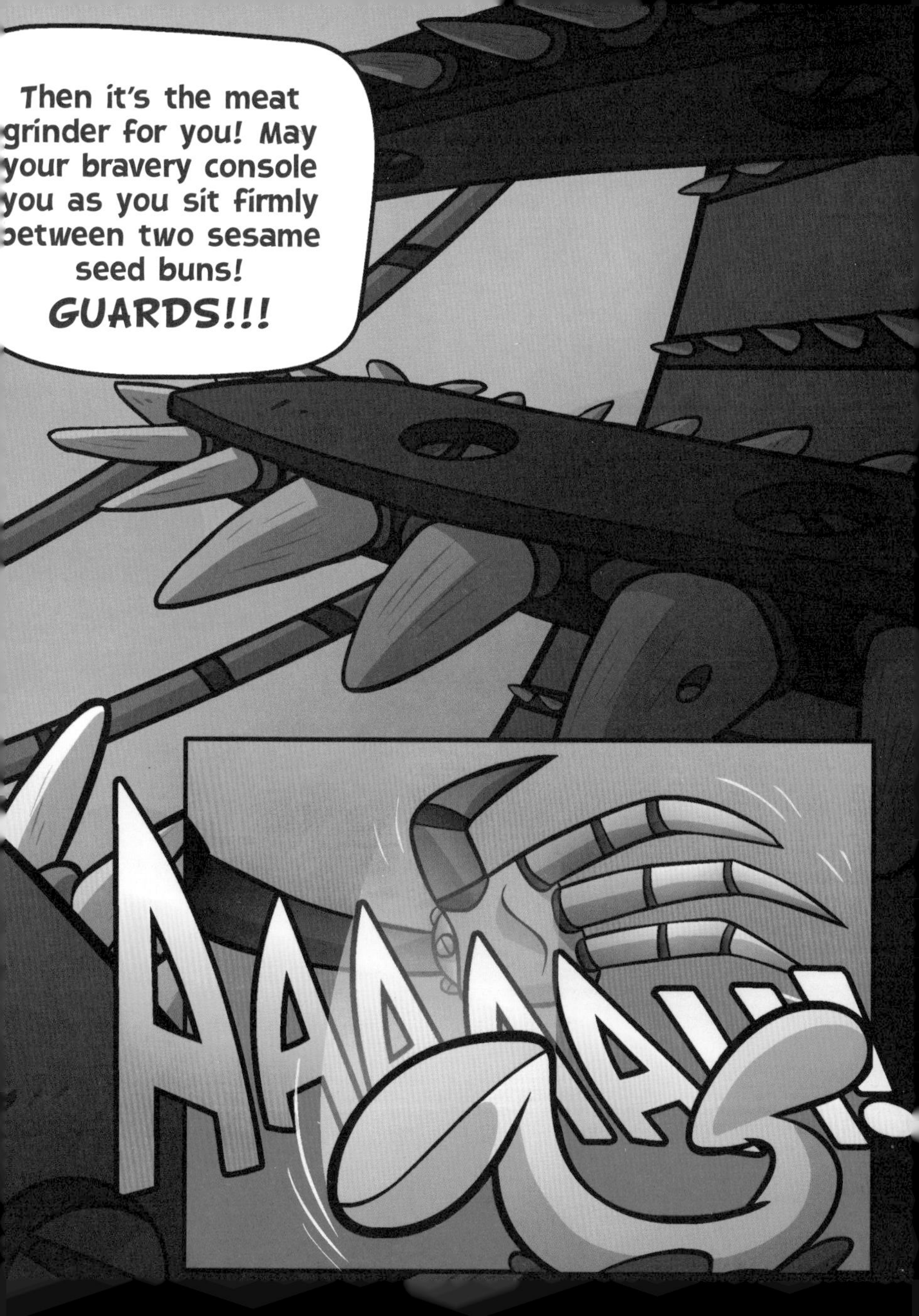
Then it's the meat grinder for you! May your bravery console you as you sit firmly between two sesame seed buns! GUARDS!!!

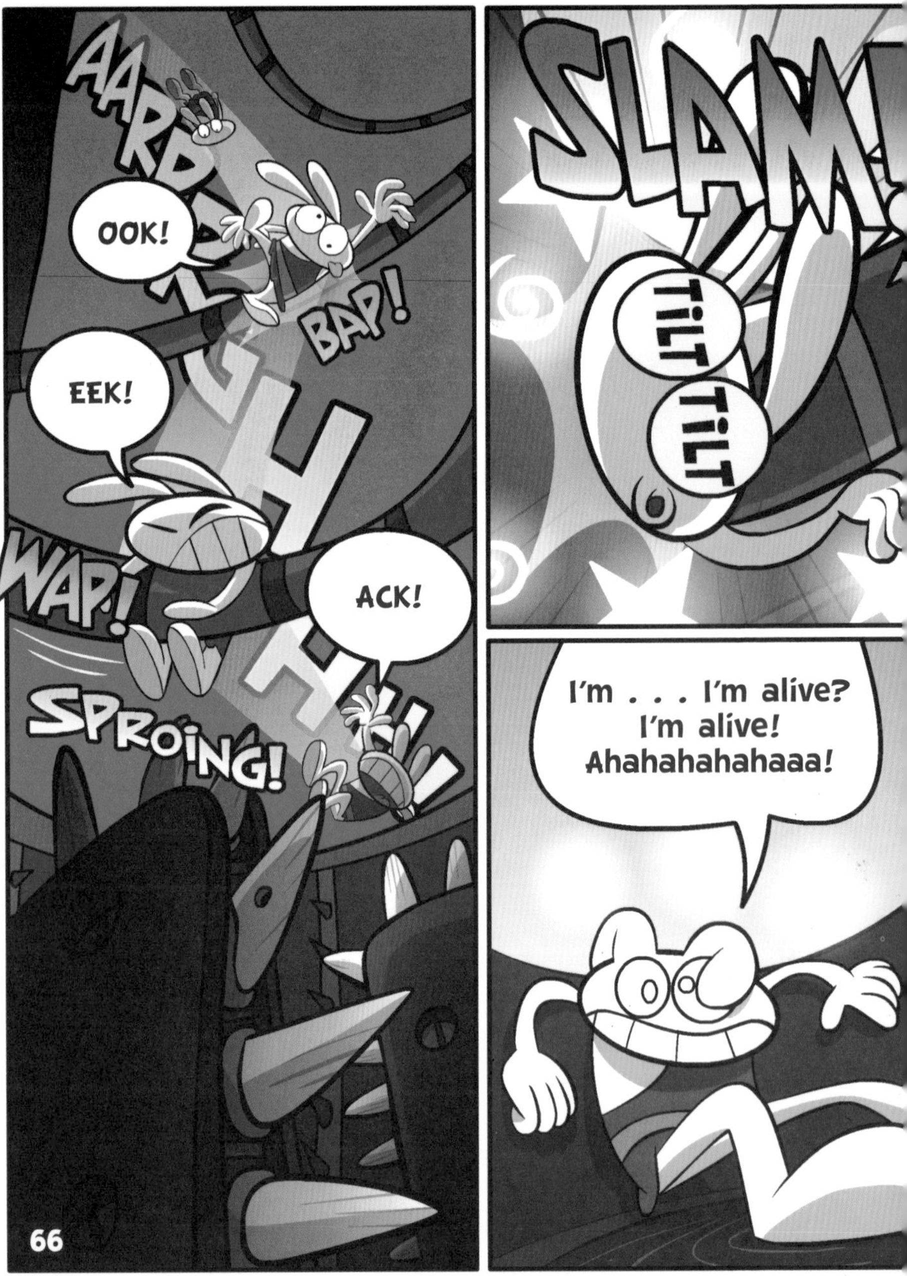
OOK!
BAP!
EEK!
WAP!
ACK!
SPROING!
SLAM!
TILT
TILT
I'm . . . I'm alive?
I'm alive!
Ahahahahahaaa!

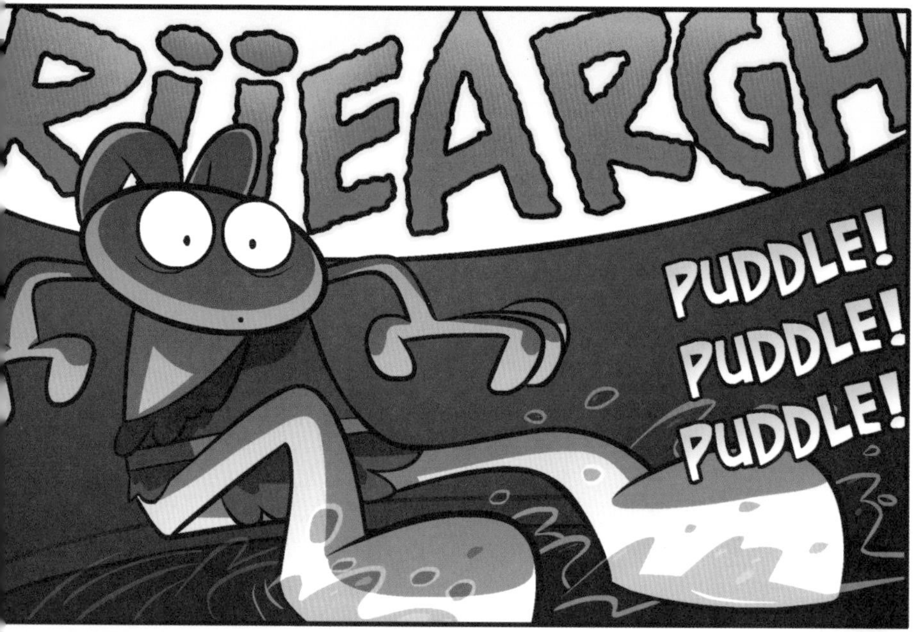
RIIEARGH
PUDDLE!
PUDDLE!
PUDDLE!

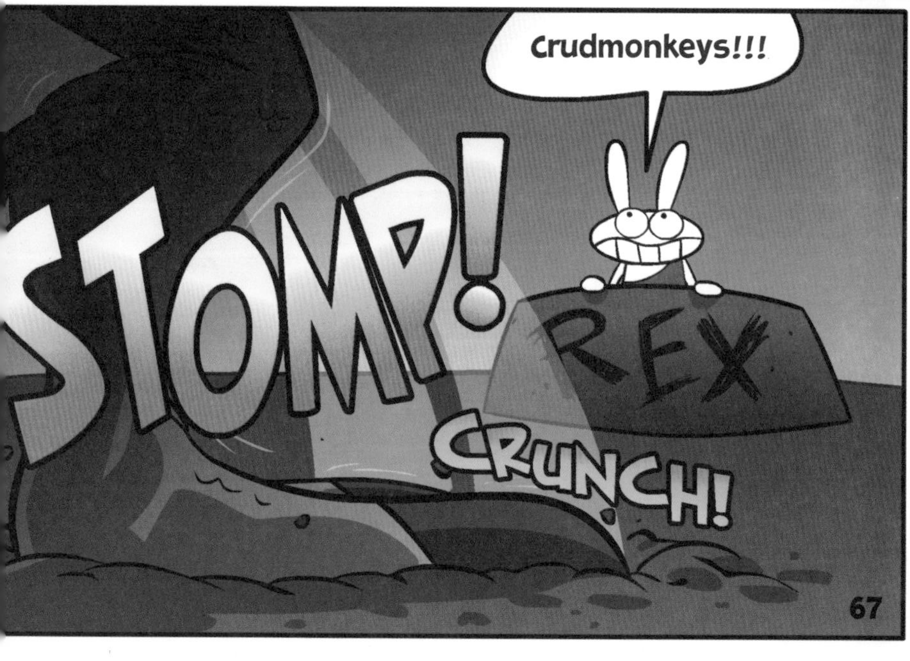
Crudmonkeys!!!
STOMP!
REX
CRUNCH!

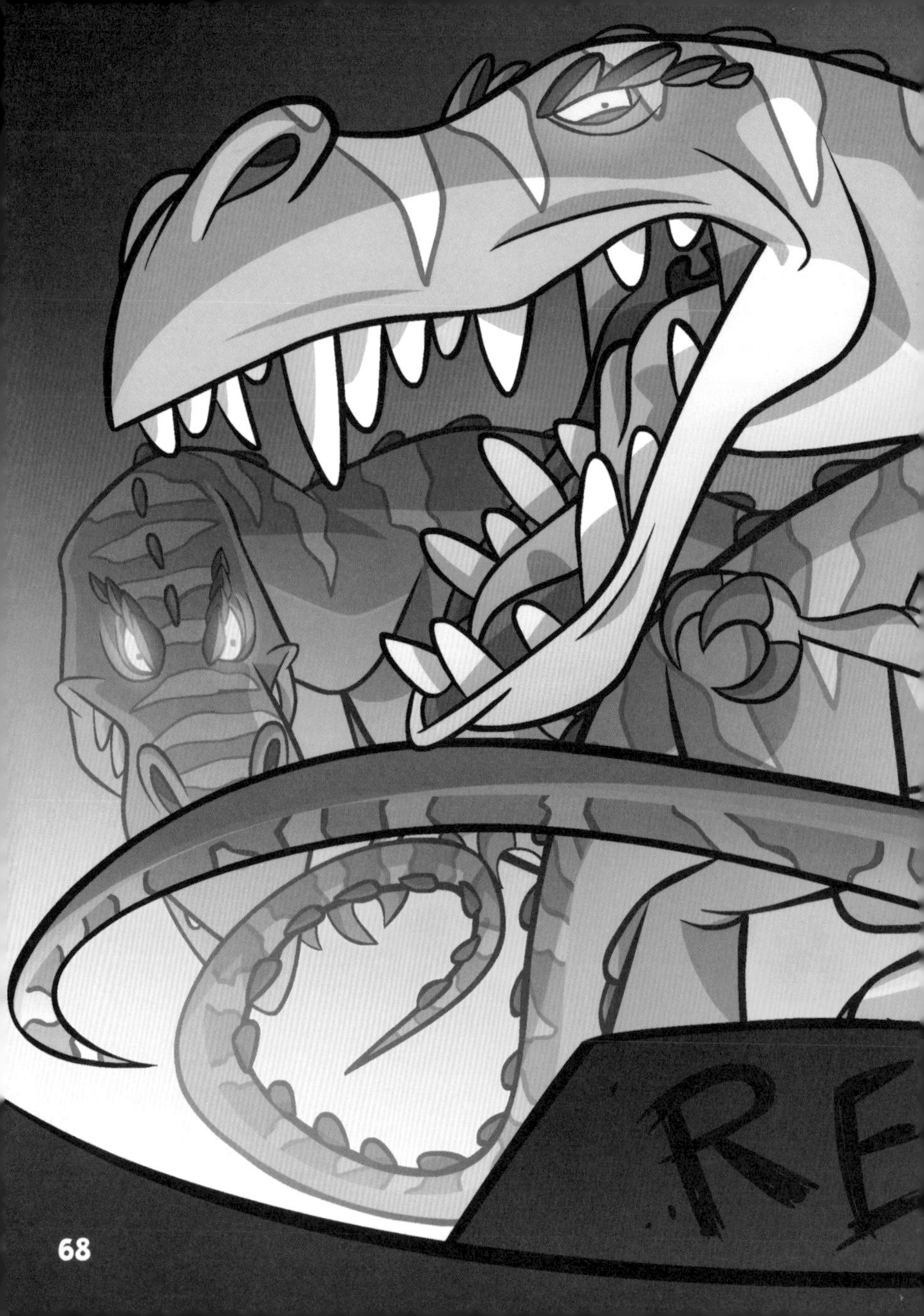
RE

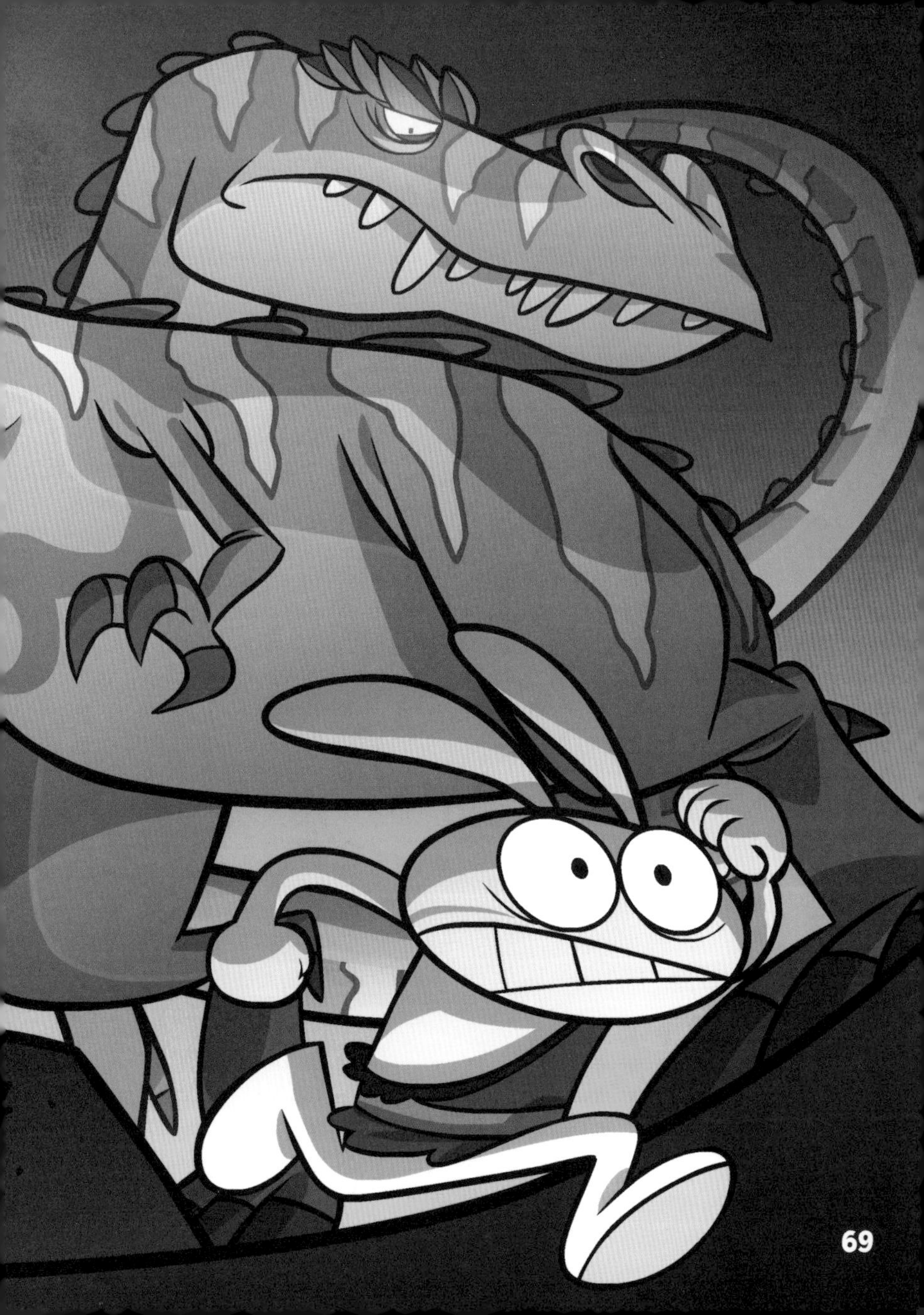

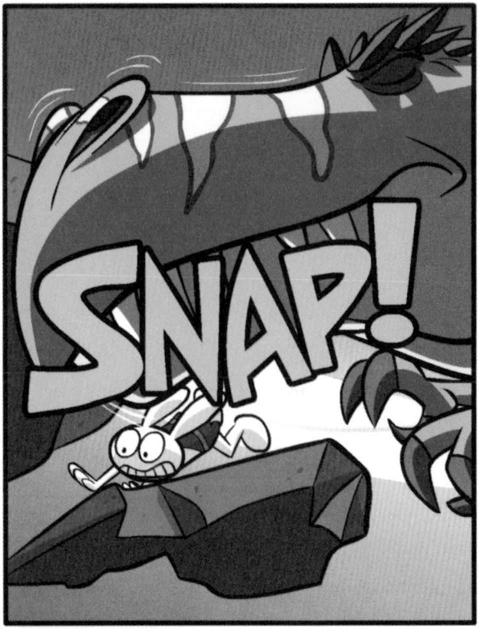
SNAP!
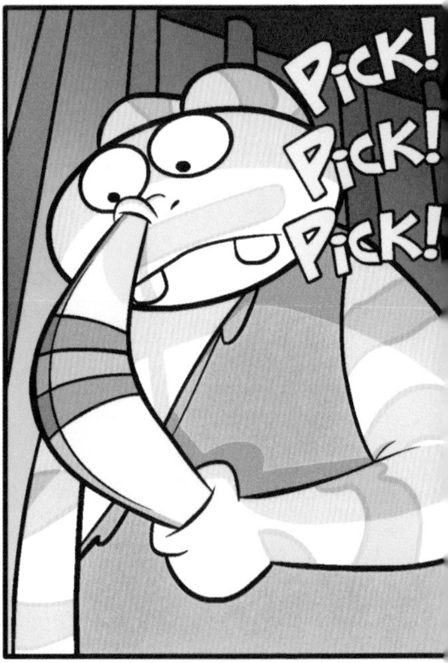
PICK!
PICK!
PICK!
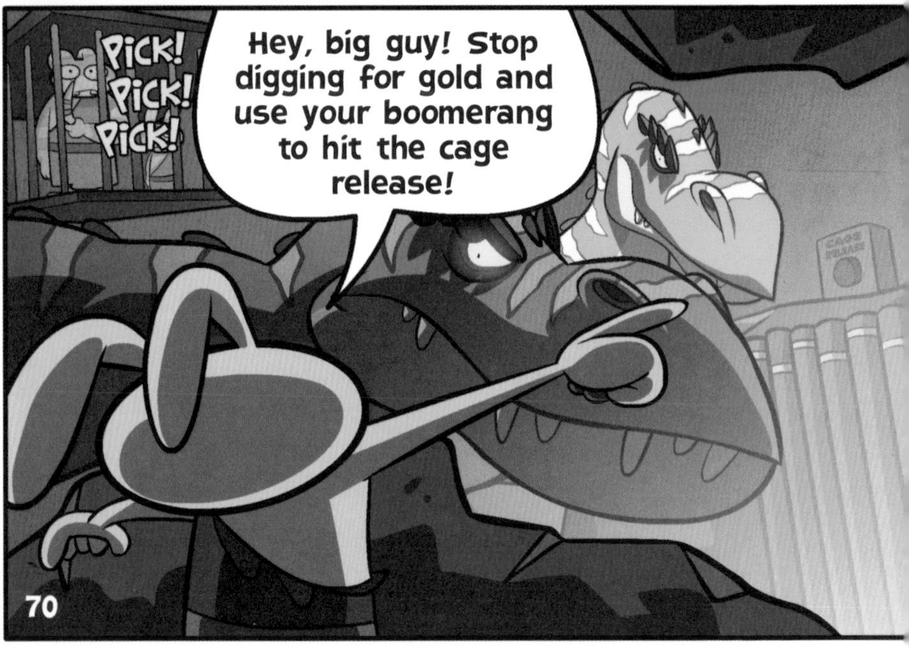
PICK!
PICK!
PICK!
Hey, big guy! Stop digging for gold and use your boomerang to hit the cage release!

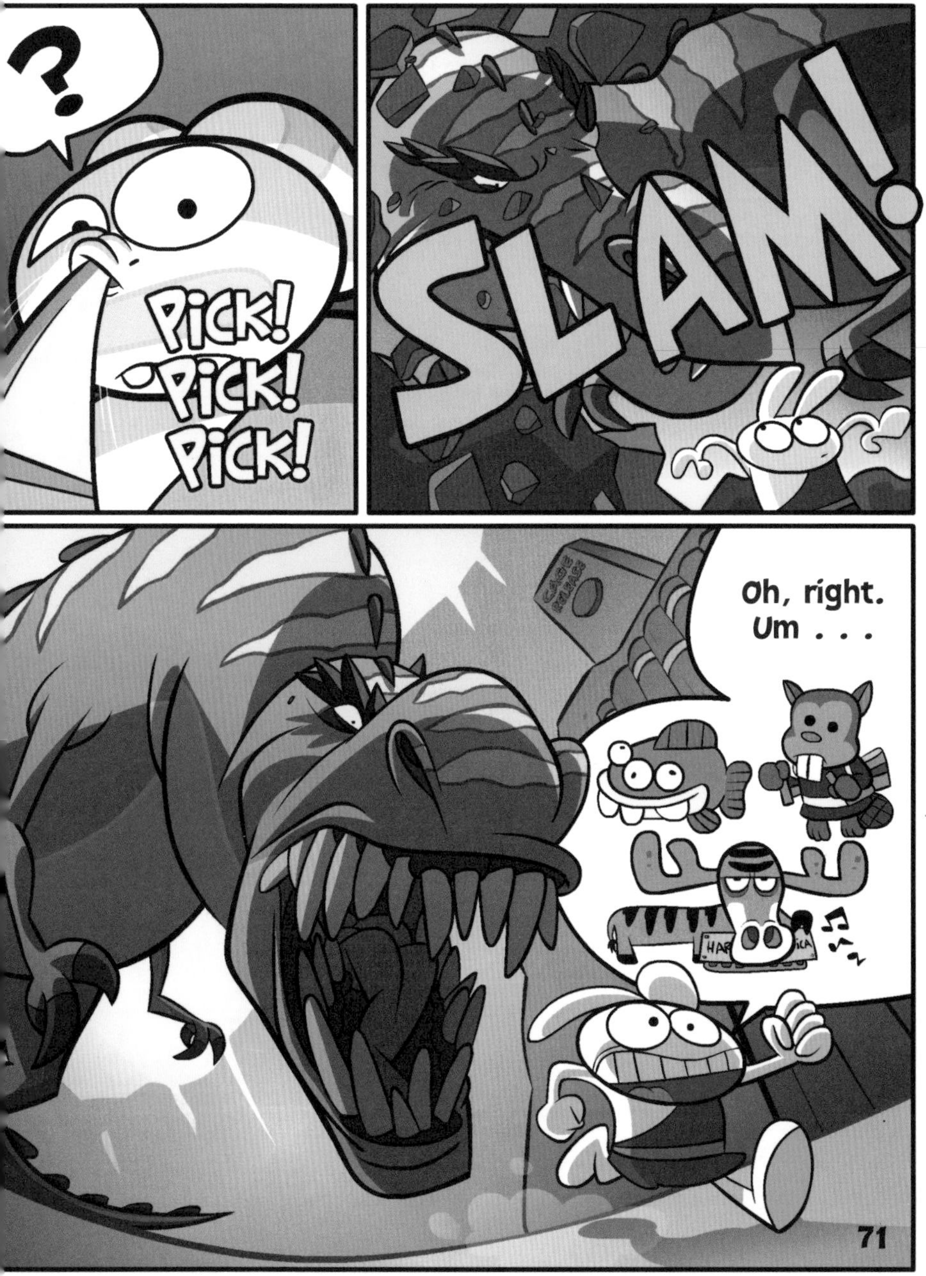
?
PICK!
PICK!
PICK!
SLAM!
CAGE RELEASE
Oh, right.
Um . . .

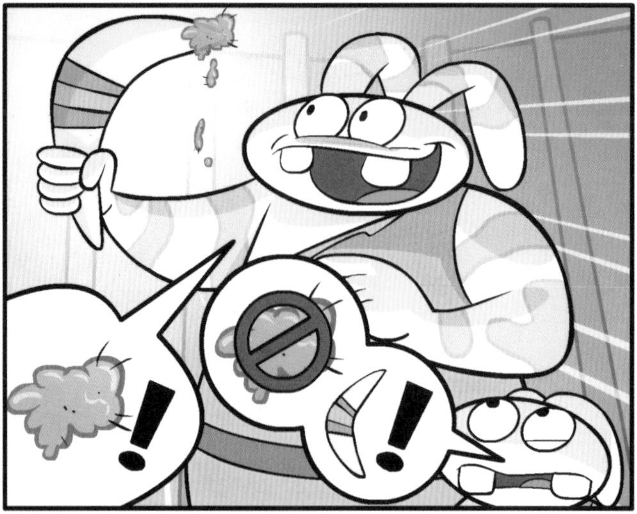
!
!
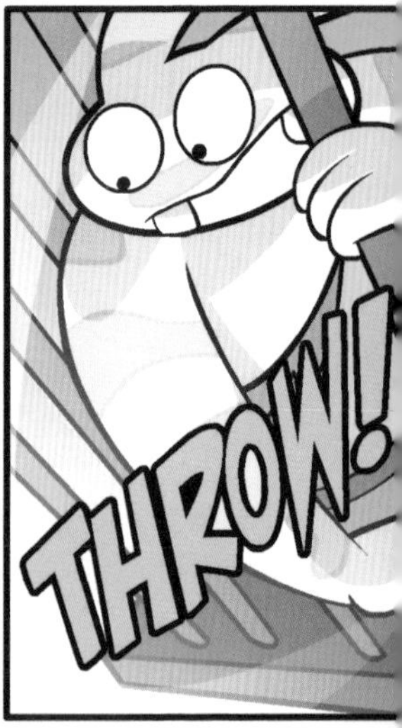
THROW!
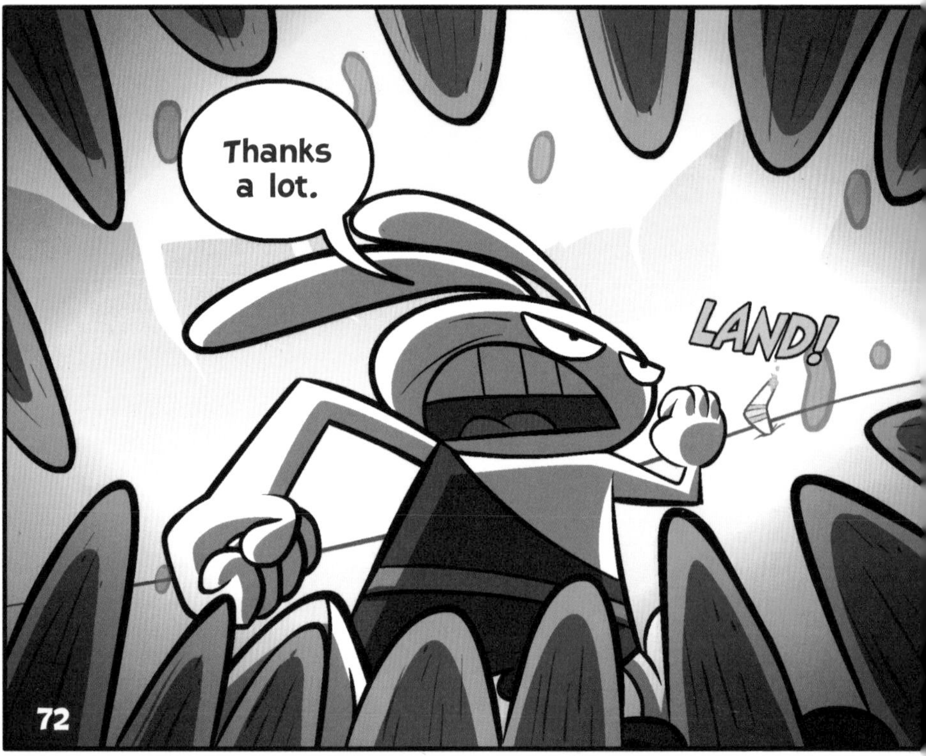
Thanks a lot.
LAND!

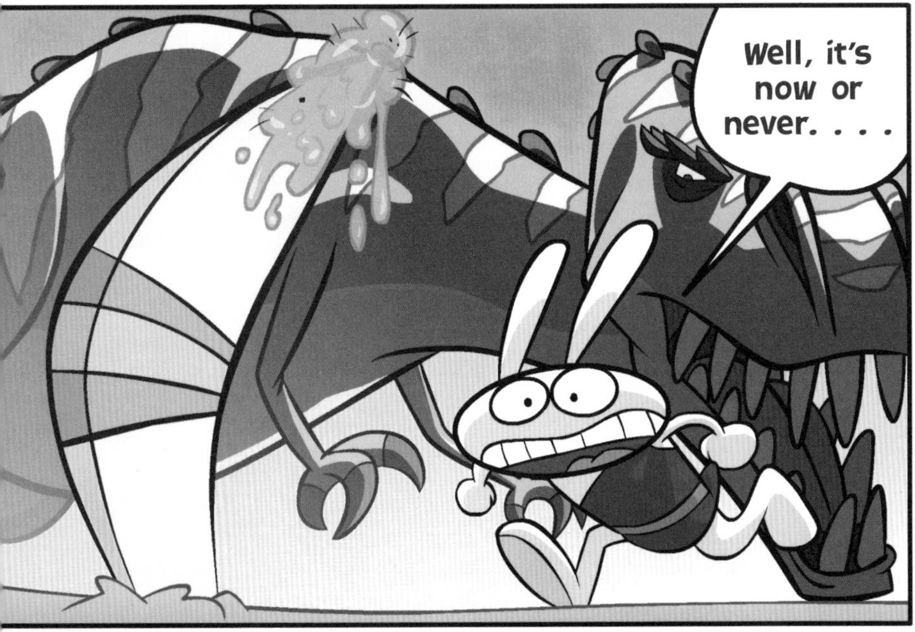
Well, it's now or never. . . .

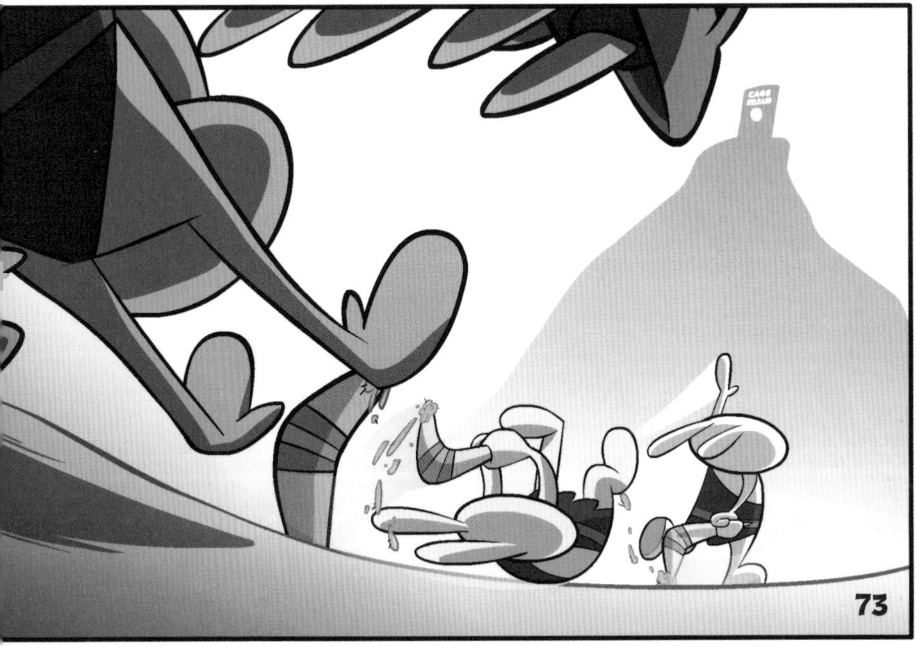

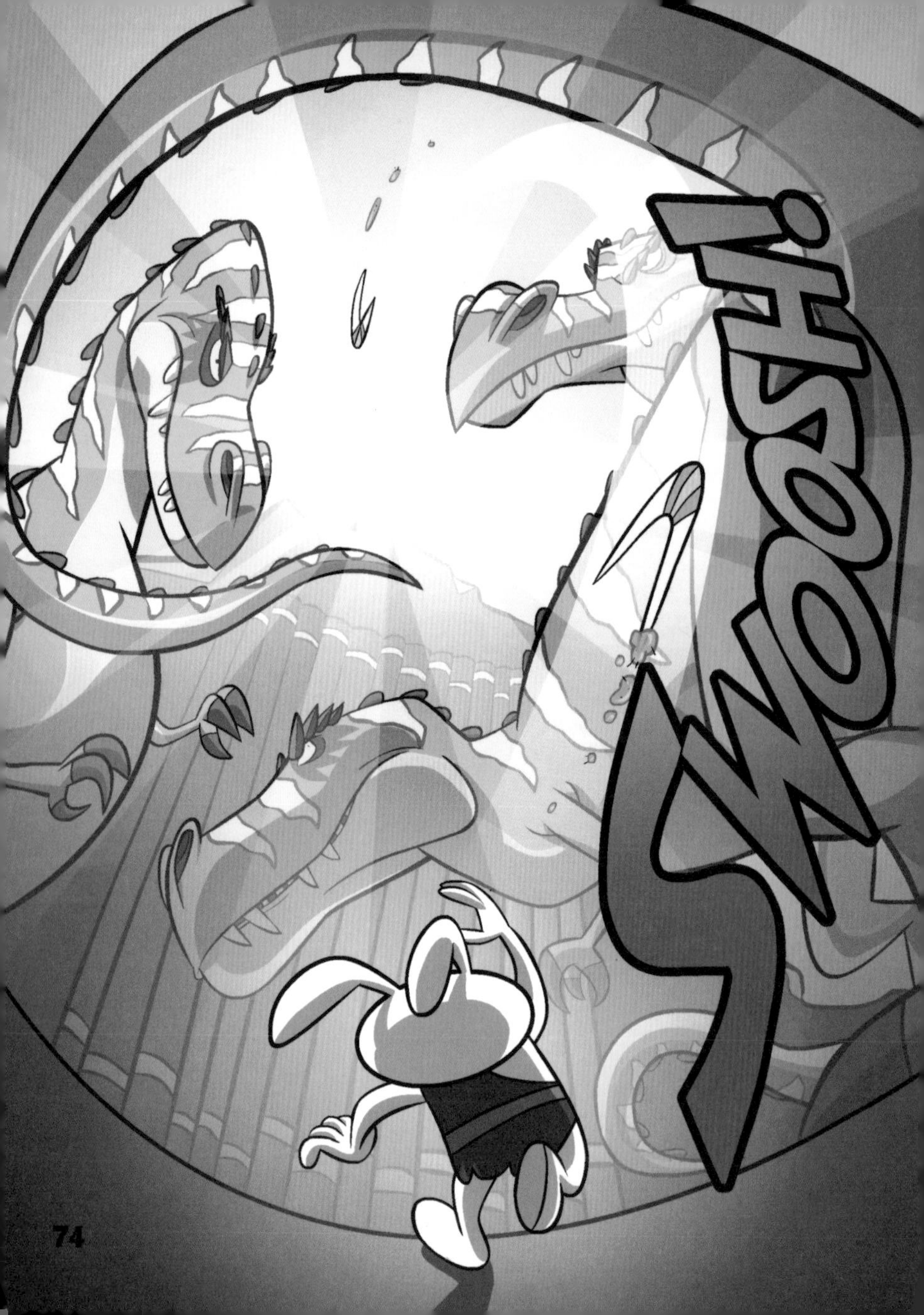
SWOOSH!

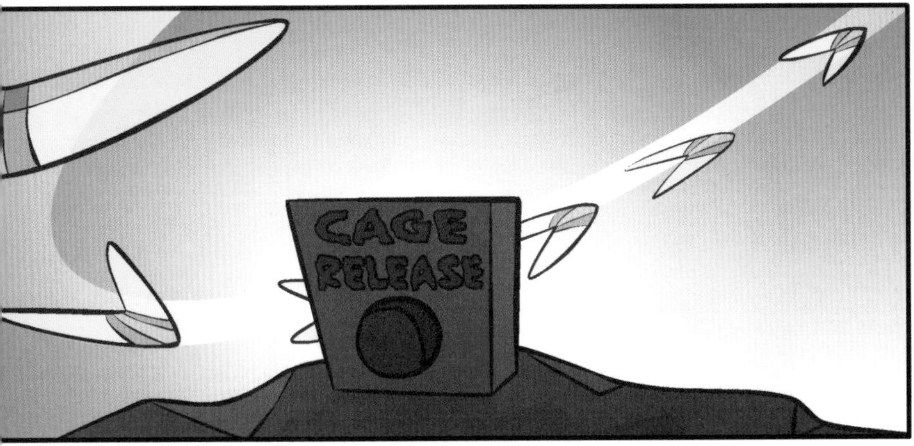
CAGE
RELEASE

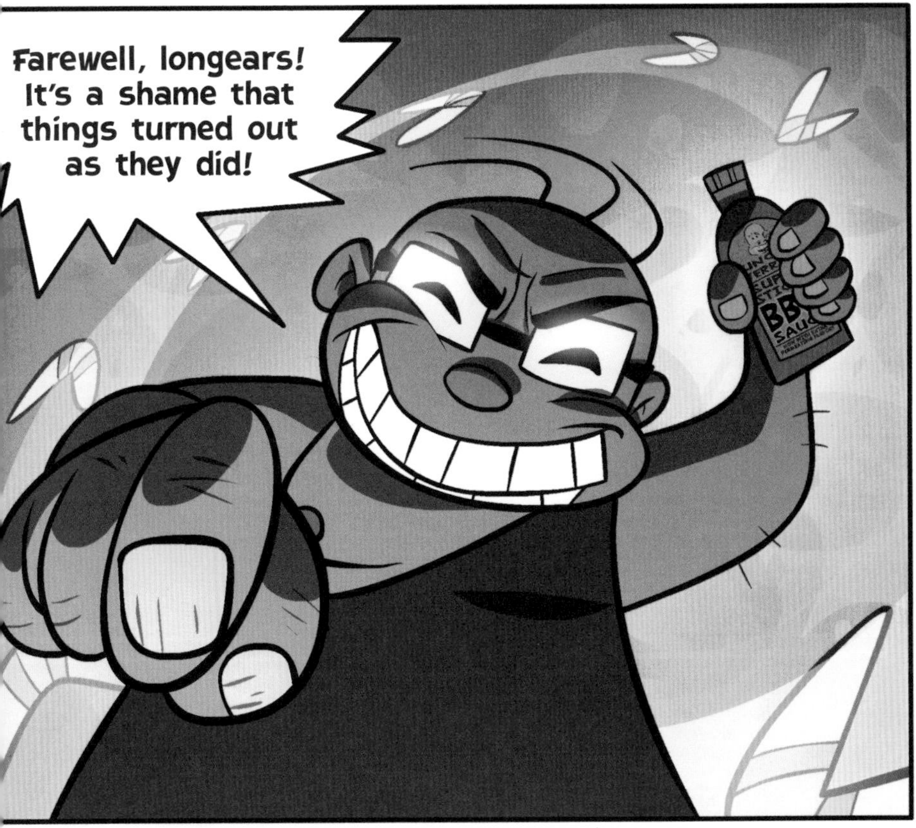
Farewell, longears! It's a shame that things turned out as they did!

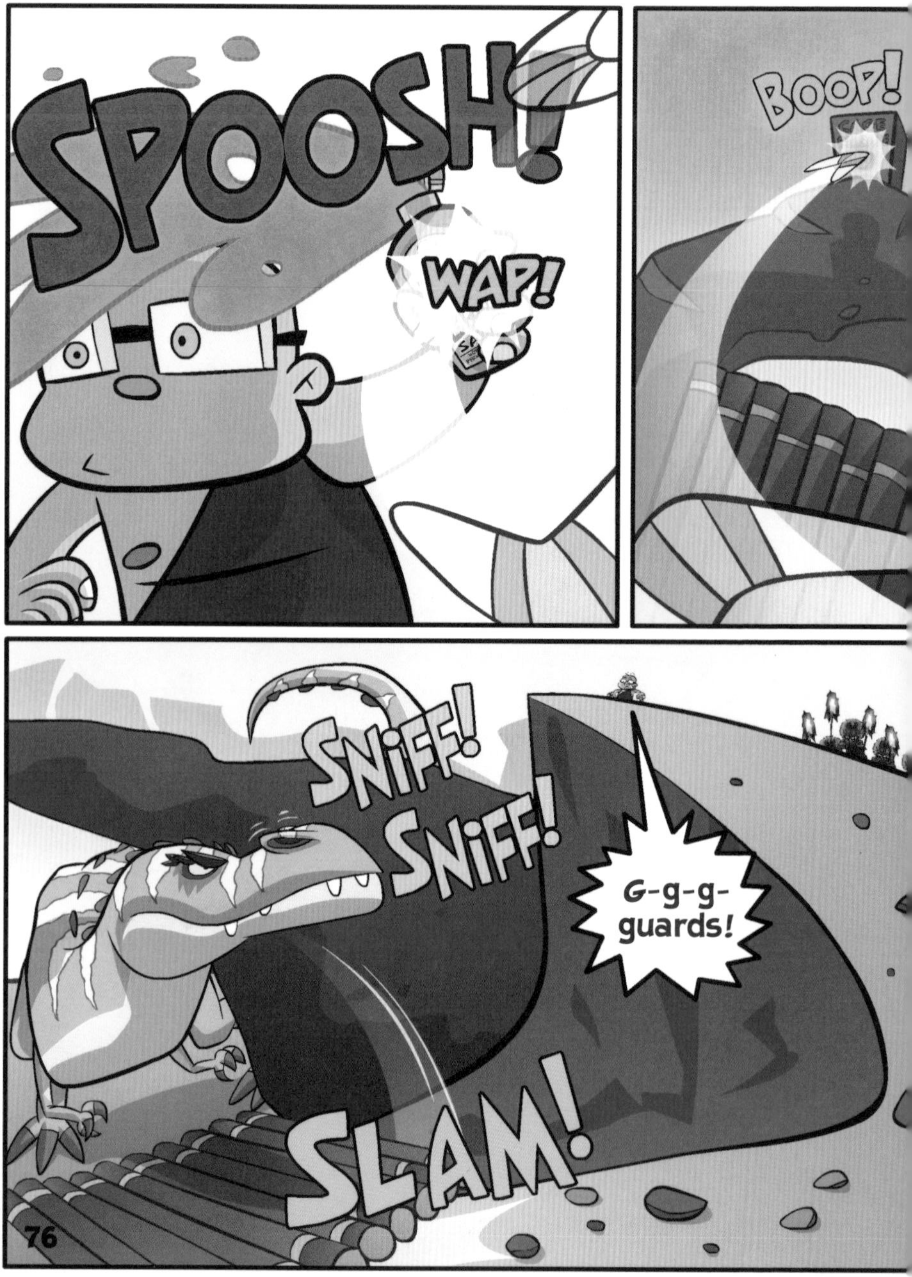
SPOOSH!
WAP!
BOOP!
SNIFF!
SNIFF!
G-g-g-guards!
SLAM!

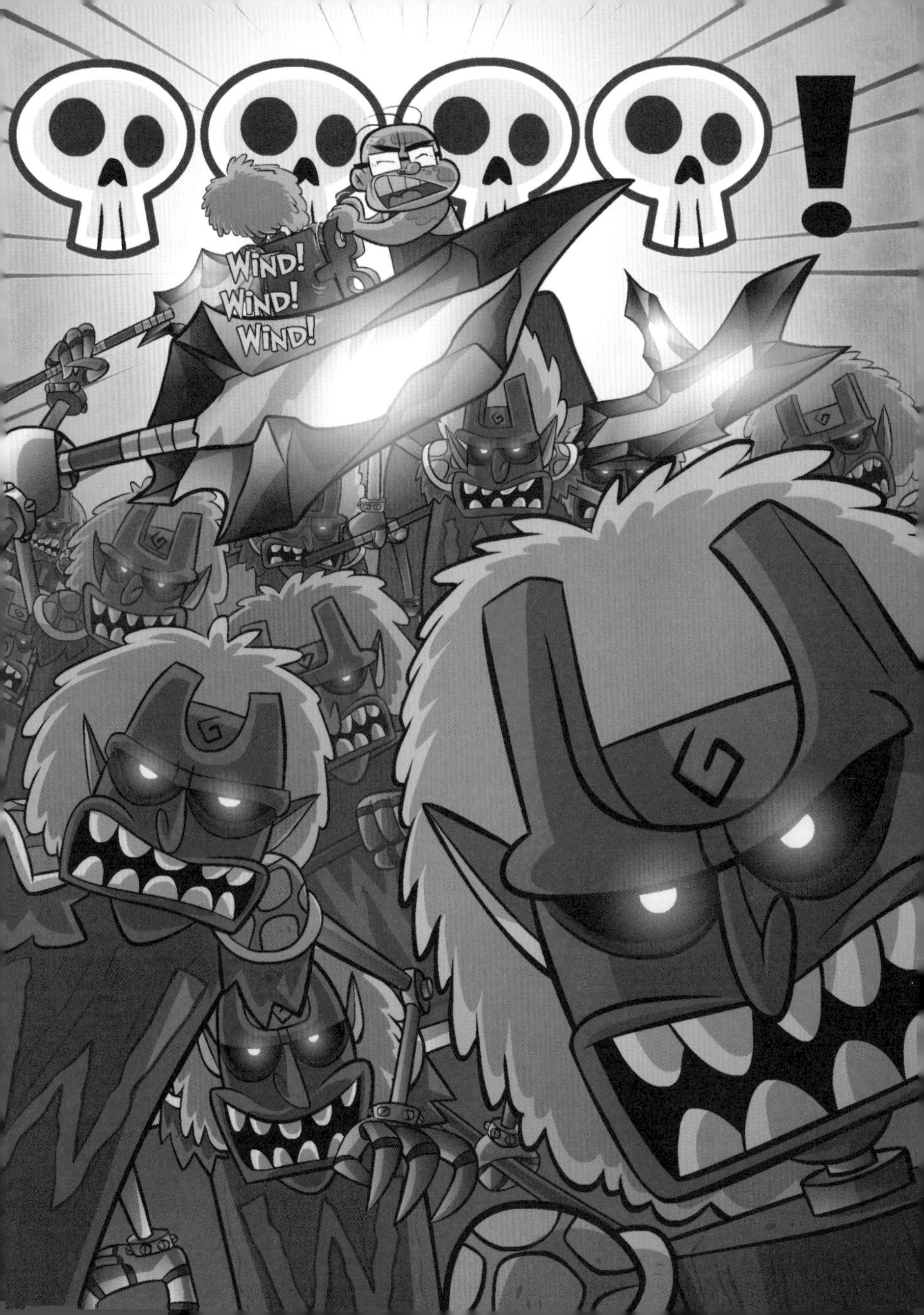

WIND!
WIND!
WIND!

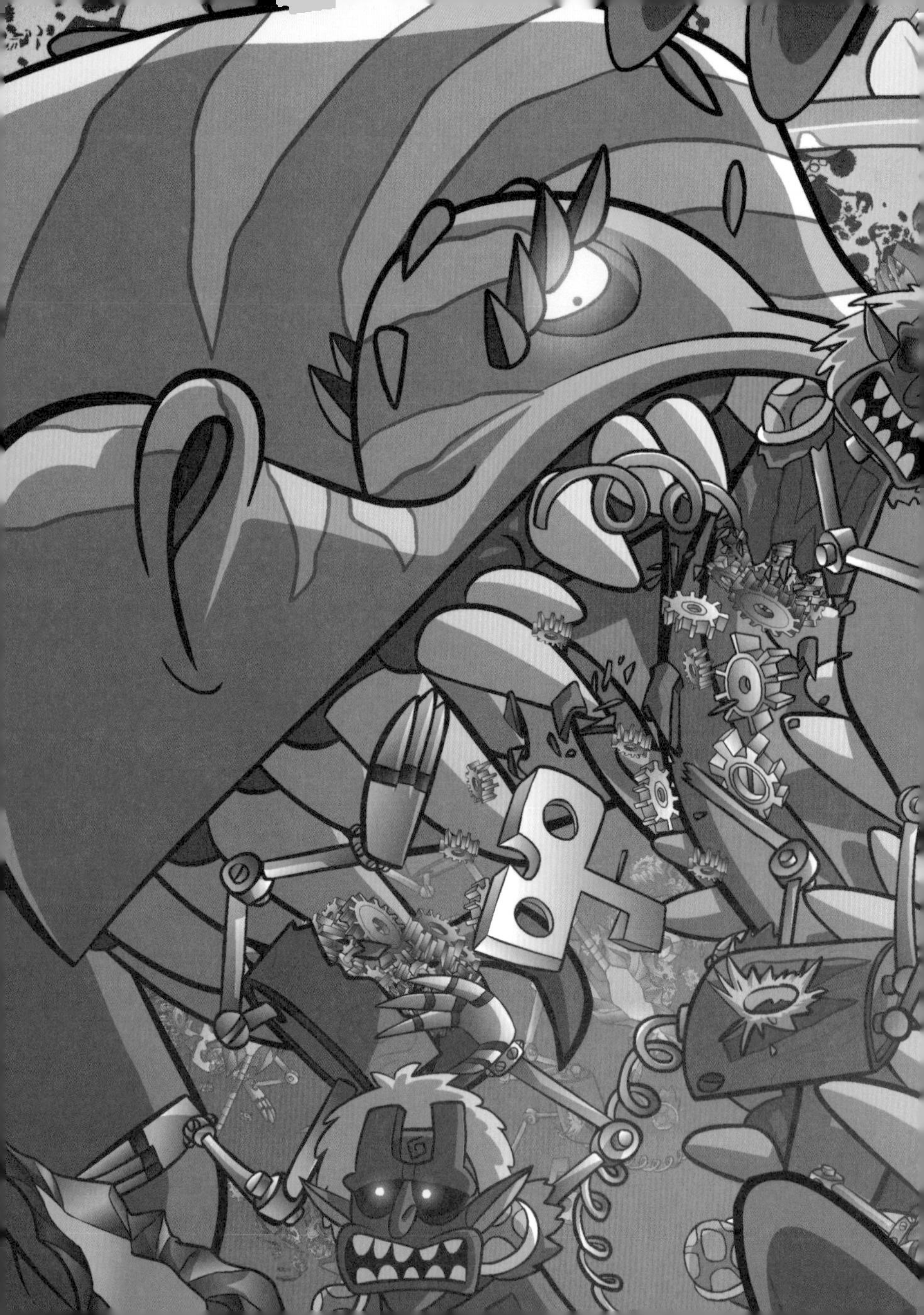

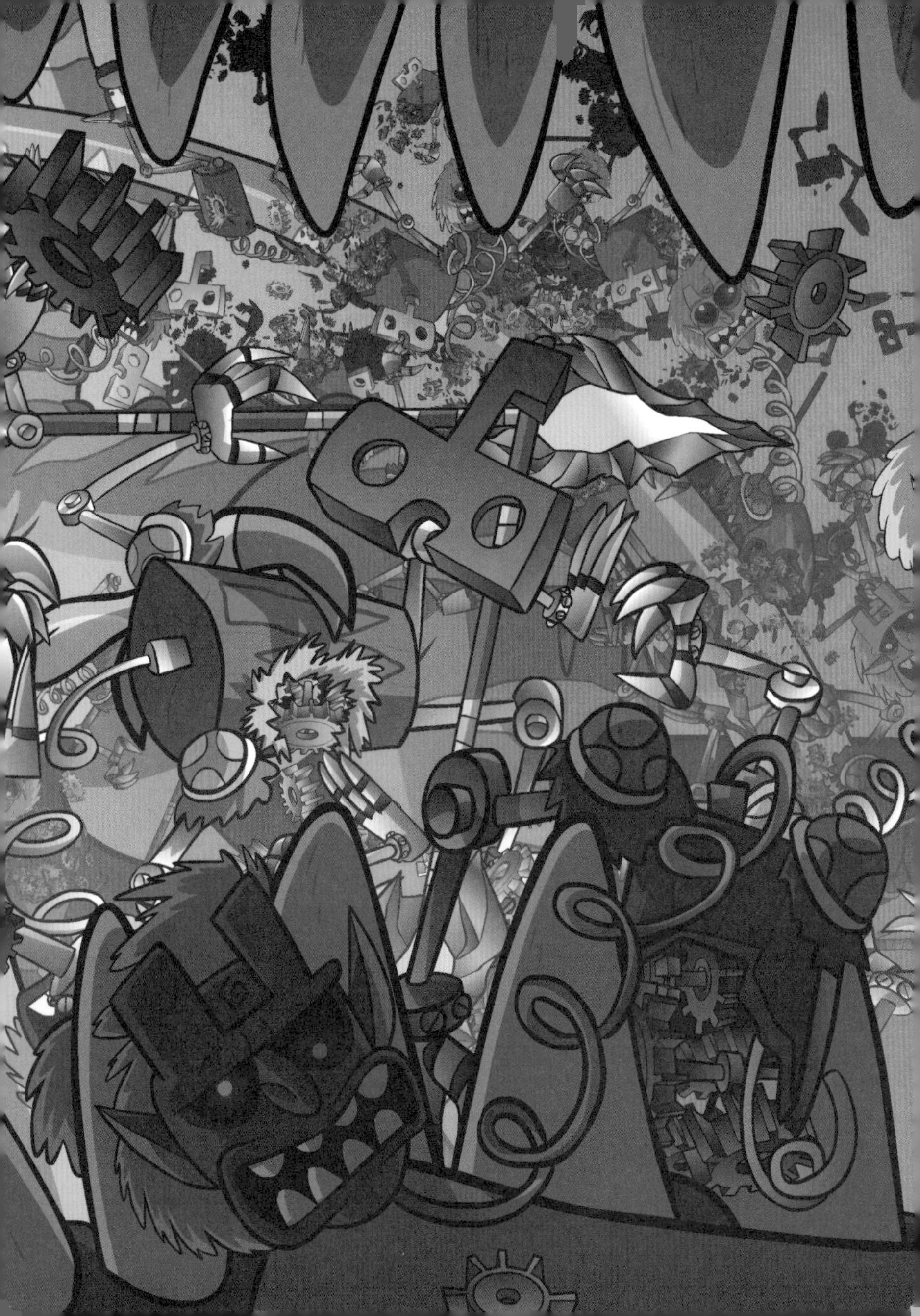

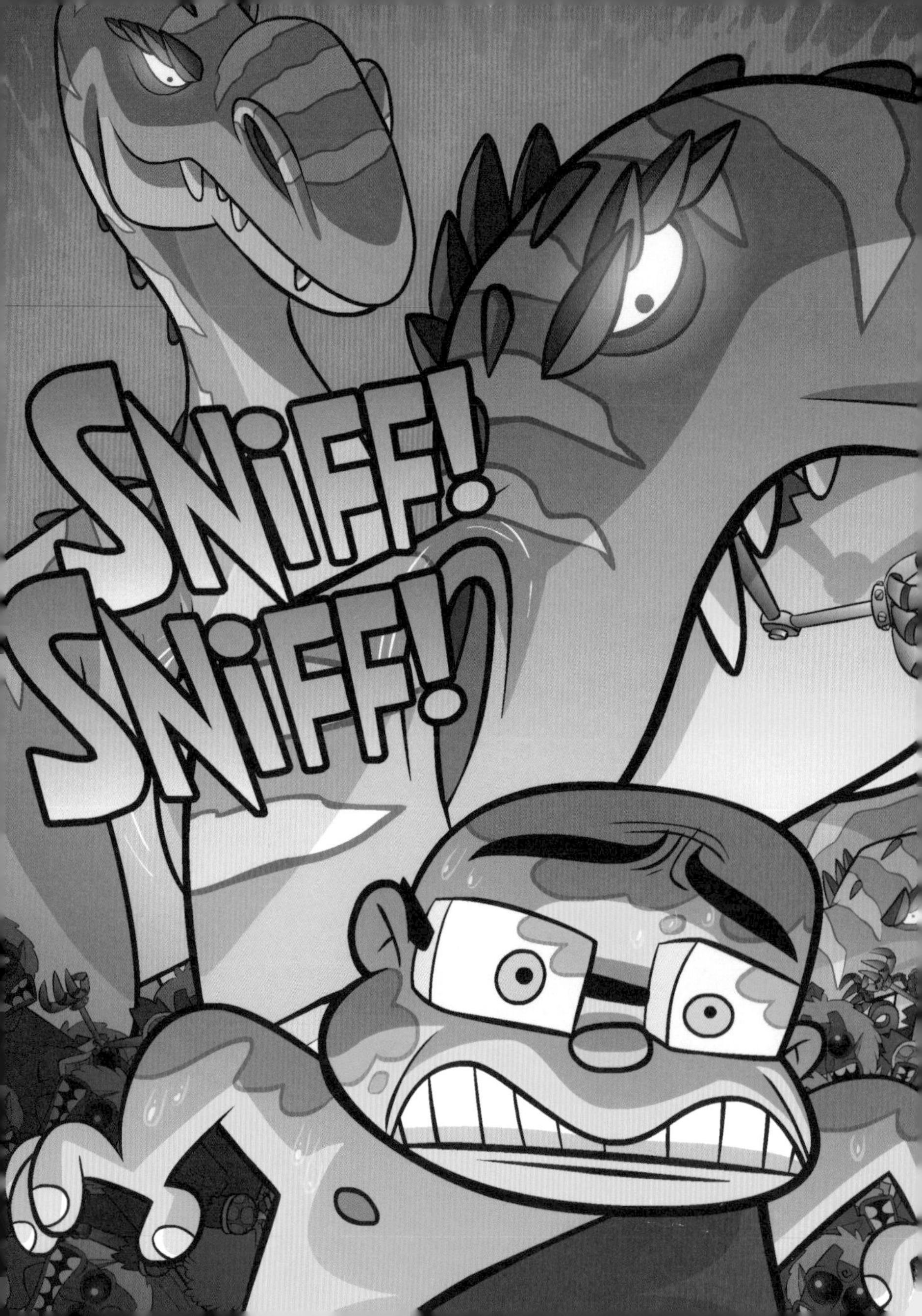
SNIFF!
SNIFF!

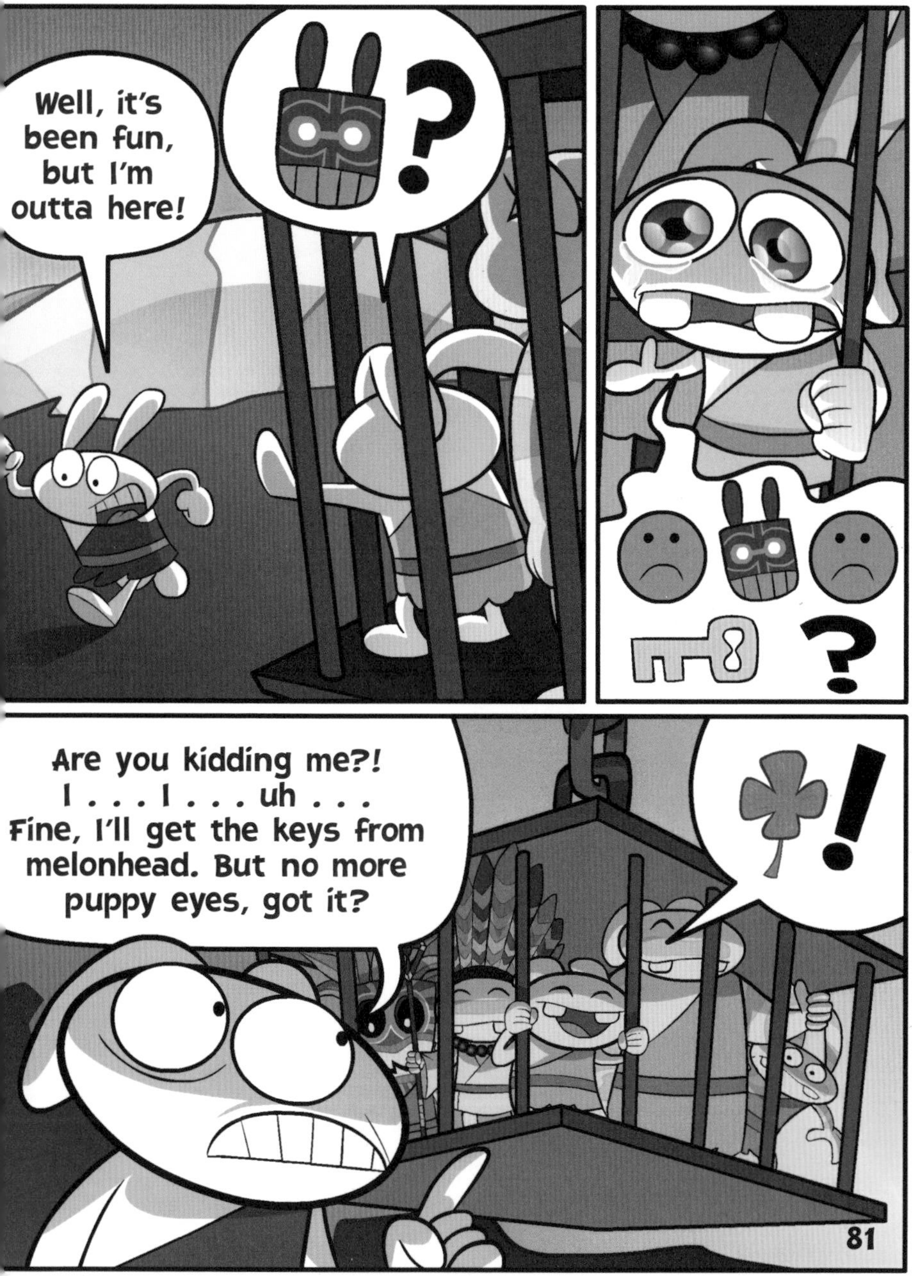
Well, it's been fun, but I'm outta here!
?
?
Are you kidding me?! I . . . I . . . uh . . . Fine, I'll get the keys from melonhead. But no more puppy eyes, got it?
!

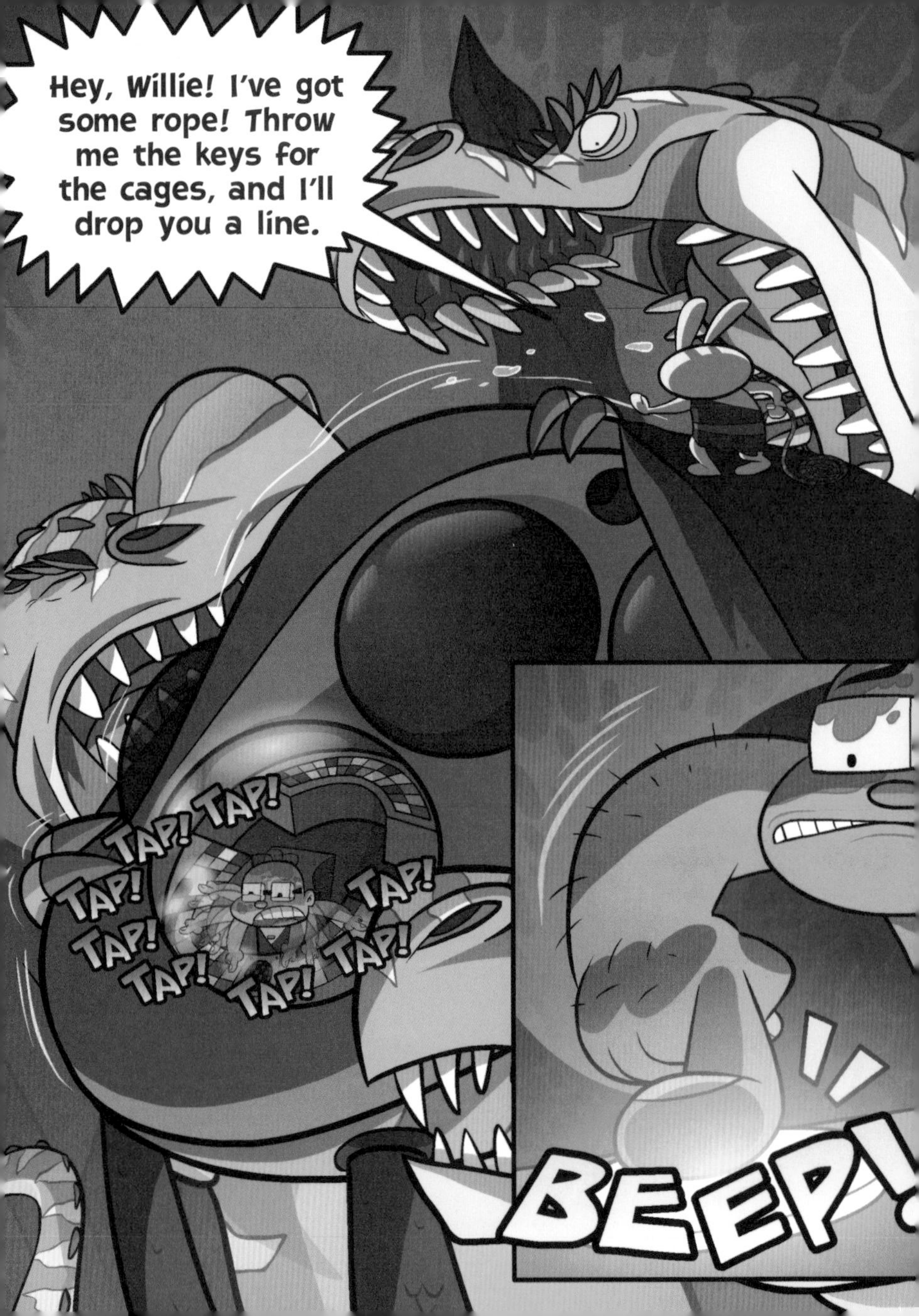

Hey, Willie! I've got some rope! Throw me the keys for the cages, and I'll drop you a line.
TAP! TAP! TAP! TAP! TAP! TAP! TAP! TAP!
BEEP!

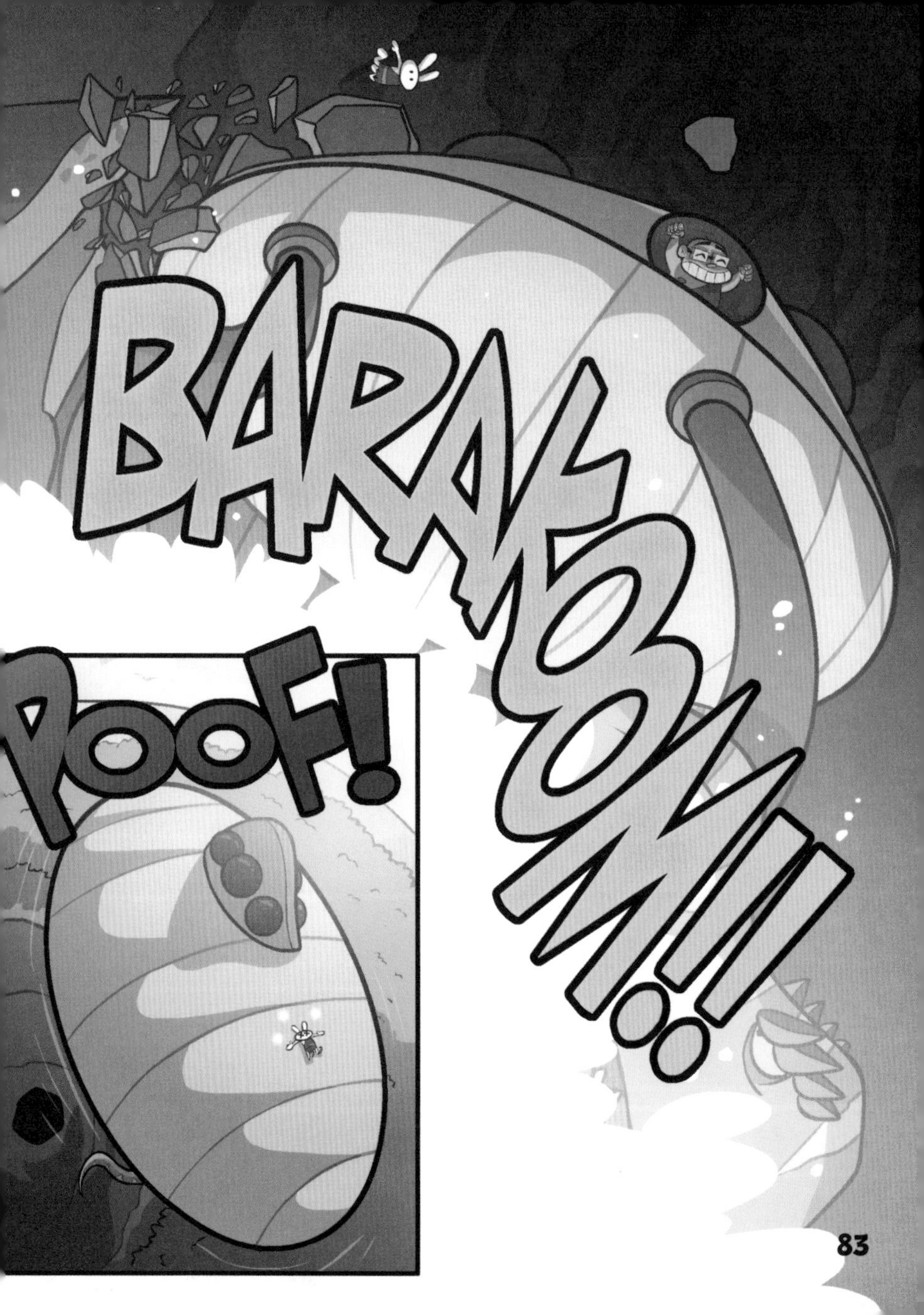
BARABOOM!!
POOF!

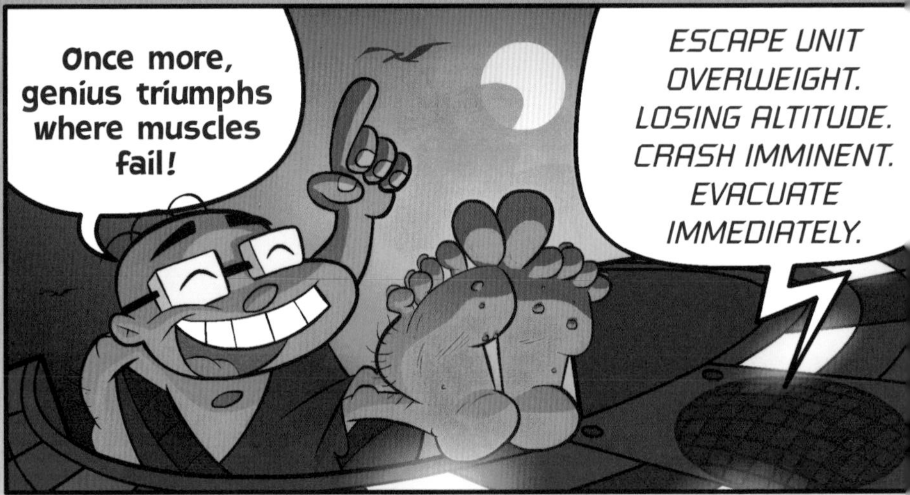
Once more, genius triumphs where muscles fail!
ESCAPE UNIT OVERWEIGHT. LOSING ALTITUDE. CRASH IMMINENT. EVACUATE IMMEDIATELY.

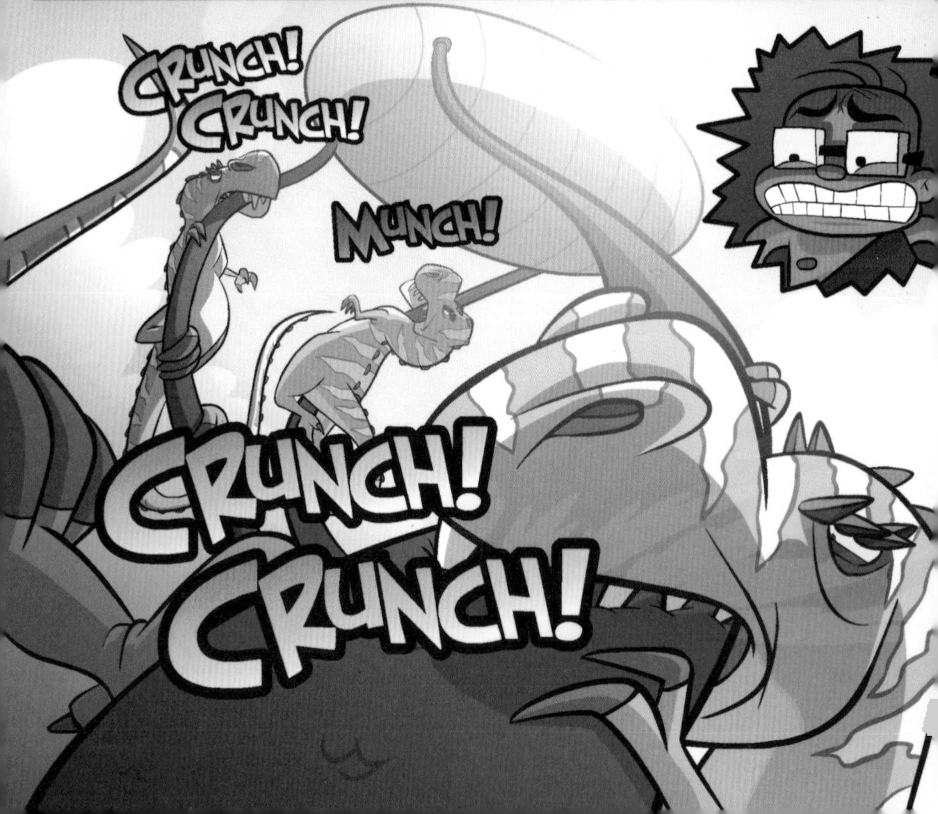
CRUNCH! CRUNCH!
MUNCH!
CRUNCH! CRUNCH!

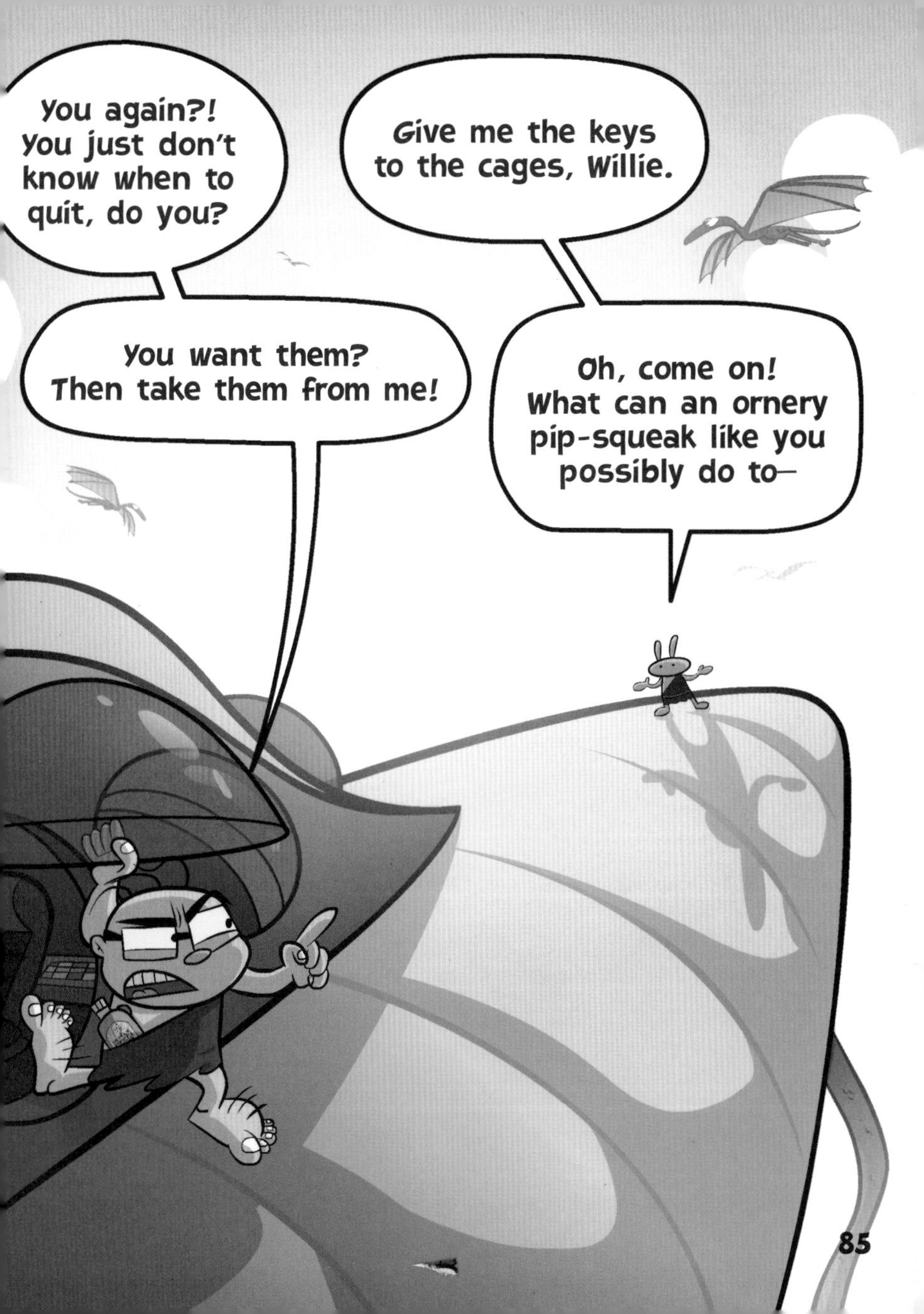
You again?! You just don't know when to quit, do you?
Give me the keys to the cages, Willie.
You want them? Then take them from me!
Oh, come on! What can an ornery pip-squeak like you possibly do to—

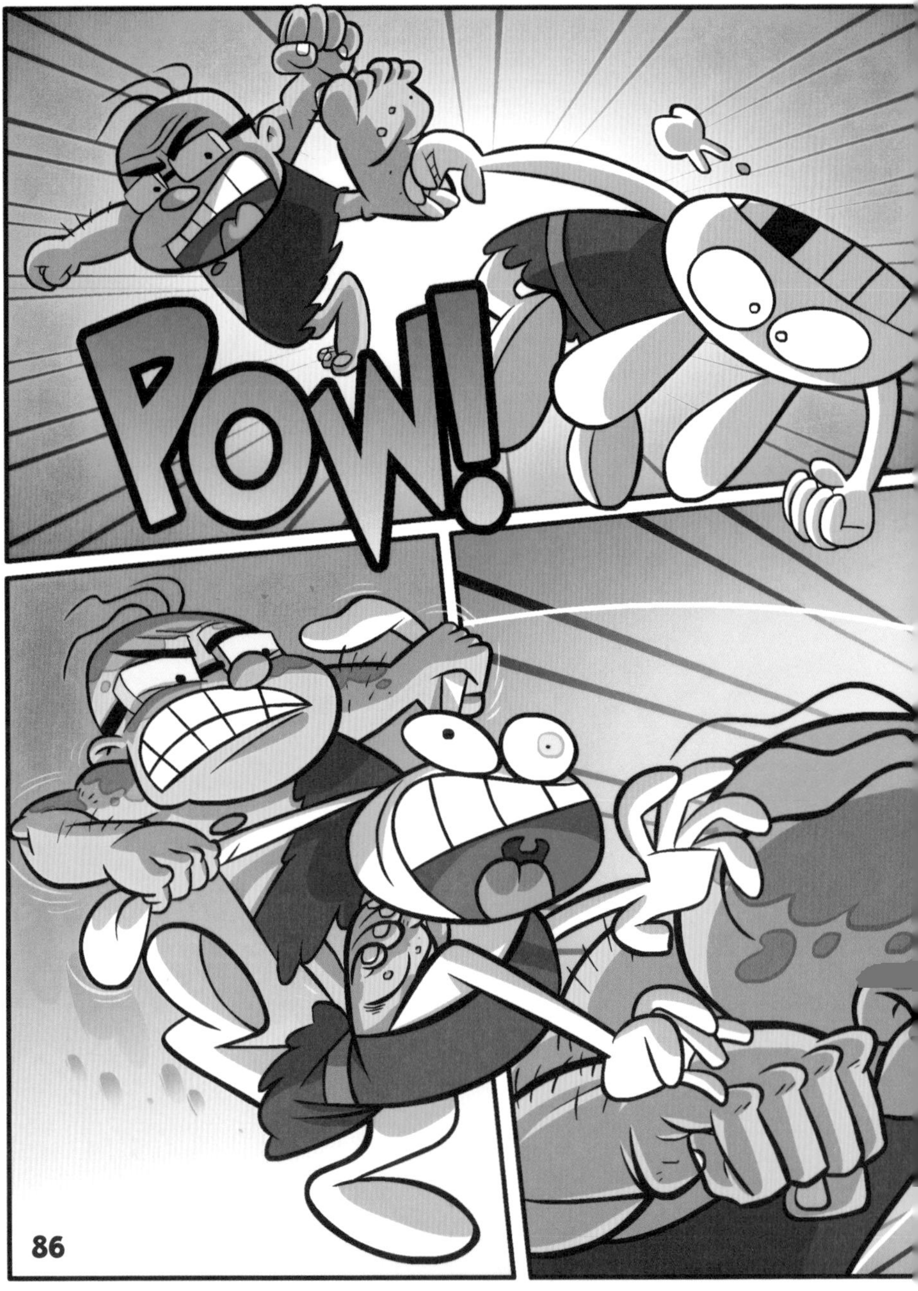
POW!

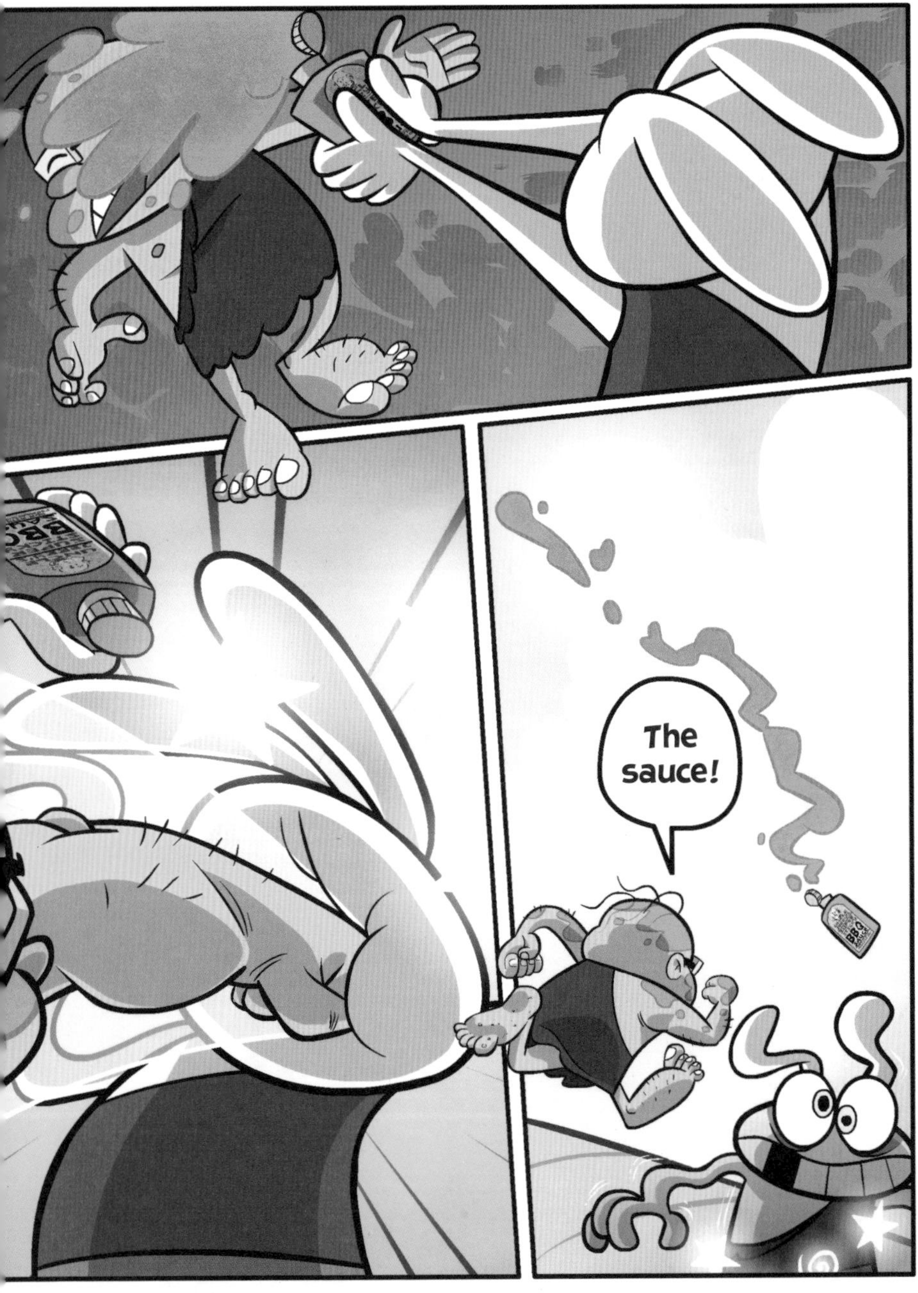
The sauce!

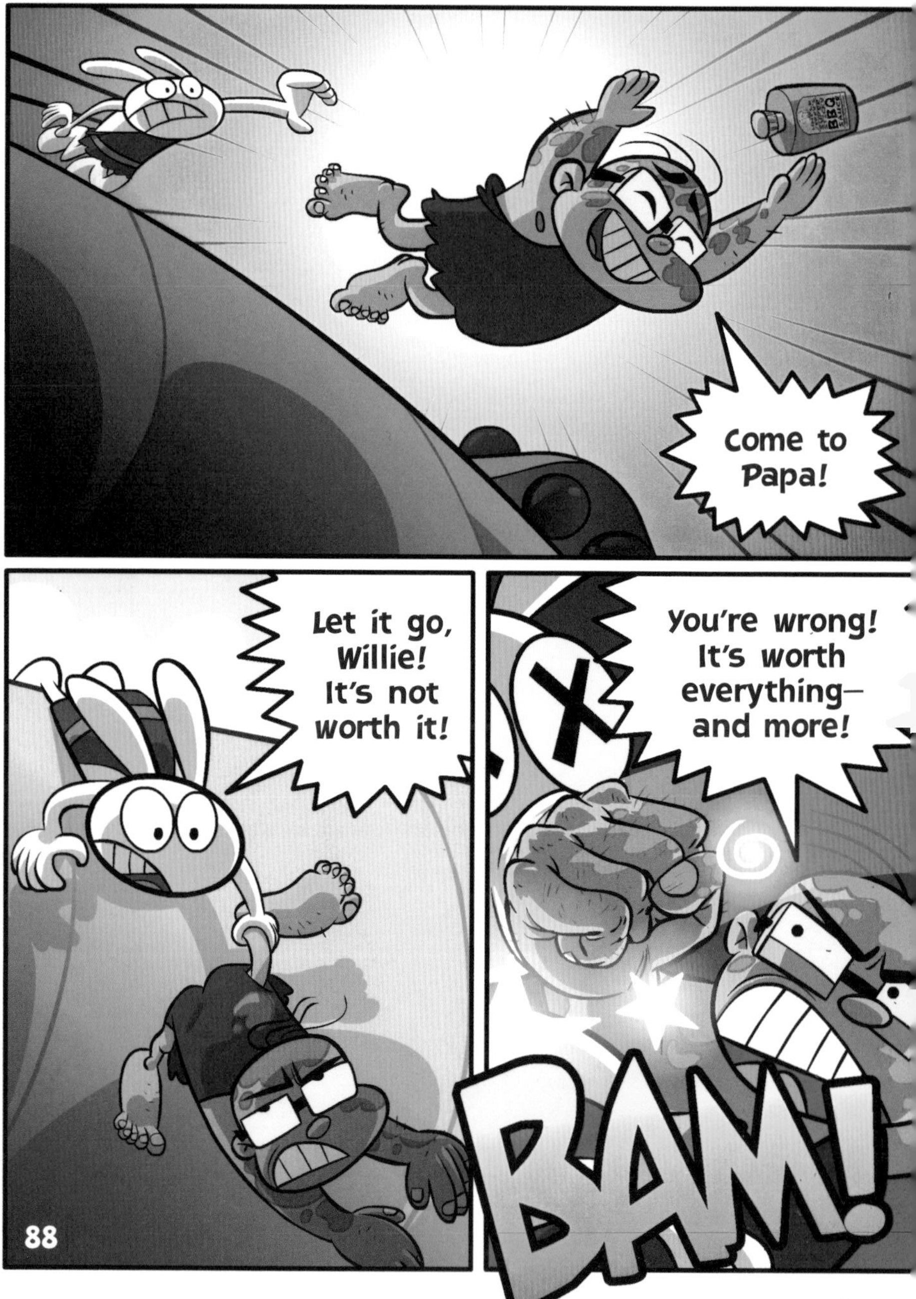
BBQ SAUCE
Come to Papa!
Let it go, Willie! It's not worth it!
You're wrong! It's worth everything—and more!
BAM!

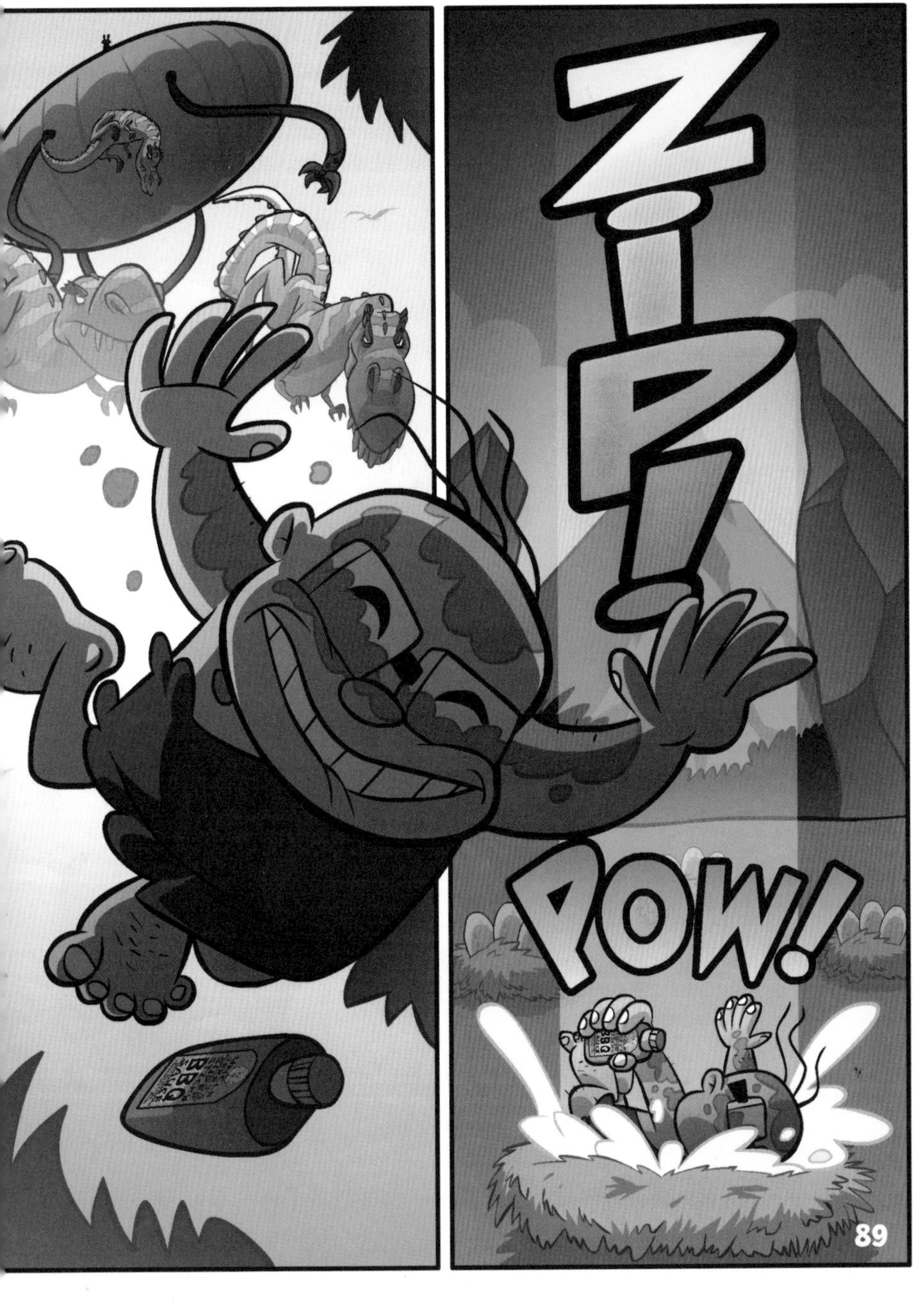
ZIP!
POW!

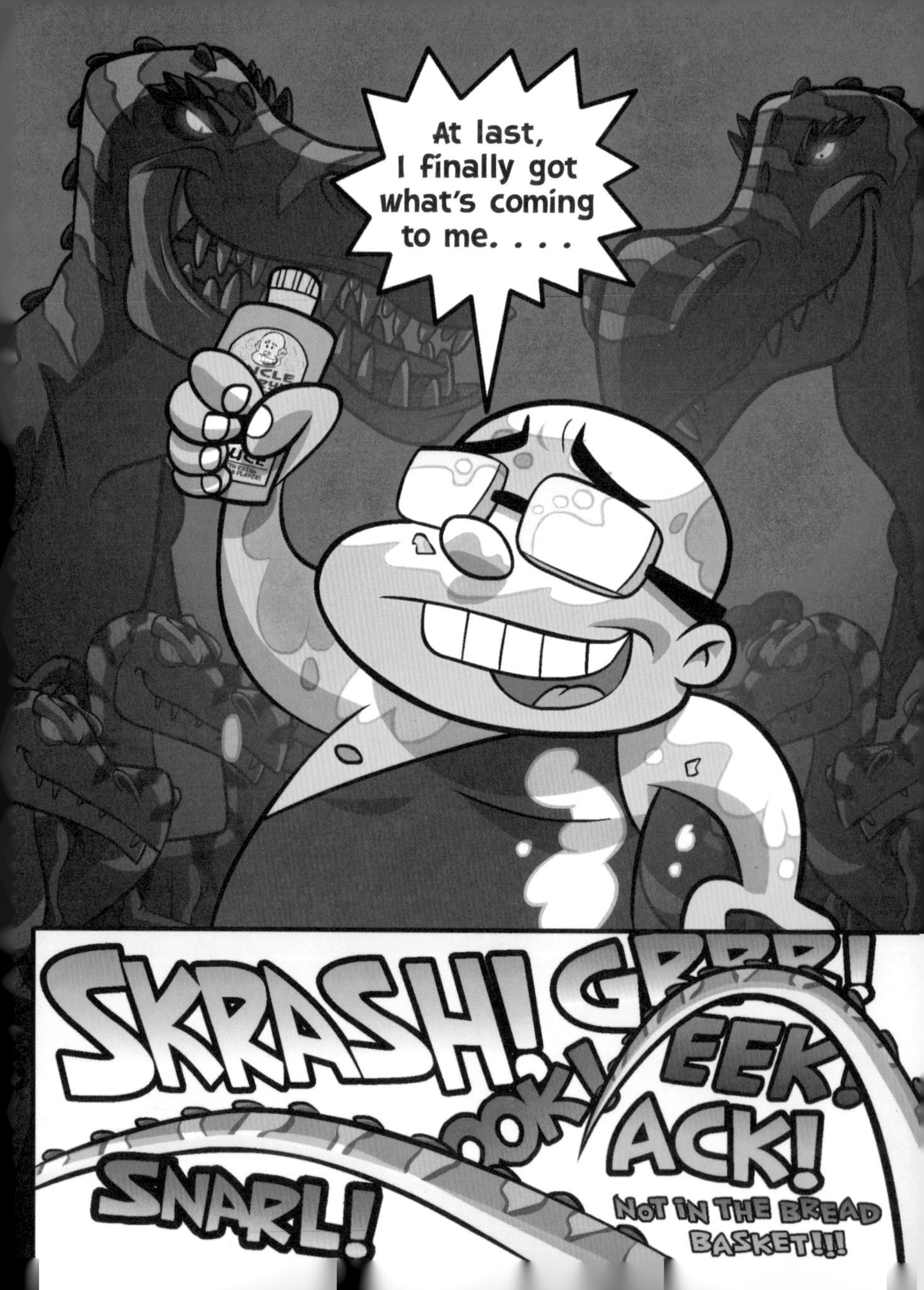
At last, I finally got what's coming to me. . . .
SKRASH!
GRRR!
OOK!
EEK!
ACK!
SNARL!
NOT IN THE BREAD BASKET!!!

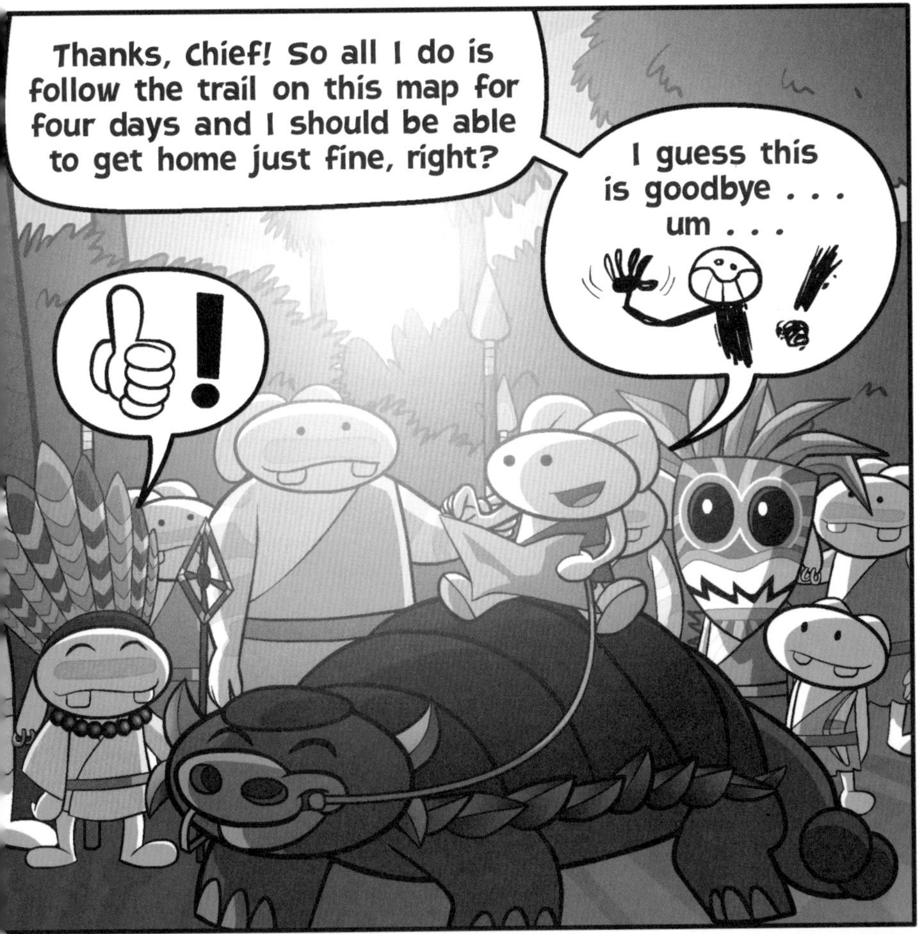
Thanks, Chief! So all I do is follow the trail on this map for four days and I should be able to get home just fine, right?
I guess this is goodbye . . . um . . .
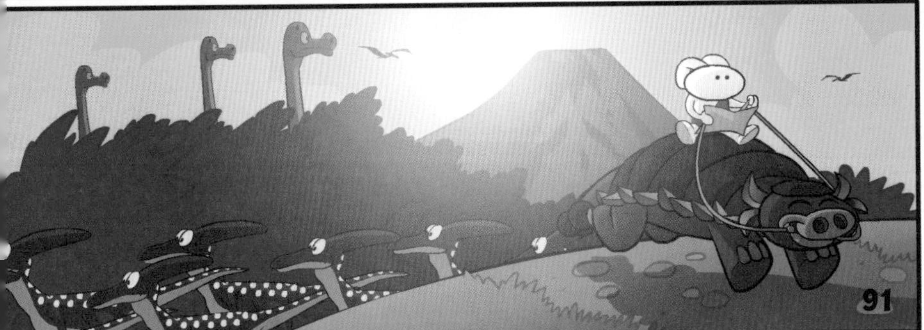

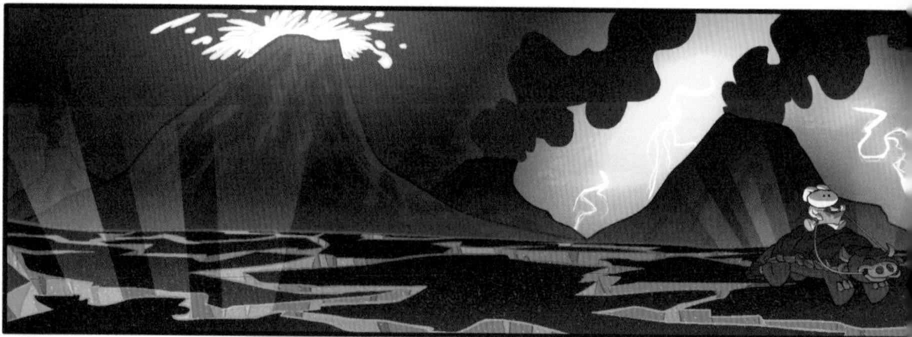

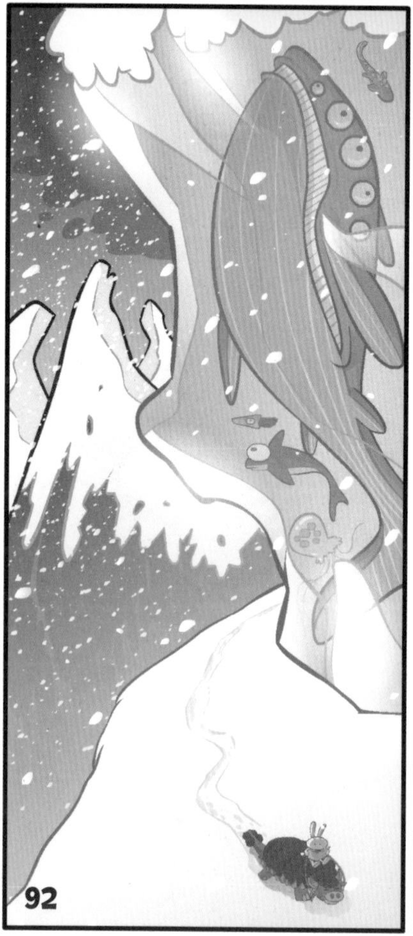

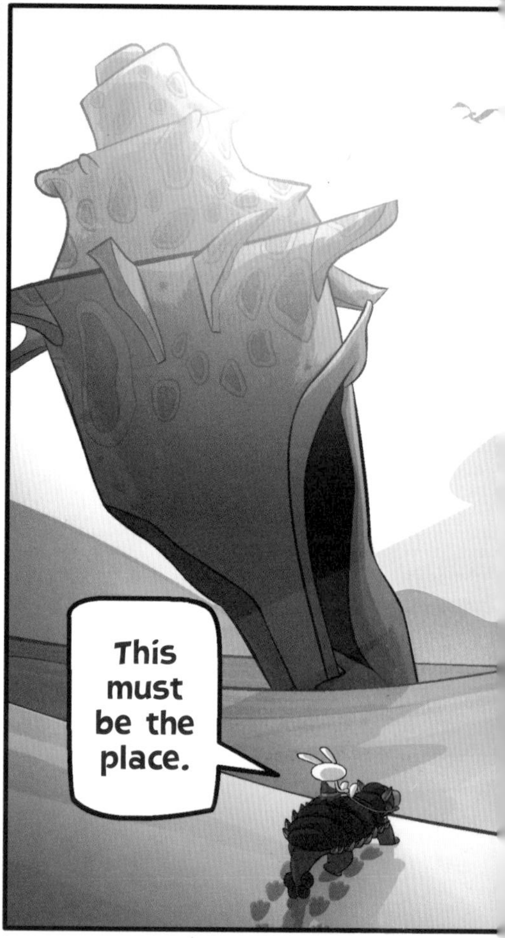
This must be the place.

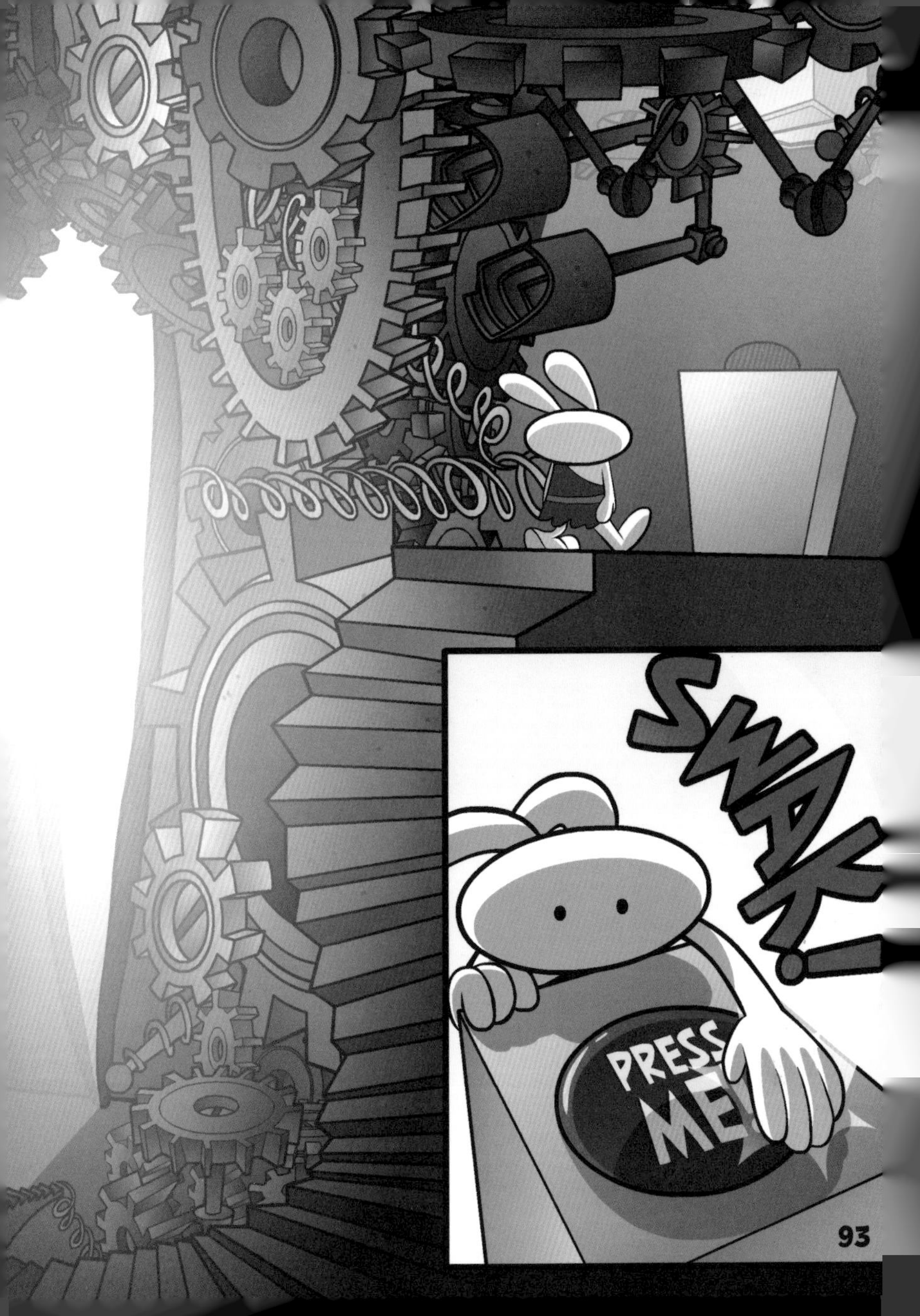
SWAK!
PRESS ME

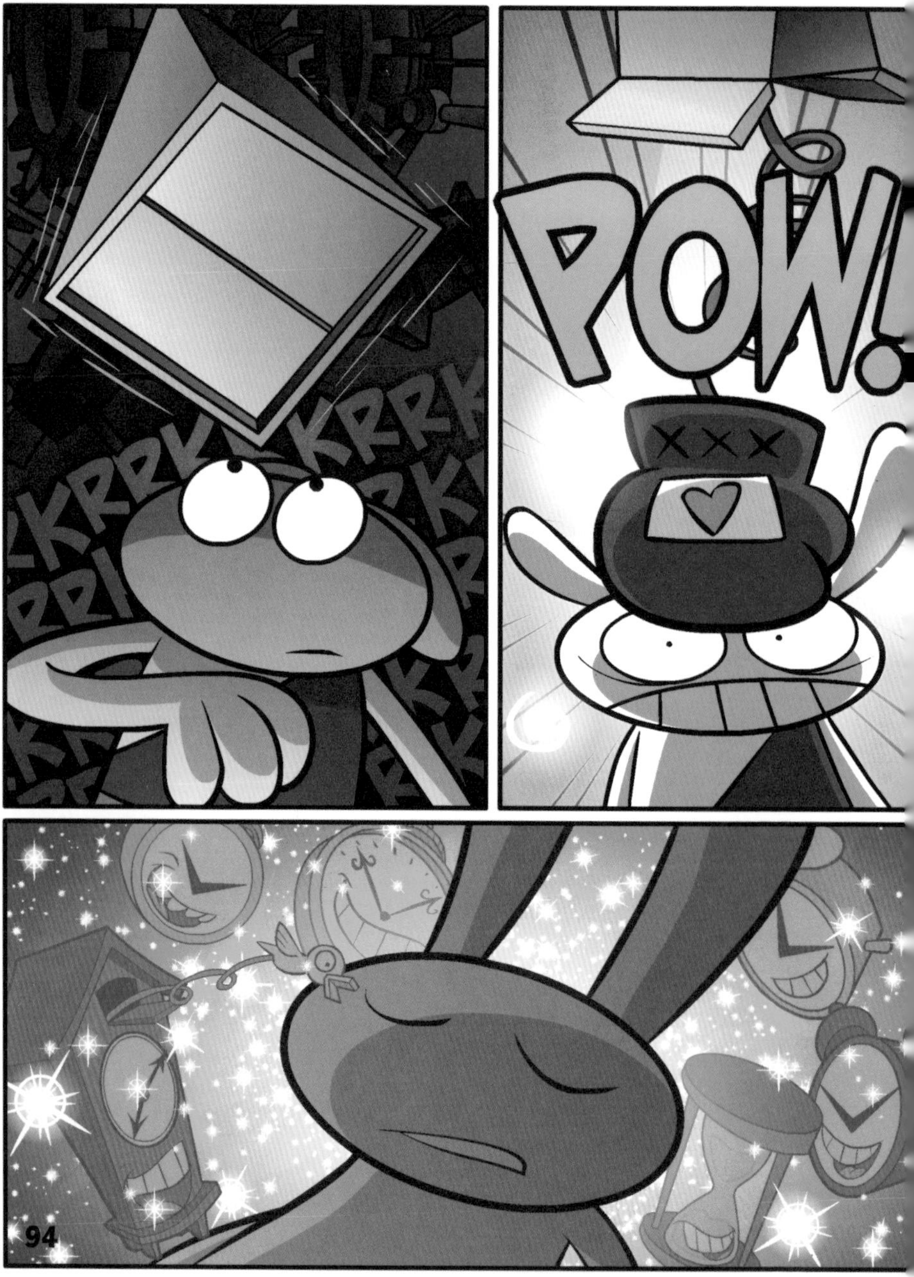
KRRK
KRRK
POW!

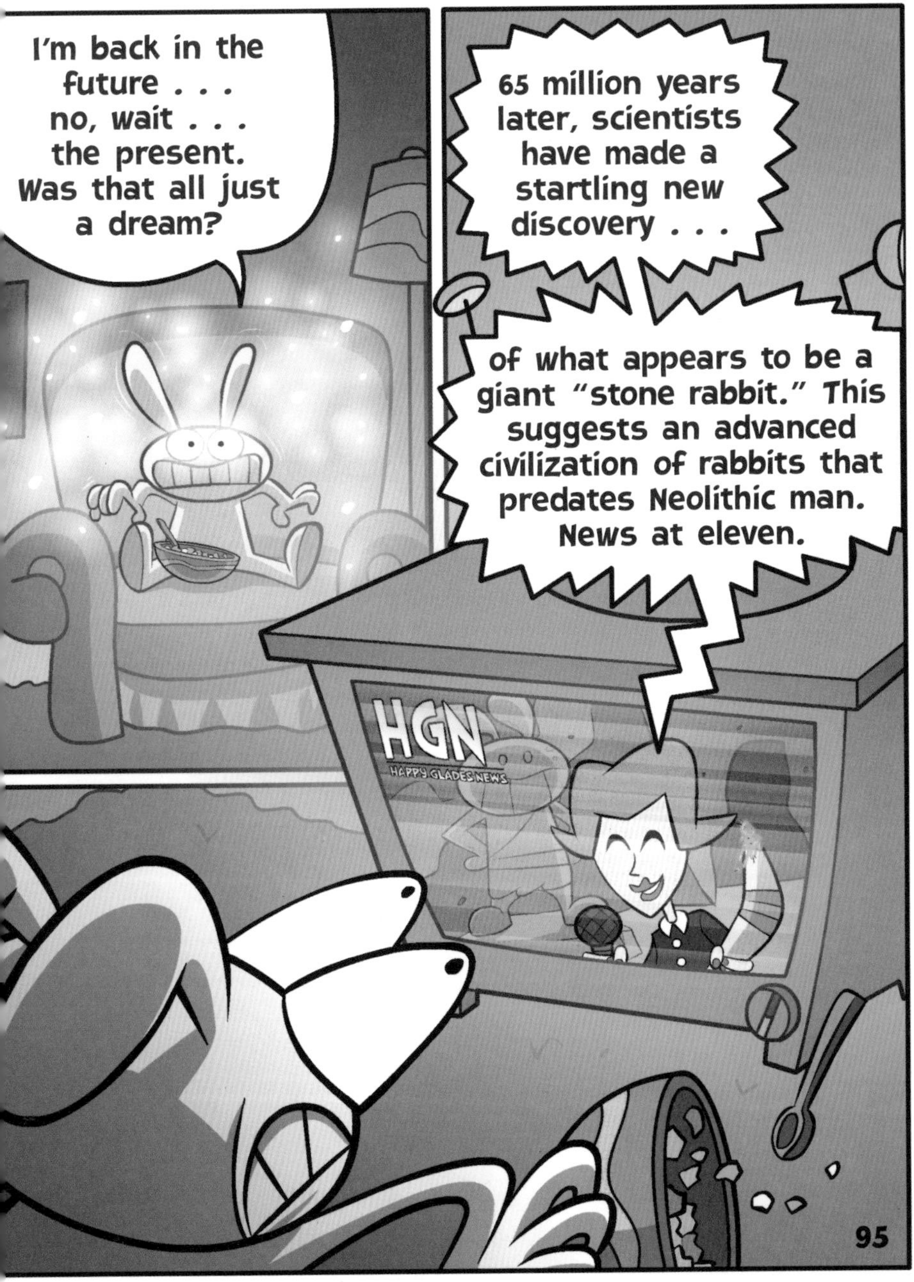
I'm back in the future . . . no, wait . . . the present. Was that all just a dream?
65 million years later, scientists have made a startling new discovery . . .
of what appears to be a giant "stone rabbit." This suggests an advanced civilization of rabbits that predates Neolithic man. News at eleven.
HGN
HAPPY GLADES NEWS

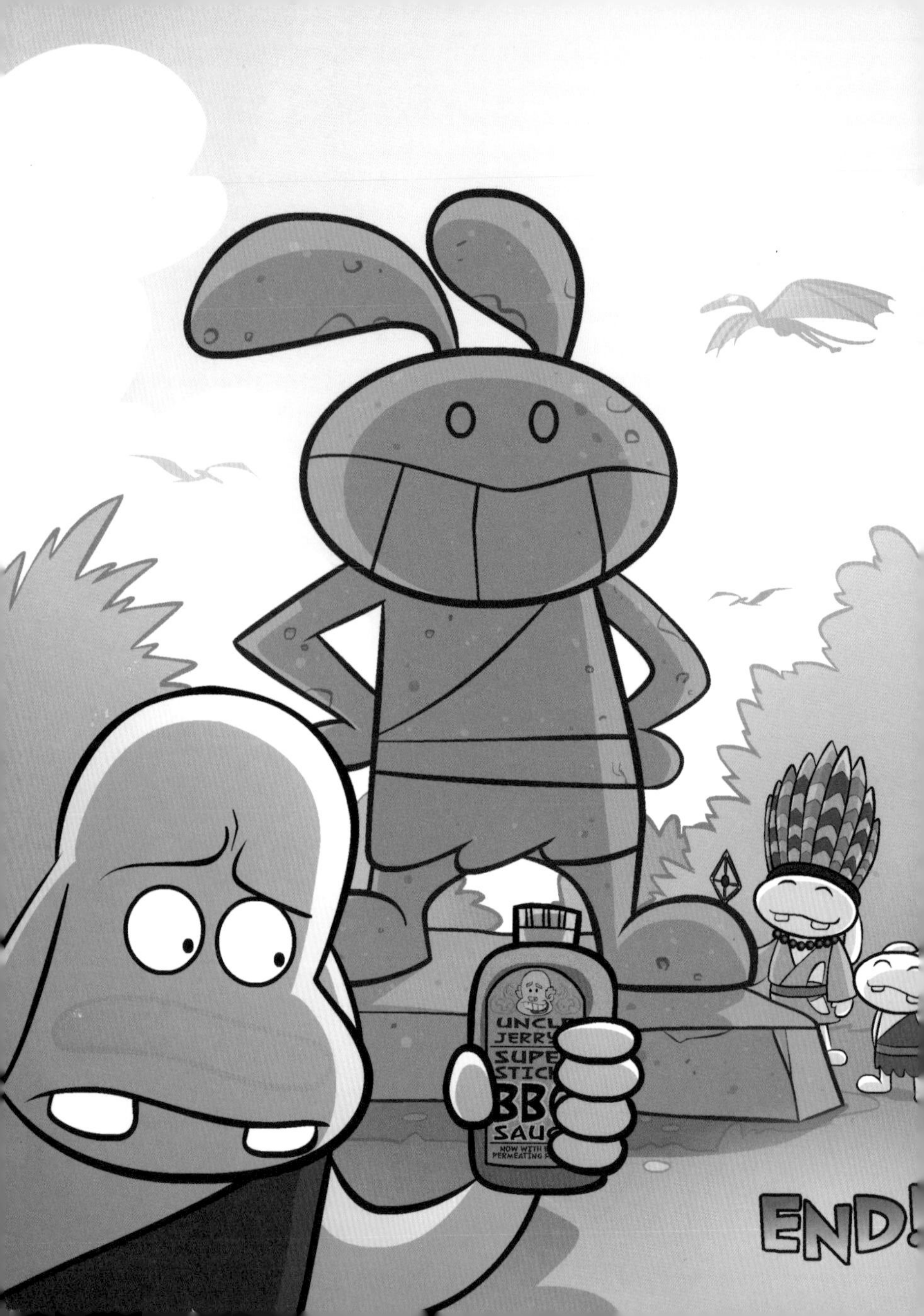
END!